Lovesong for the Giant Contessa

ALSO BY STEVEN TYE CULBERT

The Beautiful Woman Without Mercy
The King of Scarecrows

LOVESONG FOR THE GIANT CONTESSA

A NOVEL

Steven Tye Culbert

Four Walls Eight Windows
New York/London

© 1997 Steven Tye Culbert

Published in the United States by
Four Walls Eight Windows
39 West 14th Street
New York, NY 10011

U.K. offices:
Four Walls Eight Windows/Turnaround
Unit 3 Olympia Trading Estate
Coburg Road Wood Green
London N22 67Z

First printing April 1997.

All rights reserved. No part of this book may be reproduced, stored in a database or other retrieval system, or transmitted in any form, by any means, including mechanical, electronic, photocopying, recording, or otherwise, without the prior written permission of the publisher.

Library of Congress Cataloging-in-Publication Data:
Culbert, Steven, 1950-
  Lovesong for the Giant Contessa : a novel / by Steven Tye Culbert.
    p.   cm.
  ISBN 1-56858-082-7 (HC)
I. Title.
PS3553.U2848L68   1997
813'.54—dc21   96-51156
                                                                CIP

Book design by Acme Art, Inc.
10 9 8 7 6 5 4 3 2 1
Printed in the United States

*To George Cattermole, who fed us,
once upon a time, lasting things.*

The invention of men has been sharpening
and improving the mystery of murder.
—Edmund Burke

And it came to pass, when men began
to multiply on the face of the earth,
and daughters were born unto them, that the
sons of God saw the daughters of men
that they were fair; and they took them
wives of all which they chose. . . .
There were giants in the earth in those
days; and also after that, when the sons
of God came in unto the daughters of
men, and they bare *children* to them,
the same *became* mighty men which
were of old, men of renown.
—Gideons Bible, Genesis Chapter 6

PRELUDE

You pray hard, work hard, love hard, and fight to rip the mask of Reason off the face of God. The face of God is every face you see, big and little. The smirk of the punk, the frown of the angel. Bending over the river, the tub, the basin of water you wonder why your father abused you so. Looking at the sky full of stars any night, stars maybe hidden or apparent or too far away to see, you remember your mother's face before you were born, and you fall in love with Hope, Destiny, Fate, and Faith all over again because life is a yo-yo and so are all the stars. . . Make it walk, make it sing, make it spin through every thing, make it a cradle with your fingers. . . The Giant Contessa had beautiful hands and the love of a man called Jonah. . . I have regretted and forgotten more than I will ever know because why, and because why is good enough. . . They found a pair of buried hands at Cibolo Creek, south of Refugio and north of Corpus Christi, when the record rains fell thirty years after this all happened in some way, where the cement-reinforced culvert at Cottonwood Bend where

I saved U-U from the snake got whipped too hard and fast and continual by the creek-become-a-river high as the last laughing leaf of the cottonwood, and behind the farmer's culvert, in a bumpy cavelike hole six feet down, in a colored metal box of thin lead metal from long ago, they found the withered giant hands of an infant. . . The Giant Contessa had beautiful hands and the love of a man called Jonah. She was born of a normal schoolteacher mom who made a mistake. Then her mom migrated north from Corpus to start life new and earn something good to give to her daughter, who just kept getting bigger and bigger, someday. *The forehead and hands of the infant were huge. . .* The deathbed scene of the woman whose honey I stole is left out because Ernest told me to, Ernest who killed himself because he was a giant whose wings could no longer lift him off the ground so he could see things clearly and sleep the little sleep of life from which we seem to wake. Ernest of the big hands and feet who saved people's lives and was wounded for the Cross and got the Cross of War. I thank him. Real angels who don't fly in waking hours walk barefoot through the sheets of rain, the sheets of bedtime cotton or silk or black night falling without a sound your toenails make. . . The Giant Contessa had beautiful hands and the love of a man called Jonah, Mother said. The reason this is a mystery is a mystery. A spud wrench, a pair of hands, a past, a mind, a sea. Where things happen, people spin. Love, let us be true, my brother used to say from his crib, quoting his nurse who loved Matthew Arnold, and looking at me. Little things. Little women and larger men engage upon the woven string, and large women and little men will spin there, too. One trick they call Around the World, where you throw the yo-yo out hard, snap it back and up and out as smoothly and as many orbits as you can. Rarely seen: a man and woman engaged in love exactly the same height, width, and weight. Find me that. "Find me!" Eustacia called from the dark bedroom of the Giant Contessa's hut. And I did. Her lips were never mine. The starlight or liquid dust on her lips gave the mystery away in a kiss opening like a door to the sea, starved happy, though the room had no windows. The room Chet and I peeked into was the library. I laugh now, but nothing on my face changes. Remembering love and lips and cigarettes and fast cars and Beach Road with nothing on it, up and down, gazed upon and guarded in my imagination by sunflowers silver as pewter beheaded unhandled soldiers of time how time comes around. You immediately, independently, indecisively know. In youth you outwalk the pervert night and in age you are the pervert night, if the string breaks and you refuse to get another one. To those who drop their yo-yo in the sea or the lake, you can feel sorry and require of yourself as much as the sea requires, whipping and beating and kissing and coddling and loving, withdrawing and flooding and flowing around the world and flowering inside whole troops and regiments of people with fins, tails, wings, and lungs in darkness and daylight and in day that is dark, dark day. For what? For the longed-for meeting.

The Giant Contessa had beautiful hands and the love of a man called Jonah. What happened to Smokey or Whiskey the mules, the Black Joseph knows. He is a barber in Refugio who rode his mount through the corn. He is happy, looks like, and cuts my hair. He knows stories of being a self-made man, self-trained, and Bible proud. When he studies my head sometimes he drifts away, and the flab in his face becomes as stern as a tree. He will raise his hands and cut and comb the wavy air at his thing there. A faceless Happy waits for me, in a red leather chair with stainless steel arms, his melted face a noseless joy as he bursts into laughter and shows all his teeth like a retarded child practically panic-stricken to see a naked woman's picture jammed into the withered clay leaves of *True Detective*. Black Joseph says, "Let me see that," and holds it so that I can see in the mirror it is my mother. . . The Giant Contessa had beautiful hands and the love of a man called Jonah. Black Joseph is so-called because there lives a White Joseph in Dimple. Happy's nose, eyelids mostly, lips, ears, and hair were eaten by fire, and because you could not grow skin on trees or in pink little dishes in those days, his mask becomes apparent. If a Hollywood makeup artist put glasses, a nose, ears and hair, and all the skin of age upon your head, through patiently delicate unconsciously deliberate innuendoes of time, then poured kerosene over your head and set a lit match to it as you slept, your head would look like that. You would dress cleanly, every day the same gray uniform, shirt, pants, white socks, black shoes and belt, black watch, bravely no hat and your hands never burnt, perfectly clean, even as Sperry's helper. You would take pride in your uniform, attend church on Sunday, know your motto, take pride in the little things, joy in a Coca-Cola, smoke, or sandwich. A Snicker could mean the world to you, in the wrapper, frozen. The spinning chair, the spinning world, the spinning globe at school. The turning tire puckering off the wheel at Sperry's garage. Rubber George, the Knight children called him, not Happy Hutchin as did those versed in his winning ways, blessed by his quiet, whose feet he washed.

Pray hard. Work hard. Love hard. Happy said. Quoting Jonah. A shameful, beautiful thing, said the barber, and handed the picture to me. Oh! said Happy, and slapped his knee. He grimaced and a silent hee-haw came from him. For the woman bathed in moonlight, big as an embryo, Happy prayed.

William Herbert Bell, Jr. 1994

Jenny Lind: a nineteenth-century soprano and type of spooled furniture popular in nurseries.

CHAPTER ONE

The Giant Contessa had beautiful hands and the love of a man called Jonah. We called him the Muleskinner because he kept two old mules in the yard behind his house. His house was like the manager's headquarters for a junkyard centuries old, but all or 99 percent of the junk in the yard and house was removed by him to closets or sold for cash. The backyard had third- and fourth-generation mimosa trees, peach trees, pod-bearing trees, and palm trees set tastefully in the ground almost completely covered with lustrous, rich St. Augustine grass he and the children kept mowed. He called the mules his children. When I was a kid, basically, and he was a middle-aged man, I used to stand under the branches of a pod-bearing tree outside his fence, a chain-link fence, and watch the mules eat and stand around and flick their ears. When they bit at each other, flung their heads back, or spun biting their tail-roots to get at flies, it thrilled me. Sometimes in the midst of a heat-struck, sun-drenched, absolutely frozen nap we three shared, me hidden, them in the yard somewhere, but all where some sun could hit us, one of the children would snort or slowly, gently, but assuredly crank up a hee-haw, hee-haw, and I'd smile involuntarily a smile I was donated. . .

Jonah had problems like everybody. For one thing, he had no human family we knew of and he wasn't a kid anymore. It was for us understandable why he hung around the Countess Eileen so much, especially in the morning and at night, when anybody passing through could see he loved her. There's a gap between people starving to death for love, where light and darkness and things pretend to be but aren't. It was all over the Countess Eileen when he was there. The Countess Eileen was a gift-curio shop the Giant Contessa inherited from her mother who began life as a schoolteacher in Corpus. The Contessa's mother was her only family and was dead before I was born, but my mother told me for years how she was a "regular, beautiful woman who got in trouble and had to quit teaching school." The same wording all my life growing up. We'd be on the pier at Woodcock, fishing or just enjoying the sunset after a big dinner of fried seafood and sliced tomatoes with hush puppies and local relish, and french fries, and iced tea, and Mom would start talking about the Contessa's mother, how she "got into trouble and had to quit teaching school. . . a regular, beautiful woman." She would look out toward La Vaca Island seven miles away, with the wind off the bay making her look unlike my mother, eerily, and younger, and she would be squinting powerfully and say the thing she always said.

Jonah's mules had rings around their eyes like bleached-out tee shirts, but I can't remember what color they were, a jenny and a jack, or which was older or bigger, whether they were brother or sister. They confused everything but kept it quiet. They kept the confusion on track and moving, unlike dogs that bring more verve and sadness, or real kids that complicate worse than confuse. I cut my chest one time, reaching over the fence to pet them where they relaxed so rarely together. I figured what a coup, to touch them both together, to put a thumbtip on one, a finger on another. I had to lurch to do it, and think I achieved it, but when I fell back off the fence my shirt ripped and blood soaked through around my navel, like a streak or a dagger was pressed against the outside of my shirt by a ghostly knight invisible in daylight and had cut me according to its graceful form, with the ball handle at the point of entry and the pristine tip at my navel. A steel burr on the fence had cut me.

When I got home that evening Dad asked me what happened. He was quite at peace, smoking a cigarette in his chair. I told him exactly the truth, and he said simply, "Son, I've quit the insurance business."

Mom came in and pulled the shirt off me. She was doleful, slacked-out tired. She put the shirt in the sink and ran additional water on it.

"What do you mean, Dad?"

"I mean it's over, done with, son. I don't run the debit anymore."

Dad was the worst in the business. He just wasn't cut out to collect money. Mom said he wasn't cut out for anything, or anything involving money. He sat in his suit pants and wing tips, with his feet crossed like an earl. His tie was not untied and his shirt was white as snow on the breast of an angel.

"That's good, Dad. I'm proud of you," I said, surprising the entire world and all its money.

He looked back at Mom in the kitchen, hunched over the sink with her tall shoulders thinning out and the long apron bow hanging limp. He folded his paper and leaned out toward me. His eyes crazied with his dream, and he said he was buying the Hot Spring Spa.

"With what?! With what?!" Mom shouted. She looked like somebody dying to defecate.

Dad just smiled and opened his *Sports Section* and said an oo-doggie. The utterance of an oo-doggie was his way of making a patch on the blown tire of their time together, so that they could blow it up by huff and puff again, and thus the machine of dreams again, get her pumped up again, and it always worked.

"Oo-doggie!" he said again, reading.

Silently laughing and crying stood Mom at the sink. Thin Mom, pretty Mom. And I went in there, to her, and took over the dishes from yesterday, atop which floated like a man-o'-war my shirt in its fog of blood. I hung it out to dry in the yard, on the eternal wire Dad had successfully anchored to silver-painted poles with concrete plugging the tops. Then I hosed myself off to clean the wound and bathe. I thought for a minute what to do. The sun was still high and bright. I wanted to leave them alone, not to suffer, and I decided to walk to the Hot Spring.

I did not think of the Giant Contessa, or Mother or Father or seafood, iced tea, the mules or anything I think of constantly now. I thought to remember the knight who wounded me, and why.

CHAPTER TWO

Jonah's mules had names but I couldn't know what they were. So I called them Gus and Stinky. Without knowledge, this common thread runs through us all. All the way the five miles toward Woodcock, through Dimple, to the spa Dad said he bought, south across the sands of time where on either side of the road grew green sorghum and maize topped out forever without stint till it got too close to the sea and had to stop because it had nowhere to grow, I didn't hear or see a car. I didn't hear or see a person. It was a cloudy, still, sunshiny day, though, and a roadrunner guided me all the way: five miles with a bird in the lead. You could smell the ocean where we lived, and even further inland, but because it was there so close all the time, like a puddle that never vanishes, or a monstrous pond, you never smelled it or watched it after enough years.

It was love between Dad and Mom, that oo-doggie. It meant he was wrong or indebted for pretending. He could pretend he quit a job or had money, but his only real work ever was to make a clean impression on a dirty world quickly, here, now, and always. He showered all the time, and went through shirts like Kleenex. His hair was always perfect but I never saw him get it cut. I used to fear his money was gleaned from cash-made premiums physically handed to him by ignorant whole life owners who got double and triple and quadruple billed so we could eat, have walls around us, and him have his starched shirts.

I got to the spa and saw it all run down. The spa was what I called the Hot Spring inside myself. A ranch-style tract home built off by itself amid pod-bearing trees was the location grown people went to to get away from it all, the pressures of city life in Corpus. Houston had a place closer to it than this, so the people nearest it went there. I have heard the name of it but dismiss it now... Our spa was a pale, pale yellow tract home elled around a natural mineral spring heated by the core of the earth. And the spring was gray. Out in the middle was a hole deeper than I or my friend when we walked out to it just to see. It happened that same night I got cut on the fence burr (day) and Dad announced over the sports page he was quitting insurance. Before I forget or die let me say: the house front door was padlocked but thin, a cheap yellow door of veneer, and Chet broke it down (lie, he smashed it in), and inside the house was like an office with brown modern furniture Chet wanted to demolish but I said, "No, dumbfuck. It's Dad's!" He kicked the back sliding-glass door with the sole of his tennis shoe out of night-habit, and I unlocked and opened it by lifting a notched-out lever down and up.

On the patio around the natural spa sat iron lawn furniture dead in the moonlight. We had no reason to talk, but did, like human birds, little helpless owls crossed with mean sparrows, evil progeny. Chet cackled soprano like a cardinal's voice, but redundantly. It was beautiful and solid, like our dumbfuck friendship that lasted forever. We took off our clothes in front of each other and sat across a round iron table not bolted down. It got quiet. You could feel an anger in the empty tent of cicadas waiting and waiting to fuck their green brains out. Then Chet lifted his head just a little bit and the world of the spa just exploded with rattles from the pod-bearing limbs overhead. This drum beat and spun bigger in the mindless hands of God till Chet arose from his chair and sleepily walked over to the shallowest edge of the spa, into the gray newness, and yours truly followed. We walked like spacemen on the moon out toward the middle, getting quickly deeper and steadily deeper, with unclean, hard lost articles underfoot repulsive as snot spat into your ear by some chance. But it was hardened under the soles of your feet.

"Will, I think I'm in the middle where the hole is," Chet said. The water was up around his chin. We had heard rumors of all the sex that went on there, that you had to be in the middle for the true feeling.

"Feel it with your foot, downward," I said. The water was up to my shoulders and softly sulfuric.

He turned away from me and slipped into another world not unlike the sea with its animals hungry for eternity and coming to meet you. That he stayed down for a moment stirred my heart for one of the few times in my life it has ever been stirred. It was quick. A bird spinning at death into the seat of your hands. I stepped away from him, and when he came up he had something floppy in his teeth.

"What's that?" I said.

He spat it powerfully at me and I missed catching it in the water.

"Go for it, pussy," he said, good-heartedly.

I dived under and felt across sand till I found it. I carried it up and stood with it in my one hand like a man with a short, stubby carrot. The pliant softness of it was like the outside of a child's floaty and not mossy or grimy.

"Chet!" I said, because I couldn't see him. The cicadas died like a chorus of monks and I turned to leave him, when he grabbed my ankle and being stronger, not bigger, pulled me down. We wrestled to the point of drowning before he kicked me in the chest and forced away.

Pissed off but laughing, I breaststroked to the side that was deep, where the timid could stand and wave their arms in the waters, and Chet lit a cigarette in a chair.

"What the fuck is that thing, Chet?" I asked.

He drew a mighty mature manly drag off his cigarette.

"It's a dildo, you fucking dildo."

I had luckily dropped it and didn't know where it was anymore.

CHAPTER THREE

Chet had him a bellyful of beer later that night on the pier. The pier was a straight shot a hundred yards out into the bay. It looked like the most impressive thing in Woodcock toward the sea, like something Old World European, and it showed the ambition of the town. Everybody's ambitious, I think, except maybe monks. Woodcock had an antique store called the Fallen Apple or Fallen Apples across the street from Contessa Eileen's, I mean the Countess Eileen (sorry), and it was Chet's mother's. She practically lived there because Chet's dad was obsessed with junk he collected seriously and kept treasured in a shed. It drove her crazy because she had a taste for high quality she was born with. In Fallen Apples was an old picture of an old monk in Burma or some fucking place taken with a Polaroid in the '50s. I used to like to stare in his eyes and talk *to* him when no one was around. And one night when I was sleeping over at Chet's house (we were about fifteen), I got up to drink a Coke by myself in their kitchen (it must have been about dawn, because it was that night after the spa raid and we stayed out real late) and I had this auditory vision of Tung Hsi, the old monk, saying this poem from right where he stood in the picture, with the greenery around him moving as in life:

> They call you Steelhead
> and you wonder why they do—
> the frozen shutter.

I wrote it down on a napkin, with a pen off the refrigerator, and woke up Chet. We were supposed to go to work, anyway. I felt a trigger in me being pulled, squeezing. Chet looked like an old man, with his hair all ratted from sleep. His arms were hard and muscular like his mom's, stringy and veiny.

"Aw, shit—" he said, and put on his white rubber boots. I was arched above him like a human bow leaning on an arrow, maybe floating in the hands of a ghost. I told him the poem, memorized.

He took this seriously, which was always his way underneath.

"Man, you're blessed," he said, like some fucking missionary selflessly pronouncing sentence.

Chet took the napkin with the poem on it from my hand, and handed it back to me. I had the sense that, as brave and sincere as he was on top and inside, he could accomplish anything. Like his father, he could steal from the dead. Like his mother, he could use what he stole. . .

CHAPTER FOUR

I guess there might have been five hundred souls in Woodcock itself in those days. The closer-set little burgs would've added a few hundred more. Esperanza had fifty. Dimple, twenty-five. Nehi three and two dead in a private cemetery belonging to one family, mine. Cursorville where nothing happened and no one lived, where there used to be a ranch, and all the buildings of wood and stone from far away had that glamor of purity Chet's mom, Marguerite, loved. She used to go out there and stand around and smoke cigarettes winsomely, Chet said, wishing she had married someone else. Chester and Marguerite Evans had had to marry out of dignity in the town of Beeville quite young. Their progeny had no peers, my best friend. On the other end, I had two brothers, Trout and Merkel, under six feet of sand across the road.

"But we own it," Dad said one Thanksgiving. We owned the house in Nehi and the land where the cemetery was. Mexicans under a huisache tree or a big mesquite had been buried there so long ago, before the revolution making Texas a separate nation short-lived officially and ever infantile by holy spirit, that Dad said they didn't count anymore because their bodies were utterly gone: "Buried in boxes," Dad said. Chet's father agreed. *Los Dias Allegros* was stitched in pre-revolutionary iron painted white and pink and horrific lime before time sucked off the pigment down to the original rust-wish of the iron. Dad sold the Mexican cemetery sign to Mr. Evans for cash money, and Mr. Evans put it on a blanket in his treasure shed. Chet's mom lit a confiscated cigarette and folding her arm across her flat bone stomach and resting her cigarette arm's bent elbow on the clenched fist of it, leaned her spiritual belly against the kitchen sink and cried to see her husband of twelve or thirteen years drag it into the shed. Chet said he did not want me to offer to help him and his dad do the work of unloading the sign off Chet's dad's truck of artifacts and then treasuring it up in the treasure shed. Thus I stayed in the kitchen with his mom who must have then been twenty-seven. I probably had some sense I'd have to stay inside with her. She had one foot out of a shoe.

"It's such a waste to die," she said.

The light in the kitchen where she stood at the window was a changing replica of the light in an oyster shell open or shut, day or night, with flies in it or hung on a thong for a girl. She put her thumb on her eye tooth and breathed out smoke. Chet's father came in to wash his hands, and the hem of her lank dress moved like a curtain.

Me and Chet had separate low-skill jobs doing chores at THE CONSPICUOUS ABSENCE OF WISDOM OF ANY SORT bar and the private harbor, new that year, where boats of all sorts docked below it. Papa Lopez was our immediate liaison, and he told us what to do in such vague or perfectly balanced words that we got paid for a half day's work, got fed good food from the tavern, got to see pretty girls and people-watch the rich cool sailors slide in and out of the tavern in awe of the outcast misfit demigod shrimpers with hot family to go to. . . we got paid for doing, to all extents and purposes, practically nothing. Sometimes the owner's wife walked by smelling of powders and bathwater and wine, across the big chunk gravel of the massive parking lot, wearing thin leather sandals with sundials or smiling suns as buckles, and an expensive Italian sun dress that swished in her gliding arms. Even a boy sensed what to do with her. Chet saw her thighs define her skirt as she mounted the final cedar stair into the Cypress Hatch bar where people waited for tables further in, over the water, and put her pliant hand upon the padded inner door to the office, where a half-dozen pictures of seashells hung, and he told me he'd give anything in the world to count the holes in her body. Then her husband the boss man came through from the boat dock, twice her age, tan and healthy, with a solid-gold diver's watch on his thick wrist and elephant hair on the other, and he followed his wife inside.

The padded office door sighed. It had a sea horse medallion upon it. I should have reported right at first, when you saw her walk in smelling dusty sweet and looking strong innately, that the door was made of cypress off the hatch of a trawler of yore. On the side that faced you was padded red leather like on an executive couch, with big brass nails preserving the puffs in the pad thick enough that the sea horse medallion nested inside a shadow-box frame at her face level as you pushed it. Her husband and she had it custom made to swing inward. The opposite face, on the inside of the office, was pure cypress of the trawler hatch, with brass compasses and navigating tools set into it, and seashells and privately meaningful items eternitized in pockets like on the bay floor a few feet away, buried under clear yellow laminate or laminant a quarter-inch thick. The hinges of the door had place of origin (Chicago) forged within them, and off the door would have weighed as much as a baby, each. Three of them, finalizing the impression of eternity the quiet folk with money sought for, and probably fought for.

"Damn, they're clean," Chet stated.

Papa Lopez walked by, a wizened old man like the humanized bite off a stick of red jerky or the twisted-up strip off a plug of tobacco, wearing his old blue golf cap (having never golfed in his life, I bet), and picked up a trash can from the ideal shade of the Cypress Hatch men's room to empty. Chet tried to take it from his hand, but Papa Lopez wouldn't let him. He was mad about something.

CHAPTER FIVE

Sometimes the boss man is nowhere around and you have a moment to yourself. At a glance you see the waitresses are gone and the only sound is that of machines, air conditioners, jukeboxes, iceboxes, the cars on the road out front. The sparkling ocean behind you makes no sound. Sparrows dance on the balustrade across the back of THE CONSPICUOUS ABSENCE OF WISDOM OF ANY SORT bar, and sailboats, speedboats, a skimmer, and a lonely little shrimp boat wobble to a jerky little waltz. You steal a Coke and drink it proudly like a man with real responsibilities, and belch. And when you belch, the new-blossoming perfumy mimosa on the hill wobble like the boats and the little funny world, the sparrows fly away replaced by a gull sailing horizontal or parallel to the flat thick plane of the window over the dock, and a girl appears who doesn't matter, half or less than half the height and weight of the giantess.

She appears first in the casket-size rectangle of the side door of the bar, like in a camera flash or a fish falling backwards out of a bowl of silver milk, breaking from sunlight, just as you start up the vacuum cleaner to save your ass 'case it's the boss's wife catching you with a Coke being paid really for nothing, but she isn't so much a vision inside the bursting casket of sunshine as she is a girl of smell, a girl smell you've never smelled before. The girl smell is embedded in her hair of unwed curls like the hair of a girl of Pompeii. Then it's blonde and massed so thick and free and floppy with a floating comb in it the size of a harmonica that the bay below her feet (visible through the floor of the restaurant) would at its highest make a similar head of wild foam amoebic in the rocks.

She's a blonde Mexican girl your age an arm's length or Hoover's length from you, and you can't hear the Hoover running for her voice you hear not as words but voicing lips purchasing your soul as they purse and blow and pink and show teeth that have been cared for, but her nose is perfect and her hand floats up on a brown arm to hide her eyes from the sun two hours behind you. Her Little Dipper eyes make a truthful impression like she is not looking through you at something else as through a window. Her eyes were like squeeze bottles of honey you could suck on.

I turned off the Hoover.

"Papa says you should come to his house to pick up your paycheck."

"What about Chet's check?"

That didn't register right, the English sound being funny. Her brow dramatically wrinkled where she moved her fingers. I really felt thankful the refrigerator behind the wet bar was running.

"I mean my buddy's paycheck."

But she didn't say anything. She just tilted her head and looked right at me and turned away and walked back into the casket of light. It was an eternal thing. The refrigerator stopped before I could turn on the Hoover.

CHAPTER SIX

We got a ride with the King of Darts and his drunken idiot friend Sperry out to Papa's house in Esperanza. Papa Lopez said we'd know his house by the big orange sunflowers in the yard. Not the new girl, but he himself had told Chet how to recognize his house among the others unnumbered thereabouts. Sperry kept turning around in his seat (he rode shotgun up front with the King) and laughing at me and Chet, cackling and giggling with his mouth on a long neck. A drunken idiot will look at you and laugh from his passionate, peerless, pristine world.

"Oh, man! Goin' to live with the wetbacks!" he said.

I looked smart-assed at him and knew he'd never have a girl as pretty and fine as that new girl.

The King of Darts was a red-haired construction worker who hung around Woodcock in the summers. He was worldly and quiet and probably really admired Big Stud Mingus, the owner of THE CONSPICUOUS etc. I had a strong feeling like the calm side of horror that the King of Darts' real life was harder than almost anyone's. Something about true red-haired people who have to work in the sun makes them stiffen. He looked stiff as a plank of cedar the first time I ever saw him lean against the cypress bar, a slim glass of beer in his red and white, freckled fingers.

We found the house with the orange sunflowers, and Chet, like an apprentice to His Hardness the King of Darts, got out without having said a word all the way from Woodcock and he didn't thank the King. I did, though, and the idiot riding shotgun said to his master, like a human seal who could talk to his trainer: "That fucking little bastard. Somebody oughta Dutch rub that motha-fucka," and laughed with the bottle in his mouth.

The King just lifted his head.

I got out and stepped to the porch. Chet pulled up a sunflower on a wire out of the sandy loam of Papa's house. The King's car drove quietly away north to somewhere, and La Vaca Bay, our bay, paled blue under green like a chilled green face. I remembered when it turned red once, a long time ago, because a red weed floated in from far away. Tourists were advised not to touch the weed. It stayed all winter. Fish died and Woodcock went to hell except for the shrimpers who'll work through anything because they're industrious and always need money. The problem with a boat is if you lose it, it goes away. I think it's very possible that down deep the King of Darts wished he could learn to be a fisherman of some kind so he could learn a steady art that wouldn't depend on a boss and he could live in Woodcock year round.

Old Lopez came to the door and I was amazed by the way he looked without his cap. His hair was plastered down with sweat to the shape of his skull and he looked about nine-tenths Indian. The new girl skulked like a disenchanted ballerina under a doorjamb at the back of the dark front room behind him. He handed me our paychecks in separate white business envelopes with our names on them and smiled very privately, wishing to shut the door. The girl behind him had changed clothes and pulled back her curly thick hair like a Christmas tree bundled tight with twine. I couldn't smell her because an old woman had three pots of food going in the kitchen.

Coarsely, Chet said, "Come on, man. Let's get out of here," like we were not belongers and he didn't want to be.

"Gracias, señor," I said.

He shut the door and the whole Mexican world became trapped in a crack the thickness of a dollar where the door met the jamb it would probably never touch on every side. I still tried to smell what they were eating. Someone had planted a fast-growing tree for shade behind the house, and a lone cicada spun from it buzzing like an old fighter plane.

"I'll call her Mig till I see her again," I thought.

"What'd you say?" Chet laughed like a cousin to the idiot.

I must have been moving my lips. I told him to kiss my ass because we were true friends and always would be, we'd said so aloud and sober as judges on the pier one night. On the way back to Woodcock, we opened our envelopes and saw our pay was precisely the same. I felt, in the heat of the still dusk, that I had a risen brother from the grave to walk with me. The afternoon was beautiful by the bay, with Mexican hat and Johnny-jump-up-like wildflowers that nature and the State of Texas put there hot and still and exquisitely motionless along the road back to town, not ten feet from the chunks of boulders and old ruined house and building foundations and huge stumps and concrete-shrouded telephone poles that protected the flowers and the road from the sea.

We didn't talk the several miles back to Woodcock, not because we were mad or Chet was mad at me for what I'd said to shut him up, but just because of existence. We enjoyed it. It's a real common prayer when you can be silent with a friend and not worry, not mourn it, like sometimes later in life. At a bait house we bought two beers from a crippled Mexican because he knew Chet's dad owned the Circle C convenience store, and as we drank them openly down toward the Sportsman's Lodge across the road from THE CONSPICUOUS ABSENCE OF WISDOM OF ANY SORT bar, where the young Mrs. Mingus lived and drank and bathed, and which her husband, Big Stud, also owned, I just hoped against hope Chet would end up more like the King and less like the idiot, in the long run.

CHAPTER SEVEN

Chet's dad, Chet Senior, had this store called the Circle C right at the corner of Beach Road and the highway to Corpus. It was a very tidy convenience store that sold everything from Muguet de Bois to Shiner beer, dog biscuits to banana chips. "A real convenience store doesn't sell ripe bananas," he used to say to me and Chet Junior sucking on root beer bottles full of real beer right in front of him. His sense of smell was shot since he'd smoked since he was nine years old up in Poetry, where his father was a guard-orderly in a madhouse.

"Yeah," he'd say, looking over a bag of banana chips at some high school girl passing outside, "not a god-blessed thing ever happened in Poetry," then he'd open up a bag of Tom's salted peanuts and offer me and his son one. He'd pull a bag of dried banana chips off the goodies rack by the cash register and look at it like a physician examining a mole and say, "Who the fuck ever eats these things?" then slide it back on respectfully through the hole. Chet Senior was the only dad of a friend who ever cursed manly in front of me. I never felt less of him for it, and never cut him down in my mind. He moved to the side window to get a better view of that high school girl who might have been barely in junior high school, and he looked at her like a person gazing at a crystal ball or very rare trinket.

"That ain't the Woodcock girl, is it?" he said. He sounded almost crazy, and his adult eyes were hazy, like history and now were movies of flesh and blood he was living in, reeling in, obsessed as he was with keeping account and the Woodcock name. Chet Junior laughed fearfully with love and respect for his father and told him the Woodcock girl was about ten years old. He didn't know who the girl was. Then Mr. Evans looked at Mr. Evans Junior like a man dazzled by a shocking tale, and said, "Oh really?" and gave him a peanut, then me one, too.

A scrawny, suffering, sick cat walked by the store and before Chet Senior could see it, I went outside and chased it meanlike across the road where there was nothing but a field. The field was full of Mexican hat and brown-eyed Susans, and the ditch the cat had to cross to get to the field and hide was spuming with bluish purple-and-white Johnny-jump-ups. I had seen Chet's dad shoot a cat with a hunting slingshot, once, using a ball bearing, and the bullet struck the cat in the hindquarters and broke its leg so that it scurried away in a fluffy, three-legged way into the same beautiful field. I had run from the store, across the road and the ditch, into the field to look for the cat, but the field became too thick and high and thorny to penetrate even on my belly. I saw flattened cans and rubbers and toothbrush containers, cigarette butts and lipstick cases and a Lillian Vernon catalogue used for toilet paper turning into dirt, and touched them all with my hands.

It was years before the summer my dad left the insurance business and bought the Hot Spring. I was maybe ten years old and my brother Merkel was still alive. He was in a hospital for invalids. He looked like my dad in miniature and never grew. He had every problem under the sun. Being with Merkel was like sitting with an elf in a giant shoe.

CHAPTER EIGHT

It must have been a Friday night coming on, because it was Fire Engine Tradition Night and every Mexican from miles around was pouring into Woodcock. It was a new thing to keep the young people of the area from getting into trouble. On some Friday nights as many as a hundred kids, some you'd never seen before, went down to the big pier I described and waited for the antique '40s fire truck to arrive from the shed where it was stored at the firehouse, just to be able to stand around it and talk. Until the fire truck arrived, without regalia or pomp, the young people just milled about stupidly, without a clue as to what to say or do. I know this because I was one of them. So was Chet Junior. There's a certain impossibility of intelligence you feel inside when you're young. Older, you just know it but you don't feel it much anymore. The general stupidity in which all forgiveness finds root.

After chasing the living cat into the field, away from Chet's dad's store, the Circle C, I saw two Mexican kids younger than me come riding in on mules. They came from the direction of Vigoroso, a community like Dimple but all

Mexican, to the left of the store if you faced away from the sea. I have always called the bay the sea, and I always will. Simply, all bodies of salt touch each other. In sweat and tears, all bodies belong to the sea of bodies that weep and work. The mules they rode, like Jonah's mules, but not the same, different (snow white, matched) and smaller, sweated. Their beautiful dreamy eyes dreamed of food, I imagine.

The night fell slowly. I wanted to put my head down on something and go to sleep. Chet came out with a twelve-pack of Shiner and said right in front of either his dad or the tourist girl's dad escorting her down to Fire Engine Tradition Night: "Let's get fucked up," to me. I regretted it, like I have regretted so many things.

We took the twelve-pack to an abandoned clubhouse we knew about up in the live oaks, and drank it all. Chet drank six or eight beers, and I had three or four. It was two six-packs on a cardboard slat, half a case. . . I poured one of the beers on top of my head because I felt like it.

"You're a dumbfuck, Bell," Chet said, sitting in the window of the clubhouse.

"Fuck you," I said, and crawled out through this funnel-hole of vines that led to the road that shone in the moonlight. The old rickety pier that belonged to the sportsmen that owned the club back in the 1920s was still intact, and I leapt onto it from a big chunk of house foundation that was dumped off the beach road and broken, and I ran all the way out to the end of the pier and dove into the sea.

I swam around for awhile, and when I got out Chet was on the road, standing quite still.

"I thought you were dead, man. I thought you were fucking dead."

He sounded like a Mexican, but he wasn't acting. A car drove past madly, like the driver understood something more important than life could prepare him for. The windows were all the way down, and you could smell him. He was going so fast the music stretched from his radio in the aftermath of his passing. Chet lit a cigarette and handed it to me. I puffed on it.

"I honest to fucking God thought you were dead, man!" he said excitedly, meaningfully. "You scared the shit out of me, man!" he said sincerely. I felt proud, alive, and my scalp prickled with the bloody thorns of love sticking out of it. "Man, every kind of fucking animal in the world is in that water at night. Sharks and rays and shit. Fucking giant crabs and shit! Goddamn!" he cursed, happier now. I took the mostly empty beer bottle from his hand and dropped my cigarette into it. He laughed quietly and looked out to sea.

CHAPTER NINE

After that, we walked in darkness down Beach Road towards the big construction site that was supposed to be some big thing someday but which had been dragging on for years, ever since my family moved to the area from some fucking place when I was an infant or good as. The reason we walked that way, instead of back the other way towards THE CONSPICUOUS ABSENCE OF WISDOM OF ANY SORT bar and Fire Engine Tradition Night still no doubt going beyond (toward Chet's dad's store), was that Chet knew of a place where a woman slept with her window open at night, who lived alone near the construction site. He confidently asserted she was a widow who had lost her mind to loneliness and stayed drunk all the time, or doped. He said she had a good body and lay still as a leaf if you stayed quiet. I had never seen a naked woman except in magazines I found along the road, and I thrilled in my stomach in hopes it would be so.

"You can't touch her," Chet said.

"Oh, yeah, like I'm gonna open the screen on her window and reach in and feel her skin."

"You don't understand, man. She's a poor widow without screens," Chet said.

It was two miles, about, to the widow's, a cabin of dark, plain wood nailed together with shingles. The eves of the squarelike structure almost touched the tops of our heads. Chet's hair was in a grown-out crew cut, and a skinny nail sticking through the eve pierced his scalp. He hissed and grabbed his head. I laughed and grabbed his arm muscle. We felt along the walls to each window, and found each window a gutless square, a crossless hole with nothing beyond. I couldn't even smell a woman.

"Chet, you are fucking crazy, man, there's no one in there! It's just a fucking shack!"

He put his hand over my mouth. I could smell a dozen cigarettes on it he'd smoked since cashing our checks at the Circle C. I shoved his arm away.

"Listen!" he hissed.

I couldn't hear anything. He took my wrist and pulled me around the next corner of the square shack to the next window, and stood there in front of the window a moment transfixed. He pressed his pelvis against the bottom of the window like a sleepwalking person, and gazed inward through the top of the window. I pushed him away like one soul pushing another off Charon's boat, and stepped into place where he had stood. There became apparent the form of a woman lying on a bed or cot. She lay like a low mountain range washed with celestial milk. . .

Chet pulled me back. Her house was in a grove of live oaks bushy and low, so that even the forlorn construction workers who worked in the site nearby might not have seen it under the trees.

"She's naked, man!" he said.

"No, man. She's got something white on," I said.

"That's her skin, man! You dumbfuck!" he railed.

Just then, a light came on in the house and we jumped behind a tree. The woman got up from bed and put on a robe in darkness. We couldn't tell what was happening, and I hadn't heard a sound.

"We've got to fucking see what's happening," Chet said.

I told him no and pulled him back toward the way we'd come in under the trees from the road, but he jerked away and slunk toward the other side of the house, towards the sea, where the lit window was. He came running back to me in a minute, in a state of shock, and simply said, "Let's go. Right now."

As we left, the wind shifted. It circled the little shed, and I smelled mules. I imagined Jonah's mules or the Mexican kids' mules grazing on turtle grass or Mexican hat or Johnny-jump-ups under the low eves of the Giant Contessa's house. For I had seen the Giant Contessa bathed in milk, and I had fed on the very honeydew of female possibility. A regular woman doesn't look like a mountain range under a sheet of milk, with all the gold and silver and gems in the world buried under the snow. . . a Tootsie Roll washed in cream.

> Who bears a lantern
> and lights a shed by the sea?
> —the bawling of mules.

CHAPTER TEN

The Giant Contessa had beautiful hands and the love of a man called Jonah. She lived in a meager hut by a construction site, obscured by live oaks a thousand years old at the north edge of town opposite Chet's dad's store. Her mother got pregnant out of wedlock, like Chet's mom, but unlike Chet's mom, never abandoned by her dreamer, the Giant Contessa's father abandoned her. I don't know much else. I know so little, so precious little, you person, and all of it is black and white. And when what I lie about mixes with what I know, I find dead things rotting in color where the black-and-white life used to be thriving and hoping and courageous and laughing. I feel bad that the last chapter, nine by my log, is such an anemic rendition of what happened the night after we cashed our checks at the Circle C and walked past the girls on the donkeys, past the Fire Engine Tradition Night festivities (teenagers talking over Cokes and IBC root beers, red Nehis and Big Oranges crunched out of coolers thick with charitable ice). . . I feel like I failed you person, and the Lord God who made this black pen and white paper, these measurements lined in blue, La Vaca Bay, Woodcock, Chet's dad's dream, my dad's dream, our precious mothers' wombs and needs, our stupidity so colorful and gay. . .

It was all thirty years ago. The construction site became the baby blue world its maker dreamed of. All of this is too real for names. The only names that matter, anyway, are the names of heroes and the women they loved. Today, trying to decide how to continue, praying for guts, I crossed the corpses of a gull, a yellow-breasted warbler, a sparrow. I lifted my canteen to the royal palms a hundred years old where the rich folks' hotel used to be when I was young, that became the poor folks' hotel when I was not young, and Chet wasn't either, anymore. But I gave the hotel a moment's monument, a strong swig of something cold, and told her I love her. Gone. She's gone. She is fucking gone with the wind with dead birds at her feet. Nothing left but an old foundation. . . Half our town is gone, dead or gone on foot; a plastic sign flaps against a chain-link fence, troops of knightly sunflowers who've lost their heads haunt the road along the sea, and every bar and cafe's name but one has changed a dozen times since then.

But, you love and don't forget.

After we left the Giant Contessa's cabin, Chet was in shock. He never told me what he saw. But he had to have seen Jonah loving on the Giant Contessa, sucking and squeezing and smoothing all the qualities of the veil.

We broke into the Blue Bait House and stole two quarts of Miller beer and suckled those past the part of the Perry Mason beach where time and tide breathe warm as pussy, past the hulk of a wastrel craft called *Serene*, a two-man shrimper, down to where the Mexican kids were still talking, mixed with a handful of misbegotten white kids lean and happy and lucky as stupid dogs who know no hatred not inborn. We saw the two girls, *las bonitas, las guapas, las señoritas, las amores del* someday, aboard their cousins' horses called mules by me wrongly forever. . . like a sin to damage their sisterful picture with facts. . . and ever in love with me: Eustacia Lopez. My U-U.

Chet saw her and loved her, too, but never told me till a few days later.

CHAPTER ELEVEN

As I say, in those days neither Chet nor I had ever counted the holes in a woman. It was a silent source of endless mystery for us to ponder in male solitude as we went about our chores at the restaurant and at home. Because it was the summer, we had no school. I figured out just today, standing on the landlocked sandbar beside the Shotgun Lodge marina, sucking on a root beer and staring at the edge of the earth, where La Vaca Island buffers into a flatness like a mystic pancake the green sea and the blue sky, that it must have been a Thursday Dad lost his job collecting insurance money from poor people. It must've been a Thursday he lied about it to Mom. It must have been a Thursday night we busted into the Hot Spring and Chet fetched the marital aid from the warm force bursting soft from the bottom of the hole. Because the next night was Fire Engine Tradition Night, the first night I ever fell in love oo-doggie style with a girl who could get pregnant if I or someone just touched her wrong, though I didn't know how or by what entrance God would generate through me another fleck of Himself.

She sat full astride the donkey, in short shorts skin tight just standing up. On the horse she feared they might split. But women are fashioned in such a self-girdled way, this rarely happens. Even big bulky fat women laughing their hearts out rarely split out their breeches while seated on a donkey. (The Mexicans' donkeys that night were big, not burros, and thus the colorful confusion with horses. Also, the smell of a horse, the smell of a mule, the smell of a donkey, and the smell of a burro hint point blank of their similar value.)

She wore a pastel blue cotton sleeveless blouse entirely buttoned like the story life really is.

Other girls climbed on frantically, aboard the mule with my U-U. Oh, oh, oh, oh Jesus Christ Almighty I Loved Her. The other girls laughed loudly, and she smiled the smile Mary smiled before She knew anything or God. Oh God God God God God I loved her. I have tried, have this life to remember, to resee the color of her toenails hanging down in new pastel sandals plain and simple and cheap, the sandals of the meek wild poor girls all about the hooves of the donkeys in the oystering earth where the vents and caves of our hearts kept humanizing with the sea-wind-drowning ringing of cicadas in live oak yardlit and noble palm moonlit, open and shut, open and shut go our hearts. The heart of every shrimper and every king, every English queen and every Mexican virgin making the best use of laughter and blue. Her toenails and fingernails were painted pearly blue...

I spent that night at Chet's, too. His dad was out robbing graves and his mom was alone in her room. She smoked that night all night so much you saw the smoke flowing from under her door. I stood barefoot in the membrane of her smoke-embodied breath and wished the smoke was her on me. Chet had a bunk bed because Chet Senior got it for a dollar at a garage sale, and I slept on the bottom that night. Chet had a *Stag* or *Topper* magazine and handed it down to me, without interpretation. The beautiful woman in it had lips and nipples like grape popsicles and eyes like hornets. I asked Chet if he'd noticed, but he was asleep. The brown maple slats under his mattress were like the ribs of a ship. I held the open magazine to my breast and churned a prayer in my penis older than words or worlds, and maybe older than stars or any other ball of yearning dust and water but God. Not touching myself at all, I prayed with my arms wrapped around the purple-lipped priestess flat on paper, for the chance to love in a touchless kiss the new girl.

Then Chet said: "Bell, did you see her nails, her toes and fingers?"

"No. Why?"

His mother's bedroom door slammed down the hall. She blew her nose on toilet paper, and I wanted it, the tears and the self on the tissue.

"They were blue," he verified.

CHAPTER TWELVE

For years after this love happened. . .*(between me and Chet and his mother and U-U and everybody good, but not during that Woodcock summer of the Giant Contessa and Jonah, where I filtered in and out of houses, fear and work and the presence of others by walking everywhere in sunshine and moonlight and by any unmoving light, farm lights and bar lights and matches still for a single moment sheltered against my chest or a Woodcock wall or behind those Goose Island oaks, each powerful Blue Tip match flame perfect as a burning feather in breathless heavy night hungry for its stick, floating ignoring the truth of myself and my family strong as a blackbird scoring the air from the tallest sunflowers it rests upon along the road around the Motts and Nehi and Dimple, screaming his warnings skyward through the clouds and trees and earthward through the other flowers all breathing round him and waving at him and becoming still and frightening as they smell and heat the body of a snake, and the blackbird bobs on the sunflowers, then hops to the reeds and the rushes nearer the sea, and sings away the darker world where its empty nest distreasured weeps a yellow: the belly of the snake: its eggs are gone) I feared my pure soul's drowning in the hole of dreams all remembered love became. The old black and white of real love bled color in those dreams, like negative film developed by the acids of night, and only upon waking did I see clearly the definite colorlessness of pure impossible love nobody can piss on or shit on enough to ever fully foul to the point of getting rid of like bones, hair, leaves, fins, skin, scales, feathers, or pictures in tidibins, dumps or boxes or closets in lurid contact with wasted life. Real black-and-white love was the wake-up call for little gods inside us, if not inside the sunflowers, then inside the turtles and the birds and the people who were really good. The little gods are not hazy fantasies but physical inhabitants of flesh and blood bodies that somehow never age. Old fake colored-over withered-up love is like the make-up applied alone by a little girl or painted on by a paid technician trying to prove a corpse is not a murdered person hid forever in ourselves and everybody sees. . . Years after U-U and Chet and his mom and that summer, I lay in bed with my wife and in total darkness touched her colorless cave, and with loops and whorls and a warm spurting wellspring of blind love explored the entranceway to the first room of my own children. These have been and are the beloved children I have tried to love. My wife stirred and moved and the whole of the world moved like a mountain under the sea, the swallowed cave in the bone-entrenched serpentine warm and salty cavern home a man lives within. Her eyes and mouth opened like holes of ocean and shells of having known. . .* That summer, by Fallen Apples they found a curly haired drowned man dragged from the sea. In his mouth were sea horses, in his ears fiddler crabs. His open eyes were what they were in his room before he was born. For Chet's father, Chet's mother took the drowned man's picture with a Brownie camera as she found him. Chet's father nailed the curly haired drowned man's black leather wallet sea soaked with uninhabited plastic snapshot holder to the side of the Treasure Shed. All the man's pictures and money and cards and papers were gone. His belt had been torn from his waist. The particulate sand in his navel was blue and Chet's father picked it out with a stick broken from a dead willow with his wife and the sheriff from Refugio present, searching for clues.

CHAPTER THIRTEEN

The Giant Contessa had beautiful hands and the love of a man named Jonah. They were in love when I was in love and this is about our love. Everybody knows you write about things when they're gone. The most permanent love letters are written on gravestones. The real love went away with the worms, in the waddle of a woman, the heart of a gnat, the hands of the drowned man waving to the sea, and was wordless. In the song of the cicada, the rhyme for the sigh of youth. . .

Sometime that summer, before the body was found, U-U and I walked up Beach Road, searched the canopies of live oaks tortured by the south wind off the Gulf of Mexico always there, blowing, even still, in heat of summer in Texas a wind always about to blow, blowing, and we hid in trees before we could drive in cars like Chet, six months older, who stole, in live oaks up by the Sportsmen's Club abandoned many years. The club was a messianic shack of cum and rubbers and broken history left by sportsmen, all their glory gone to teenagers and vagrants needing peace and quiet and a place to lie down, for instance, on a hollow door that used to hide a bathroom, now a bed for anyone brave enough or stupid enough to crawl through the secret door under the hair of the live oaks mossy and forlornly wondering, always, always wondering about live-oak things I couldn't understand. . . the hollow-core bathroom door the sportsmen used to shut for privacy in the 1920s and '30s was now our bed, our cot of love. There I just smelled her pimpled cheek and watched her teeth clear her lips because she smiled. The smell of her cheek was corn before you bite into it, her tongue pink as bubble gum, her lips the juicy cob from which water is sucked. She kissed me first, her head tilted like the curly world turned sideways. We both sighed and laughed, already married by all the law and the prophets.

We walked up Beach Road to Shotgun Lodge where Mrs. Stud Mingus had just placed a family of three deer made of statuary stone. The deer looked over the Cypress Bar and THE CONSPICUOUS ABSENCE OF WISDOM OF ANY SORT tavern, toward the bay. The color of the bay was chalky blue like the pastel finger of a hop-scotched child. We sat on the creeping hopeful patch of St. Augustine grass sandy at the feet of the deer and wished we were hitched by human law before Adam and Eve lost the touch, followed by a billion names and holes full of ribs in groves of trees. We ourselves never voiced the wish, which meant we were already married. Above the deer bent live oaks a hundred years old, their crowns touching above the deer and us and the Mingus house which was part of the lodge that was leased to Mexicans and whites and anyone who could afford it. Most could.

Right then I wished we were older, with a family, and owned Shotgun Lodge where people stayed and dreamed happy, like Stud and his family. Then Eustacia elbowed me in the ribs and said, "Look!" It was getting close to dusk and the first lights in buildings were coming on. With the deers' heads not moving, nor Eustacia's, just her eyes, I turned my face to the Mingus's kitchen window and there saw Mrs. Mingus holding a statuary fawn in her arms. The fawn lay folded like a lamb, but alert like in life. Mrs. Mingus moved toward the kitchen door to the path of stones that led to where we were sitting.

U-U was laughing.

"Come on, let's go!" I said. She held my arm down. Her father worked for Mr. Mingus. Or was Papa Lopez her uncle?

"Come on, Eustacia! We don't belong here! This isn't our land!"

Eustacia mocked me and lost the almondness of her eyes. The cicadas in the oaks blew into a chorus of lust as the kitchen door opened and Mrs. Mingus emerged cradling the deer. Her feet were bare and white and she wore a flowing nightgown. She did not see that we were seated among her family of deer facing the faithful sea, and she placed the fourth statue where it belonged at the heels of the doe.

CHAPTER FOURTEEN

F. Brundetti was the drowned man's name, which hasn't got a goddamn thing to do with anything. The sheriff from Refugio came down to question Chet's mom at Fallen Apples and to see where the body was found. I remember he lay stretched alongside Fallen Apples like a man taking a serious nap, or a poverty-stricken day laborer drunk on Thunderbird. His attitude was that of a conscripted sponge diver in blue cotton slacks and a short-sleeve plaid shirt surfacing empty handed. His eyes were opaque memories milky from the sea of Time. But his name hasn't got a goddamn thing to do with anything, a single sunflower growing out of the shrimp boat Serene.

The sheriff from Refugio, a blonde, green-eyed Spaniard with a silver-handled .45, excellently groomed in khaki, badge, and manner with Mrs. Evans at the antique store, stood by himself about noon the same day, eating Mexican peanuts and caliente jerky at the Circle C. He gazed out the window onto Beach Road, his feet widespread in rich brown boots. He was the only nonemployee in the store. When he had finished eating, he tossed the empty packages onto the floor. As if the sun was changing places with a cloud over the refrigerated world of the store, he turned from the window and moved toward Chet Senior carrying a sack.

Chet Senior had parked his truck outside somewhere nontraditional for him, and walked up the front steps of the store, carrying a sack, but I hadn't seen him till he actually passed through the door and the sheriff stepped toward him as he entered, as if to apprehend him.

When Chet Senior produced the valueless (empty) black wallet sun dried off the Treasure Shed wall, the sheriff looked at the hole in the leather made by the nail, fingered it with a tanned forefinger as well groomed as Big Stud Mingus's, and glared at Chet Senior. I opened the cold drink machine and handed the sheriff a root beer. He opened it graciously, manfully, his perfectly engineered fist bulky as a coconut. His shirt was heavily starched, and he wore a heavy diver's watch of some metal I didn't know the name of. He looked out the front window of the Circle C at the vacant field of flowers where the cats hid, and smelled the wallet the way you'd open a lovelorn love letter and smell it. He flapped the wallet like a child playing with an old blue wallet from his father's drawer. It flipped and fluttered the way it might have in the sea had it not been in Brundetti's pocket. Then he waved it slowly without a sound.

"I knew you at the Academy in Harlingen," he said to Chet Senior. Chet Senior circled calmly back behind the cashier's stand, keeping his hands visible to the sheriff playing with the billfold now like a toy in a dream.

"No sir, I went to high school elsewhere."

The "elsewhere" was brave. I made my young presence known by simply moving.

"Beeville?" the sheriff said.

Chet Senior coughed into his fist. He smiled wistfully. The sheriff relaxed out of his official dreamstate into the everyday.

"Play any ball?" he said, meaning football.

"Some," Chet Senior said.

A suntanned tourist girl in high school or younger wandered in. A daisy chain of struggling cicadas broke in the new world. The sheriff pursed his lips politely like someone tasting a plum, as she walked back out with a package of Tom's peanuts.

The drowned man's name was Brundetti, he then told us. He had been seen in a bar in Aransas Pass, either the Blue Nickel or Hairy Buffalo, three days before he showed up facedown in the sand at Fallen Apples. He had spent a night at the Boy on a Dolphin tourist lodge in Aransas Pass, alone. He apparently was not homosexual because he had tried his best to get sex from a barmaid at Hairy Buffalo's or the Blue Nickel, whence the law got his name.

"He had told her that all his life he had wanted to have sex with a southern girl," the sheriff said. "She did not comply, and he went away angry, forlorn."

Chet's dad hadn't said anything in a while, and the men went outside. You could see the wandering girl up Beach Road by the Woodcock mansion, which was occupied then. Both men looked at her longingly, ruefully, brothers in the trade.

The sheriff put on his Stetson that he had placed on the seat in his car, and got in. He shut the door and Chet leaned on it stiff armed. They exchanged words and the sheriff drove away toward Aransas Pass, then U-turned a quarter mile up the road and drove in the direction of the mansion, of the girl. Chet the father watched all this with his fingers in his back pockets, and when the sheriff from Refugio finally passed the girl and the driveway to the mansion Chet Senior stepped up the concrete stoop and entered the store. When he saw the wallet on the counter where he had set it for the sheriff to begin with, he picked it up and pressed it between his palms like a woman increasing the size of her bust or strengthening her arms. He put it in his back pocket that had no wallet in it, then took it out, opened the cash register drawer, put a dollar in the wallet and dropped the wallet into the same drawer with a ring. The ring came from the tongue of a bell shaped like a basset hound.

"What did he want, there at the last?" I said.

"He asked me what I knew about the giantess and the Muleskinner."

I looked right through him like he was a clear thing. He put a bag of peanuts into his shirt pocket and went into his office and shut the door. I took the phonebook from under the counter and hunted down a Lopez in Esperanza. Using my own money, I walked up the street to Fallen Apples and telephoned U-U. An old woman answered who spoke no English. I asked her in Spanish if Eustacia were there. She very sweetly told me that Eustacia did not live there.

"Donde vives?" I asked.

There was a pause. Nothing inside Fallen Apples made a sound.

"Con el papa, in Dimple," she said.

She said good-bye in English and hung up. I put a dime in the basket of change beside the cash register. I remembered

Eustacia laughing on the mule and her oceanic eyes at the bar. Maybe the girl at the Lopez house in Esperanza wasn't her, a virgin in a headscarf.

"Fuck!" I said.

Then I looked at a female clothes dummy standing beside a pile of old dresses stacked in the window. The dummy moved an arm and turned her face toward me. She had the wan look of a warm woman of plaster. The must of the old worn world captured all flesh and blood, and she asked me to look away.

I looked away. My mouth, chin, heart, and stomach were all one piece. I shut my eyes, and Mrs. Evans walked past me. She did not smell like cigarettes but like an old dress soaked in roses. She took my wrist and opened my hand and placed a tiny hard thing in it. I opened my eyes and looked into hers for the second it takes an apple to fall from a branch to the ground, all the time it takes for everything in the world between two people to drown. Her eyes were the color of every body of water at night, and what was in them was in the need of the waves. A huge satin rose hung from the rosebud-buttoned bust of the garment she wore. She plumped it in her hands. I looked at the object she had placed in my palm and saw that it was a petrified rosebud.

CHAPTER FIFTEEN

It's hard to say what was happening in Woodcock that summer. With all the pickup trucks and radios, you had a lot of noise. But then there'd be a boy on a Sunfish, a girl fishing, a family of old and young gathering shells, a man and woman holding hands at THE CONSPICUOUS ABSENCE OF WISDOM OF ANY SORT bar. If I had had a dog to run with, or some brothers, or a vehicle to escape in thoroughly, things like the petrified rosebud and the spa and Brundetti would have rolled through me like food at a picnic casually eaten, or past me like acorns off the feet of statuary deer. Living as much as I did around the Evanses changed me.

Woodcock was two miles of hurricane ruins along four miles of gun-barrel sea. Inland, Nehi, Dimple, Huisache Mott, and settlements with names only privately or even personally known, existed like the tatters of a rag or peripheral visions in a mirror passing through. But, I lived in one: not actually Nehi (named for its hills), but a simple house across the road from Bell Acres where Trout and Merkel were homesteading facing the sky. Dad said Trout Bell was the cleanest individual by nature he had ever seen. He said that even when he was little he would stack his soldiers in rows on their backs in their fort-box (a metal fort that folded for night storage) and place his toys into tiny townships in his room. Part of his death was caused by rheumatic fever that was never diagnosed. Mother and Dad would go to his room and watch him lie still, loom, leer, and smile, sink and rise for days on end. Dad said he was happy in there, and that it was a comfort to know he had a full life. I think my dad was insane, too big in his dream. In one of the few times Mother verbalized her true feelings, she told me how she and Dad would go in together to check on Trout ("poor Trout"), how Daddy stood in misty delight looking down at his first-born son sinking and sailing with gray bulbous eyelids hiding his oceanic purity, and how my father sometimes laughed so hard he had to take his starched arm off her shoulders to squeeze the tears of joy from his volcanic eyes. He cried with joy so much at Trout's purity continually guaranteed by fever, she said, that his eyes when shut looked like boils.

To get the feeling of the sea, you had to go there. To get the feeling of the sea otherwise, you had to be there. Only after walking from Bell Acres the five miles to Woodcock, did I get it. . . Sometimes (once), Chet stole a wretched old antique pickup and saw me walking east of Huisache Mott, the seven-mile way to Woodcock. He honked his horrible horn like a mule choking on a kazoo, just laid on it, and slammed on his brakes like knuckles of iron in the dust. This dust was powdered sand from the Sea of Time married to pleading glaciers mostly ghosted, bleached knuckle dust of colored skin, huisache pod pollen and mesquite thorn anciently shedding, the reverberant slough of skunk ("a gooder smell than armadillo" —Merkel) and dinge of gull, the slow boat of turtle stopped eternally in the road... You smell where you walk and know why the wind matters so much. It's like at home when there's a pan of spaghetti simmering and you open the door to tell the world something nourishing. Probably the very birds salivate.

"Huisache Mott is the asshole of the world," Chet said, lighting a Camel with a stranger's Zippo. The Zippo came with the car. He laughed and blew smoke through his kiss-pursed lips emphatically the way Sperry the Idiot used to riding shotgun with the King of Darts.

I didn't respond. I knew he wasn't a criminal, but it wasn't my truck, and I didn't respond. He had a Coke between his legs, and sipped it. He puffed his cigarette more normally and shook his head. He already knew not to ask me by any means why I didn't want to find out why he, Chester Evans Junior, concluded that Huisache Mott was the asshole of the world. But he wanted to know. It was something I had.

I rolled down my window. I rolled up my window. He sucked his stolen Camel and did the Sperry blow.

"Man, you are fucking weird. Weird as grandma's weenie. Weird as a monk's duck," he said.

I rolled down the window and let clean air vacuum the cabin. Chet got really quiet and didn't say anything. Huisache Mott was far behind us, and the silver ranks of headless sunflowers everybody loves flooded the ditches to the road. It seemed so narrow a shoulder running beside them that only armadillos walked it. I would have been the sole human wayfarer there had not Chet picked me up. The headless old sunflowers were the awfully old robe of a king.

By happenstance, the vehicle had, of all things, air conditioning, and Chet had her going full blast. Before he took it upon himself to roll up my window for me so the machine could do its job, I reached across him, myself, and rolled down his window all the way. My arm brushed him. In our friendship, we rarely ever touched each other. He actually flinched. He looked at me as if threatened. For a moment I was scared. To the south-southwest, across a square mile of green cotton making good behind the wall of sunflowers, a settlement of houses with a personal name looked unpeopled.

"Let's go there," I said.

CHAPTER SIXTEEN

We drove up the white sand farm road through high green cotton to a set of chipped-gray quarters a hundred years old. These were hot-looking places, low to the ground, with sloping roofs. Dented roofs like square old cans of pancake syrup. Chet shifted into neutral and slowed to a stop. We had stopped in the middle of the set of four houses. Chet started to light a cigarette, but I asked him not to.

"They'll smell the smoke," I whispered. The words were little rafts shooting round the bloodstream of my soul.

"You are a fucking monk," Chet said.

I got out, too, and you could smell nothing human in the breath of cotton. Each white ball in the sunny shelter of green was the head of a child, the whipped, unhandled crowning.

"Look at that shit!" Chet said. I saw a large, dusty turtle, its feet sugared with sand, marching across the road in front of the truck. Had it been four times bigger, Chet could have ridden it. I hunted the blue sky for sun or trees, but a mile of cotton is a lot of cotton. It got so quiet we heard as if amplified the footsteps of the turtle. It was like a goddamn battalion of

Necessities. A cicada clinging to a house burst out crazy as a Roman candle and flew into the cotton. Chet tried to light a cigarette, but I jerked it from his lips and put it in mine, unlit. Chet looked at the house in front of him and said something childish and delinquent about how the truck was on loan and he had to get it back.

"This on loan, too?" I said, and stuck the new cigarette in the brown valley above his ear. His hair was freshly burred by his father. (Every year, the last working day before Independence Day, my father took me to Aransas Pass to get a burr to last till school the first Monday after Memorial Day, or Labor Day, the first week in September. We did almost nothing else together, but he took me there. A beautiful girl named Misty showed her legs while Earl cut it.)

This was the last week in June in the Unknown Settlement south of Huisache Mott, 1964, three miles inland from the Gulf of Mexico. I then knew what day of the week it was Chet stole the car; I do not know now. I craved shade so hard and badly, I would have killed Chet just to crawl under the turtle lost in the cotton. It wasn't so hot out in the morning, yet, but the sky seemed full of needles pointing down. I heard a chunking sound from behind the house in front of me, and walked around back to find the Muleskinner loading a cart with household items timelessly plain, some of them iron. He carelessly, expertly threw them into place. The board walls of the winged cart shuddered. His perfect honesty and coldness in the sun were breakfast for me. The veins in his arms and head were rivers to wench them up and down and sideways through every year.

I went back around front and told Chet Jonah the Muleskinner was there.

"Oh, this must be a Negro place," he said, relieved, formal and polite like his mother would from Alabama, but quietly ambient with the holy regard you feel with only a rickety house separating you from what you worship but never touch or truly know, but you are holy too because the unrehearsed regard is hatched out like an egg without intention of itself but from its mother the old turtle now trudging through the cotton. . .

The mules Smokey and Whiskey were hitched to the cart, and they broke into bawling hee-haws at something. My mouth, heart, lungs, and belly formed into that worm that contracted big mouthed sucking for soul. Chet started for the truck, but an old loving woman behind the gray door groaned, "Jonah! Baby! Baby!" limp and desperate. A door slammed in the back and a pressure built up magnitude within the world of the house big enough to burst the heart of the worm, the shell of the tortoise, the walls of the hovel if anything else moved.

Chet turned the key and emphatically begged me to come on. Without talking, his torso begged. I knew what was in the house not by face or name, but by scent. Fish, sweat, soap, bleach, sand, sawdust, blood. Water, salt, Time, Sex, vigor, Death, and Love. Duty, blame, fucked Hope, and pristine kerneled Faith. God raised my arm to tell Chet to go but he was already gone. No one came out. Noontime came without an animal attached to it, just the kind sun afloat. Jonah, aboard his plain board seat nailed somehow securely to the front of the flappy cart I knew he constructed himself, pulled out from behind the house, drawn away towards somewhere by Smokey and Whiskey. Bundled up in quilts against the iron and china qualities of life was the old woman with wispy hair watching the world like a gull. Her feet were shod in sandals over thick socks cornflower blue. I waved and nodded like Tung Hsi might have, but she didn't recognize me. She just stayed folded. She looked all ready. Determined and cool with a "this time" expression.

I had to move or lose my mind, and went into the house to see it. I was not a criminal like Chet, and I wasn't going to steal anything. As soon as I opened the back door and saw the bar across the back of the front door, I knew I was just like Chet. If I stole anything or molested anything, we would become identical. I had that strong, needy, wormy feeling again. Up against the no-window walls of the house were many pictures and, for some reason, the framed cover of an ironing board impressed with the faces of different irons. "My goodness," I mused. I went outside, out back, and with great effort rolled a rain barrel on its end up to the back screen door to hold it open. Nothing else would do. The only other things heavy enough were a bed and dresser. An oval, frameless mirror hung outward on a wire and nail above the dresser. The possibility of being seen in the mirror made my face crawl like maggots of horseflies lived in it. With my back to the looking glass I shifted on sandy boards to beside the valed bed and studied its making and posture. "Too old to be called a twin," I said. "Looks like what they call a standard or double." "Proof ghosts talk," I said. For more light, I shuffled across the room to the front door to open it. Putting my hands on the bar to lift it away, I couldn't bring myself to, and just closed my eyes. I swear to God I saw myself loving U-U and I didn't know how. She lay on a cloud of mottled marble, as on a picnic blanket, and her curly hair was how it was the first time I saw it. I was inside her eyes but not there.

The Hoover started up and a chorale of cicadas rang me like the sea ringing a bell, so that I could find about chin level pinned by a pearl hatpin or doll's hairpin to the back of the door an old photograph snapshot of a handsome young man in shirt and suspenders, smiling well, his hair parted on the side and plastered down thick like a bush run over by a car. His hair was painted red by color added after the picture. Depinning the picture, I took it off the door where I felt it had been for years. I left the pin in place exactly in its original attitude atop the picture paper so as not to increase the size of the hole. For some reason a scrap of aluminum foil that had been at one time wadded up, then torn away from a bigger piece and folded into a crude butterfly, fell from behind the picture when I took it down. It had old black ketchup on it. The back of the picture in violet ink said "Jonah (Baby) Hutchins Mott Refurio Revival Picnic," with an *r* for a *g* and a date I forgot. She spelled like people talked. The hand was lovely, as natural as wisteria. I felt it was the love-schooled hand of a mother but did not know.

All the pictures on the walls had faces in them but I didn't care. Relaxed, I repinned the picture and walked to a shelf on a wall. It was a slender board shelf nailed on brackets around the entire rectangle of the house. On the shelf was one jar of honey still liquid. I took the lid off. It had the rank black smell of whole honey. I held the jewel to the sun of the backdoor and put it back on the shelf, took Chet's dad's army knife with a spoon out of my pocket, the one he had used to help his wife and the coroner inspect Brundetti, then given to me instead of Chet, his boy, and I opened the spoon never used (its stiffness) and dipped a spoonful of honey from the jar and ate it. It was wild and garlicky. I licked off the side of the jar and twisted the lid back on exactly as it had been tightened before, and stepped outside. The jar was where it belonged. I rolled back the rain barrel and let the door shut quietly. For a little while, I couldn't really remember whether the actual backdoor behind the screen door had been shut when I first went inside to inspect the house. I lied to myself that the person who came and went at home there would never remember. . . In the open air, I tasted sea horse on the honey and stood in the tall cotton away from the settlement, afraid.

A sick horn sounded. It was Chet in the truck, and I ran down a row of cotton, through the ditch of tin soldiers, to join him.

CHAPTER SEVENTEEN

Pre-Fourth of July, 1964: People I still knew: Chet. Mules who still knew me: Smokey (Gus) and Whiskey (Stinky)... Things I rather knew: antique army knife with cleaned folding spoon given to Chet Senior as valuable storied artifact by Mrs. Evans, named by great-aunt in Tuscumbia, Alabama, "Glory T." (for Tuscumbia and Tuscaloosa, Alabama, and Tejases Seriosas in Mexico, not for "Texas, My Texas," the song we learned as part of the love of One Texas Under God Indivisible from Texarkana to Matamoros, as Chetty, she called Chet Junior, claimed), on their sixteenth wedding anniversary... (You wonder what Brundetti's lint meant to her, and why she took the name Marguerite at the time of Fallen Apples. Maybe she was trying it on, like a dress.)... I knew the eyes of sea horses and the eyes of mules, the human innards of fiddler crabs playing quiet songs, the drumming of the sea, Brundetti's hair asweep and bare feet smelled by catfish, and the hermit crabs having to wait like Nautilus for fucking ever... I had the rosebud in my pocket opposite of the knife, the last week of June 1964 in Hutchins Mott (called Unknown Settlement inside myself then). Refugio Revival

House had no green door like the one painted softly behind lone Jonah (Baby) in the picture. That was the door of the cotton-picker house I raided and plundered, the green front door pickled gray by the cottonball sun... I knew of a dog Chet Senior loved and killed with a slingshot before Chet was born. Chet Senior was a boy up in Poetry, Texas, or Beeville, and the mongrel a sire called Bouncy. This La Vaca County told Mrs. Evans in a report: "A steel pellet or ball-bearing shooter in the left eye at close range." She used the report to absorb coffee stains beneath her cup at Fallen Apples...

These were knowledges like clues to existence I had consciously taken hold of by the time of the dead Brundetti's appearance beside Fallen Apples, June 1964. Till thirty years later, they were pocketed in me like shells in which the worm of my gut found housing; but secret deductions and treasured sundries, too, that I wanted just for me, to which and whom no one else was privy...

"The Contessa's mother was a beautiful woman of normal size in Corpus, who made a mistake," Mom said directly, aloud, but normal voiced to me, with her face facing away into the wind off the Gulf, one hot night that summer early on, on the pier in the glorious, incessant wind with practically invisible Milky Way-infinite pollens on it, spilled from the wind's basket. It felt like a little girl of titanic size was leaping or dancing back and forth over the bay from La Vaca Island to Woodcock in a long dress of immemorial size, monstrously huge but beautiful. It felt across my sleeveless, beer-anesthetized torso like a dusky blue tattersall check fabric of a feminine skirt dragged across a baby's face or a grown man's face as the girl made of wind, carrying a basket of flowers from La Vaca Island, jumped back and forth the seven miles over the bay and dragged the hem of her garment near the skin of the sea, touching the man-baby's face, and next to him his mother's face, dusting both with pollen... *How can it be a little girl with a basket, the hard-blowing breath off the Gulf of Mexico? And how much harder and bigger the girl and her basket, like the Giant Contessa herself, across the buffer of the cattle island, upon its gulfward shore? Can't be. Was. Is...*

My mother's voice at dusk, that dusk of the pollen so solemn and serene, my mother's age-bleached face so painted by the sea that it looked ageless but still was young, just not young to me back then, my mother's gun-barrel blue greenish black gray cloudy eyes foamy with flecks of Shiner, my Shiner beer I shook toward La Vaca Bay and La Vaca Island for the full-grown hamburger cattle and their milkweed-spangled doggies enstalled at the Ranch House barn for veal, for tenderness, bawling really quietly so you couldn't hear their cries for mamma that the Gulf gold dusted at night with her infinite pollens: precious sundry...

I shook a beer and let it explode on the wind and upon us for the Contessa whom I had never touched and never known like a man and baby touch and know, like Jonah touched and knew. The beer I shook and exploded over me and Mother and the sea, I exploded for her, for the Contessa, not for Jonah, not knowing why. Because why is fucked. It never knows. If the titanic girl picking sundry flowers upon the island had ever asked why, when told it was impossible to leap across the bay from La Vaca Island to Woodcock, we would perhaps never have inhaled and been dusted by the slightly golden pollen that impregnated our lungs and hair and made us some better than why.

Unsurprised by the spray, my mother laughed. I had said nothing in the way of a toast, and she probably knew *why*. Because I was not quite sixteen and the sundry house of secrets was just Mother's and mine and still locked. My room was mine and her room was hers and *the Giant Contessa had beautiful hands and the love of a man called Jonah. . .*

Mother had a moment before spoken her story of the Contessa I knew by heart and mind like a middle name everybody else but Mother and me and maybe Chet knew just as a letter, an initial. She didn't talk more, but, calming unlike the wind against us strengthening, looked sadly at the sea, a soupy green and salad monster scooping at the legs of the creosoted phone-pole pier beneath us, as I looked toward the unpersoned un-yet-lit bait and ice house at the shoreward end and saw my father marching white as a ghost toward us. White shirt, white pants, white socks, belt, and shoes. Tan face, slick hair, gold watch. He did not say hello, but walked past us to the end of the pier, to a sheltered area where a shadow stood, and he kissed it. The shadow was boxed inside a covered fishing station roofed by Woodcock to hide the sun and rain like a narrow doorless closet you could stake claim to and romance all night if you could take the wind, and thus I could not see the gender or age of the shadow the man in white bent over, surrounded, kissed, and lifted. . . But then I knew it was not my father: he wore the wrong pomade and was too tall. Scrubbed-clean men in solid white at dusk look much the same, marching down a pier, dissolving as they bend over a shadow cloistered over the water. . .

My fear is to get drowned in a dream and to never live. At the funeral of another or the witnessing of a corpse, you know for a certain, frightening moment that they were dreams. When my brothers, Trout and Merkel, died, they became like inseparable dreams, and I like a dream they had had. I remember, that summer I was almost sixteen, on the pier at night, or at work raking gravel, emptying garbage, or pushing the Hoover, feeling like my Steelhead second self was a dream-vision the monk in Thailand had had, or some shit...

Brundetti's dream. Brundetti.

You cannot go back and kiss that dream in place of your father's face. Your brothers are dead, no matter why, and not a dream or dreams, but, yes, as a dream or dreams flee upon waking or get smothered when turning over in bed or vanish into the ground or on the sea like when we die and all our remembered treasured dreams housed in our selves just vanish like flowers, maybe, carried away in a basket by a little girl.

You would not if you could, perhaps, go back and kiss the face of your father.

In remembering the strength of the railing of the pier, plus the strength of the wind, to withstand the humanity of the man in white's and the shadow's rendezvous... I remember that the shadow had a smell. The man and the shadow formed a noselike mass sniffing atop the railing. Her shadow blew back with her hair I couldn't see, and he was buried in her, tall enough to stand and strong enough to lift her. Imagine the whipping the pier took, the wind at the pier's head, the waves at its ankles, the slapping pelvises. *I know that smell. That clothes-dummy smell.* I stood downwind of Mother to block the faraway man and his wrap of shadow away from me. Then Mother moved leeward of me and took my foam-sticky hand and dragged me home.

I was drunk as a skunk on Shiner. Mother had let this happen. I do not remember how. I recall reaching into a giant blue cooler and extracting a disintegrating cardboard carton of Shiner. Don't know where. We were thinking about Dad and dead Merkel and Trout and trying not to think about them. I knew this was true because we were no longer talking and sharing and Mother and I were never afraid to talk and share. We took a long, roundabout way home, through the Motts and Dimple and Esperanza, and drove slowly through the parking lot of Shotgun Lodge without talking, just to look and see things like the King of Dart's truck and not to talk, like window-shopping the night, and when we got home to Nehi Dad was there. He had bought little executive reading glasses that rested impressively on his nose. He had changed clothes from his usual suit and tie, and sat in a fresh laundered shirt in his reading chair, smoking, and when he saw me walk in uncharacteristically ahead of Mother, and smelled me drunk on the exchange of air, he leaped from his chair and screamed as loud as a man still in the insurance business could scream, with all the weight of a salesman:

"You fucking bitch! You fucking dreamless bitch! He's fifteen years old! Can't you pick 'em any younger?!"

Saliva frothed one corner of his mouth. He wiped it off with his thumb.

"Mamma just watched me drink some Shiners, Dad. . . We went to the pier."

Mother stepped forward from behind me and slapped him in the face only once. I had seen her arm draw fully back and watched her whole weight blow into it, with the swift movement built upon a screeching, groaning sound. It was like the fluke of a sperm whale striking a shark. I looked down at her arm to see if it was broken. The hand was quivering, all alive. Dad's reading glasses spun into a corner. He collapsed into his chair, with his paper in his hands, blank as a palmful of pomade. His feet would not cross, and as he began to try to cross them like always, he seemed to be swimming backward from a crouched position.

I backed away, outside the house, and stumbled over to Bell Acres gate and puked shrimp and beer acids, then I crawled over to my brothers' graves and slept between them. The cicadas in the graveyard oaks rang true and loud into rosy rings, with not a real rose flower in all of Woodcock, Nehi, Dimple, Huisache Mott, my newly personal Hutchins Mott, and only one coral rose in far Esperanza. The cicadas rang true and loud into rosy rings of noise tilting in and out of each other in my drunk-but-safe-on-the-ground-asleep-with-the-Mexican-dead-and-my-two-dead-brothers holy family around me. In my sober soul I had a vision of my perfect invalid brothers then years dead, Trout and Merkel, and of my sick mom and dad in the bleached kitchen of another house. . . I wept moisturizing tears for the graves of my brothers and the fucked-up flower of me between them. . . The cicadas' deafening music beat from the sea-blest, heavy air two thin crowns like wedding rings shining in the bent horizons at dawn and sunset, shaping the golden settlements of one eternal day and one eternal night, over the ghost of sweet Merkel's head. Then both sat up in their graves like brothers in their beds.

"Trout was murdered," Merkel told me there.

Merkel looked happy, like a holy elf. Trout seemed half asleep in his sweaty pajamas.

It was news for me to take away, eternal news, like the flowers in the girl's basket, the night I got drunk with my mother, the summer I knew sundry things. . .

CHAPTER EIGHTEEN

"Women know why. . . When they cry. . . Men don't lie. . . When they sigh. . ." were four homemade signs I saw on Pentecost Road between Woodcock and A.P. the day after the Hutchins Mott raid, when I was hitchhiking to Earl's for a haircut. It was nine miles from Woodcock, past the carbon factory where white egrets waded shin deep in black water, waiting to snatch the black frogs and black crickets and black grasshoppers that lived there, to the city limits of Aransas Pass. U-U was there, in my mind. I kept wanting to give her something. . . "I just want to give you something," I said. "I just want to give you love."

The carbon factory didn't move. The white egrets didn't move. The plain grasses and naked world of sand haunting the flats to the sea half a mile to my left didn't move. A car pulled up behind me, and stopped. A woman in curlers reached over and pushed open my door and I got in. I just sat down on a blue vinyl seat in Heaven. She didn't say anything or look at me for a moment. She looked concerned, directly ahead over the wheel. Her fingernails belonged to a gut-busted beauty I longed for. She asked if I had a cigarette. I shook my head.

"Shit," she said, and pulled a cigarette from a pack in her purse open between us. She said "match" with it in her lips, angrily, comfortably, searching the seat and her purse, reaching into the glove compartment at my knees. . . "SHIT!" she said. She did not yet look at me. She pulled the cigarette from her lips and put that hand back on the wheel. The curlers were tight all over her head. She got a fresh idea and pulled over at Strangers.

When she jumped out to go in, I saw she was barefoot and her buttocks miserable in cutoffs. When she came back out into broad, blinding daylight, in a coastal world where it hadn't rained in thirty days, I saw she had on a blue-and-white sleeveless checkered blouse. When she got to the car she put two beers on the roof and pulled out the tails of her blouse which she tied beneath her breasts. She got in the car, lit her cigarette, and nervously unbuttoned the buttons on her blouse above the knot.

She gave the beers to me and asked me to open them. I didn't know what to do, how. She opened a zip pocket in her purse and gave me a bottle opener. I opened both beers and held them open in my lap. She rubbed her chin with her thumb.

She pulled off Pentecost Road (that was buried under the new, wider road we were on, a road with a number) and up a grassy lane to a coppice gate overgrown by vines at the mouth of a migrant cemetery. She took one of the beers and sipped it, looking straight ahead at a tall white cross of timber leaning away. Then she turned her head to the left to see a field of tangled things.

The worm in me wanted to suck her legs. Her painted toes played on the brake pedal.

She had not yet turned off the engine, and she clutched the key in the ignition to do it. Then she looked at me.

"Gonna drink your beer?"

I was dead. A dead worm. A horsefly or housefly maggot stillborn.

"No," I said. "I'm only fifteen."

She shifted into reverse and swiftly drove back up the lane to the highway that did not have a name. A furious boredom uglied her face as she reached across me as I had Chet that time at the Unnamed Settlement Hutchins Mott, and she levered the door open and pushed it out.

The car was still barely rolling.

"This good enough?" she smiled, and I got out.

I still had the beer in my hand. I looked up and down the unpeopled highway slick with mirage, and set the bottle at my feet, on the asphalt, for a possum, armadillo, or lucky dog to suck on, something realer, and walked into Aransas Pass.

CHAPTER NINETEEN

Earl was gone. A paper clock with a red hand in his window said "Back at Noon" but it was afternoon, then, and the place was empty. The two red chairs looked glamorous, the one never used. A note in the window below the clock said Earl and Misty were gone till the sixth of July. Sorry. Come Again.

A sun-blistered shrimper drunk on his ass in the sun, barefoot and filthy, asked me for assistance in locating a cigarette, match, and men's room I wouldn't fear going to myself. I told him what you'd expect and that the only place to take a pee or shit I ever used was Earl's, and Earl's was closed. He looked shocked, and walked from beneath the palm tree wherein whose split shade he was standing on black feet, over to Earl's window and beat on it with his fist. It rattled like a bomb went off wrong in gunnery practice at sea, and he shrank to his knees on the spot.

I walked over to him. He looked older. His burnt-black freckled skin looked like dead catfish crossed with spotted trout. He was laughing and his teeth were rotten. There seemed to be a picture of nothing in his hands.

"Mister, do you know where I can get a haircut?"

"I always get mine cut here," he said.

I noticed his hair was bleached and dyed many colors, like watercolor paint tossed on grass that had grown out. He drew his fingers from the picture of nothing and covered his face.

I wished I had that beer to give him. He began to sing behind his hands "Where the Buffalo Roam" in a jerkily comical mock-serious way I can't write down, and I could see he had talent. But if I said anything the whole thing would go on and on, so I walked away. I was half a block away when he shouted from Earl's, "I can *sing*, man! Can't you hear me *sing?!*" It drew me to turn and look at him, whereupon he froze, his bravado burnt off, and he turned his back schizophrenic. He faced Earl's window like a ward of the state, and scooted flat footedly around the side of Earl's. A giant palm tree grew there, between the barbershop and the mattress shop, forcing the buildings apart. Their buckled roofs were patched with tin, and the palm tree brilliant in the sun. . .

I found out the only place open for a haircut was the barbershop at the old Tarpon Inn where Jean LaFitte slept, out on Mustang Island, so I asked a pink-faced old man and his tasty-pudding wife if they'd be so kind as to give me a ride to the ferry. I imagined he was glad to be old, he was once so baby faced. We didn't talk the whole way to the ferry, and once we got there he gave his wife something which she turned and gave to me: Five Dollars. She peered sadly at me and tilted her head like a dog, like a dog my mother could have been had she been happy. I thanked her and got out of the car.

The ferry in those days was free to ride and owned by the state. It travelled constantly, day and night, from Aransas Pass to Port Aransas, usually packed with cars and pickup trucks. Once you got to P.A., it was a little ways to the beach where as a kid I found sand dollars and watched the locals surf the waves that were big enough off the Gulf. In the old days there were some hotels and motels, bars and beach houses there, but not a billion like now. Upon the ferry I stood beside a ferryman with long white hair and watched a pod of dolphins they call porpoise playing in the sea. The three of them darted, wove, and drilled the channel before and beside the boat, and they seemed very happy, like the boat was a sow they couldn't let go of.

Once on the island I went right to the Tarpon Inn and found the barbershop closed. The lobby was newly air-conditioned and I froze in my clothes all sweat soaked from the day. The clerk looked at me like I was out of my mind when I asked him where I might get my hair cut. But he pointed with his thumb out the back door to the alley.

The alley stunk direly of kitchen garbage and hotel trash bins burgeoning with refuse. Further down the alley was more of the same, with restaurants and motels backing up toward the never-ending mystery that is alleys. But behind the motel I found a stack of cotton bales tumbled over, probably props for the melodrama, and down between two of them a fold-out panel of five old photographs of a white man and black woman making love. They were not tame photos for the time. Though you might imagine them, yourself, I'll tell you what they contained, briefly.

The first showed the Priestess holding the Cowboy's gloved hand. The second showed her holding her headdress across her privates, and him looking dapper fully on. The third showed her fanning the headdress off to the side and the Cowboy in his chaps and hat. The fourth card showed her from behind and him gasping at heaven, and the final card was blank black with a big white question mark on it. I folded the antique and put it in my pocket that was soaked with sweat, but I couldn't carry it publicly.

Sad music came from down the narrowing alley and I went to find out why. I had become increasingly tired as the day wore on and I had left home without breakfast. Worn down like a meatless oyster, I found a blue door ajar a few inches and opened it more to the width of my foot. The sad music drew me like wind from a cave, but I was blind by the sun. A few little red, yellow, and blue Christmas lights blinked inside above my head, or the level of it. A deep, soft, tenderly womanish voice asked for identification.

"Will Bell," I said.

A foot inside a bulging shoe the size of an arctic mitten came toe to toe with mine. Then a meaty hand twice the size of my father's took my shoulder and welcomed me in. On the hand was a black cuff, up the cuff a black sleeve, and on the shoulder a veil. Behind it was a woman's intelligent face like a Spanish nun under wrought iron. The veil was peaked. She took my hand and led me to a little round table and chair at the feet of the musical source, a man on a bench whose neck looked broken, pigeon-toed for his guitar. The stage of his bench was lit but nothing else was. People just had to know their way around, like initiates.

Suddenly a man I knew from life came up and sat down beside me. I cannot remember if he took part of my stool or brought his own. The light off the guitar lit his face to show it the sheriff of Refugio.

In that light his head thrashed and tongue flashed as he talked *sotto voce* and told things he could tell to ruin lives:

"Muleskinner. . . Evans. . . the wop. . . the right goddamn people. . ." Many of his words got swamped in fatigue, scuttled in music. I glanced at his face ghosted with rumor. It shook like a skein full of oil and his eyes were slick as a cat's. He didn't look blonde in his face and head, anymore. He looked golden, extra-virgin olive-oil golden. . . "We know," he coughed in his neat fist, "what the fuck's going on w' you little friend and you little gir'friend and yo little half-pint Chocola negra ova hea and his big ol fat mama white as a mag-no-ia. . ." He sounded more southern than anyone I'd ever heard speak from Refugio. Without Spanish tone. He paused in his tirade and glanced away at a man I couldn't exactly see. Then he disgustedly clicked his teeth and stated: "Cock strong pick'ninny." The sheriff looked around like his neck was stiff but it was only sin that stiffened him and slickened him and glazed his horrid eyes. He gripped his knees over the deep creases of his sheriff's pants and hunched his shoulders, rolling his eyes and rocking his head, and then he shoved his face up close to mine: "Bofe Evans." *Both Evans.* His hateful eyes held solid knowledge, solid as the history of things I could smell he had eaten. He throttled back some words and swallowed them like a chunk of corncob coated with snot and hissed between his showing teeth and dug a business card from his shirt pocket and jammed it into the front pocket of my jeans, put on his Stetson and left.

The music dwindled and became like a rat scratching on a wall. I arose from the little desk and stumbled over someone toward the alley. But the alley wasn't there. A massive heap of human was there where the door was. My face and hands pushed into her like a puppy or infant would in blindness at a hungry breast, and she took me by the neck back to my table, that was a little desk, and made me sit down. All gently. The rat music tinkered, toiled, and toyed with bent-necked sadness; no one made a noise, and I had to put my head down on the table.

When I raised my head the room had grayed, lighter, and no one was there. Five or six tables like mine, the bench, and a bar backed by burlap.

With everybody gone, the place had become lighter.

I just wanted food, a place to lie down, and a haircut.

I walked back to the alley and lay on a bale of cotton. The stars above the island had no alibi, no job, no ambition, no money, no hot spring, no hair, and no name. What would a giant mean to a star? No alibi, no job, no children, no love, no mules, no horses, and no name. . .

CHAPTER TWENTY

If stars could be rhinestones rocking in a cradle, I could show you what that night on the cotton bale was like. The soft hot Gulf a few yards to my right. . . the love-tuber dolphins possessing the passion of tugboats to my left, where in the slow deep channel between Aransas Pass and Port Aransas stingrays flapped and crabs flowered to signal corps of jellyfish umbrellaing the higher way before the ocean meets the air. . . could be called the color of my first runaway night (not *wholly* night yet, but gauzy dark, stretched on the bale) away from home. So, you can see I wasn't worried or sad, awake. The sheriff's talk was like sugar in my sleep from before, the taste of a loaded beverage in a dream. . . On the bale, I heard a banjo tenor through the thin back of the old Tarpon Inn Playhouse wall, laughter, an Oomm of air conditioners, and applause. Then two boys shot out the backdoor off the lobby where I'd ejaculated earlier in search of the Blue Nickel and a haircut and found the nasty pictures of the Cowboy and the Priestess. The boys lit a hoard of firecrackers strung like the spine of a whale down the alley. The Black

Cats cracked and fizzled and snapped as the boys whee-owed, laughed, stomped, and threw out hollers shaking rings of smoke meaty as snails the shape of Nautilus, and I watched. There must have been a thousand firecrackers strung by hand from Hong Kong celebrating independence by those parentless tykes the night of Thursday, June 30, 19 fucking 64, Port Aransas fucking Texas, back of the old Tarpon Inn dumpsters, where my raft of cotton was moored.

The smoke from the early firecrackers floated above Tarpon Inn and blew away. The wind off the Gulf was always strong.

One of the boys saw me on the raft and said, "Nice haircut," without perfect tone 'cause he was young.

"Fuck off," I said to him.

He ran back into the hotel with the other boy. A big-haired woman well dressed looked afraid out the back door window, the day clerk's replacement.

"Mom's probably smoked a carton of Winstons by now, worried about me," I figured.

The woman in the window, wearing a dark suit with buttons, turned away. The disturbance was over. I lay back and listened to the cypress-muffled dialogue of actors. Jesus Christ, nothing'll make people stop play acting. I was fucking glad of it. Hot mist rose from my eyes I wiped off and jumped to the surface of the alley. Just like the bay at night, you could explore without fear there.

Back down the alley to the blue door I walked past cats integral and trash from a shoe store and the sea. The door was shut, no crack with a mittened foot in it, and I knocked on the fucker. Knock Knock Knock. The giant nun pulled me in. It was cold as an icebox. A musician sat on the stage bench, reading a book. She sat me at the burlap bar made of old trawler hatches lacquered deep. I pitied the ships gone away. She brought me a cold drink of mint and syrup that I drank for the be-Jesus gist of green that drove it, drove it like a nail to my wooden soul, Sweet Jesus-Baby, and when that shit hit my lungs and stomach it was like a dove hitting a window in a church.

"Please, another," I said. A perfectly groomed black man with immaculate hands and impeccable hair brought a glass of the same. Not being sun enslaved, I could see things as my eyes adjusted. Colored spotlights so dim they looked like dying stars hung at angles from the ceiling. Ten people sat at five tables. Every man wore a suit. Where I had sat earlier, a man sat on a woman's lap. He was small as a child; her arms were locked around him. His two sleepy hands were joined as in a fallen-asleep prayer on his lap, and one of her hands covered them hugely, like a mother's hand over a baby's two learning-to-pray hands just falling asleep over the Bible. His sleepy head drooped from the block of her starlit head to the shadowy vale between her neck and shoulders and rested there, his whole face lost in the shadow of her neck. She released her grip on one hand and stroked back his floppy, loving hair. . . Her hand was a white, heart-shaped feather off the body of the Dove of Love that comes and goes. It alone defined all the beauty and duty of the female world. . . The little man so sleepy, a boy who got lost hard at play, kissed her neck with his liquid eyes flickering as she stroked him a fifth or sixth time.

The guitar struck a strong chord like heat lightning with noise, and the mood-changer sang, "Chartreuse, Grenadine, the Grand Drambuie. . . My dad was a shrimper named Louie

Louie," and that was it, and everybody laughed and clapped. It was meant to be funny. Then the musician just played quietly some Spanish music like exercises among the classics.

The dinky man seated on the woman's lap arose and drifted to another room. He was neat in a suit, negro, and not so dinky standing alone. The Spanish nun approached their table and began to talk on friendly terms, as with an acquaintance, to the lady with the feather-shaped hands. The two embraced, and the seated paramour's white face looked gently happy over the Spanish nun's shoulder. Its whiteness had the tone of a pale pansy blossom. The gentleman returned and approached the bar, but now he wore a hat that slouched across one eye, making him look entirely confident, debonair, and slick.

"Blue Nickel," he said.

The bartender fixed the same drink I had snuffed and guzzled, and set it on the cypress before the man who sipped its bulging unspilled fullness, smacked his lips quite unselfconsciously, grinned into a squinting grimace showing a gold dog-tooth cap dull with Time, and told the bartender it was good.

As he returned to the table, he took off his hat and the woman stood, depressing the wrinkles from her dark linen suit. She walked off box ankled in high-heeled shoes big as boats or fat gravy dippers, but her massive femininity meated up any ugly abstraction I had floating around in my brain concerning what disproportion the world had given her. The musician raised his head and looked at her. . . "Some Spanish Dream" he sang. . . The man accompanying her darted forward and opened a door. He waited.

"Goddamn, she's big," I, the uninitiated, said.

The world we were born in took offense. The bartender iced my glass and life with a look, the mean-sure look of the Pagan.

"The Giant Contessa," he said.

. . . I cannot say why I did not recognize her. I cannot say why I did not know. The Giant Contessa had beautiful hands and the love of a man named Jonah, was the anthem of my life. Mine and my mother's. And it might have been the silent anthem for Chet and U-U, like a song for their personal country, for I never spoke my mother's magic words to anyone, and cannot know. But it was likely the anthem of others who didn't know or couldn't see the fleshed-out meaning of true love close at hand, early at home, or ever at all. . . if not the actual words I've recited, then the melody in the elicit lovers' unheard, imagined, prayed-for laughter and the rhythm in the mules' clippity-clop, marching feet around the precincts of Woodcock, Nehi, Dimple, Esperanza, Huisache Mott, Hutchins Mott, and the God Only Knows Unnamed Settlements where turtles trod looking for love, some old folks died knowing it, and sunflowers followed the sun. . .

We knew of their colorless love but refrained from putting it into black-and-white words at all, for fear of the envy green in those who saw color. . . And in youth, thirty years ago, our souls awoke deaf and dumb from sleep deaf and dumb and worked deaf and dumb in the talking world where everything meaningful was uttered simply in looks, just like now. . .

It was like living by the ocean all your life but never touching the urgent water, never tasting it on purpose, past a certain age or at any age. The dolphins' ballet and the death of a pelican: where?—I could have been living by a prairie sea of grass, or in ten thousand miles of sand, or under the snows of Kilimanjaro, with the true world of real love the Contessa and Muleskinner fleshed out large, quiet, private, personal, and almost better than human, of which I sing. . . and still I may not have seen the prairie or the desert or the tallest mountain in Africa. . .

You reached to pet the junkman's mules but never shook the junkman's hand; you window-peeped the giant girl like a Tootsie Roll mountain dipped in moonlight whose valleys watered the junkman, but you never shopped in the Countess Eileen. . .

Your treasure-hid anthems of precious sayings from the world of people talking became a verbatim, factual, almost genetic inheritance, then or ever a dependency, a melancholy mantra advertising the service of your soul, but first you came to life silently, then, later on, in noise, the treasure-hid anthems and precious sayings became a caption under a picture of how things should be—a woman smoothing a man's loving hair, a man who loves her so much even his hair loves her and her hands matter more than her weight, her weight and height like nothing, like words you can't remember exactly except just to say: the Giant Contessa had beautiful hands and the love of a man called Jonah, again and again, but aloud to someone else now.

CHAPTER TWENTY-ONE

Everything gets blurry, especially the links. How you get from one house to another, one plate to the next, river to river, grave to grave. Your hand is lost in your mother, found in your father. Family means everything but no one sees it around you.

I don't know what took me from the back of the Blue Nickel to the front of the Tarpon Inn, but something did. A road, an alley, a raft, the shoulders of a giant? The players had finished and Romeo stood outside the hotel entrance with his arm draped over a nice placard framed on a tripod nailed to the floor. The wind blew so hard off the Gulf, you had to nail things down, like signs and waste baskets. Surprisingly, the old tasty-pudding couple who'd given me the ride to the ferry were taking his picture. The placard said, "P. Charles Darling and Vega Cleary-Rothschild, *Shakespeareans*," and in the cardboard slip beneath it: "Here Tonite," which the Tarpon Inn could do (be vague) because it was the only first-class, dressy place on the island. Truly, no place except a Catholic ruin no longer used for gatherings, up in Shotgun, was any nicer or prettier than the old Tarpon Inn. The man dressed as Romeo put his arm around Mrs. Tasty-Pudding, kissed her forehead, and said, "We had a world, did we not?" In a flurry, she kissed his cheek and huffed (like my dad's oo-doggies) and her jealous husband pulled her off. Romeo laughed. It became shallow and calm as the old people left and Juliet came outside onto the porch to fetch him back.

The sea nearby hissed and thundered and worked away the wishes of its life just like Shakespeare. . .

The next thing I remember is being back at Earl's in the night, that same night (6/30/64). I had not gotten a haircut or seen the sun come up on Port Aransas. If there were dolphins sewing in the bay, they must have been under the water. The signs up at Earl's were still there: Back July 6.

I looked between Earl's and the mattress shop for the shrimper, but found only the cat-shit stack of old newspapers where he had lain. No one moved on foot about the main street of Aransas Pass, but only a few cars and trucks. Round about my head, from the eves of Earl's and the mattress shop and the places thereabouts, the whirring beat of love-incensed cicadas hard from their armor blazed like a zulu of sound or a thousand thousand kicking beads rolling in a black tambourine.

"Jesus! Shit!" I thought, and started north.

North was up Main Street that became Pentecost Road just outside town, at the city limits, and both Main Street and Pentecost Road were buried under six inches of asphalt already crumbling they called 35.

At the edge of town, a black Lincoln Continental slick, sleek, heavy, and clean pulled over in front of me and rolled down a window. A billow of cigar smoke poured out and a young sexy blonde with a cigar asked if I wanted a ride. I'm fucking this all up. She was on the shotgun side, not the driver. I think the windows were electric, but wouldn't swear to it.

I got in the back door and sat by a window, behind the woman. The man wore sunglasses at night, a suit with cuff links, a huge black cigar. I knew it was Big Stud Mingus on a date with a floozie. She put her bare arm on the back of the front seat and looked back at me and smiled, chewing something. Big Stud looked quietly upset and slumped and changed hands with the cigar that looked like a stick bomb.

"Honey," he said, "quit chewing that sardine, baby. It's making me sick. Please!"

He sounded like a young married man talking to his young married wife, trying to stay married. But the man was married, a married man with a little boy named after him, already, to beautiful sexy Mrs. Mingus who had lost some aspect of her gardening mind, for now she gardened statuary deer. He slouched uncomfortably again, puffed diligently on the cigar, made a decision.

"Give the boy a sardine, Esme."

She put one in her teeth by the tail and stuck her head over the top of the seat to give it to me. The worm inside me writhed and paralyzed all at once. Mr. Mingus snatched the sardine from her teeth and stuffed it in her mouth and made her chew it. She was laughing. She put another sardine tail between her teeth and offered it to me, and he slapped her. She still laughed, and he laughed.

About a mile past the migrant cemetery, as we passed the carbon plant, a great white bird flew across the road toward the field of nothingness that separated the blackened world of the bird's feet and the dead tomb of the factory from the moon-loving sea. It got as still and dead and mirthless in the Lincoln as an adulterer and his whore can get. You could almost smell the wings of the bird as it crossed over the road in the headlights of the car.

She had handed me the open can of sardines, and I was eating them. They tasted good to me because I was so damn hungry. Big Stud was like a lot of rich people. I don't think he saw me.

About a quarter mile to where the road peels off to Woodcock, he said, "Where to?" It was dark in the back seat, but his face was lit well into heaps of shine and valleys of shadow, richly masculine, and he looked back at me in the mirror.

"Oh, anywhere," I said.

Esme was drifting away inside herself where everybody really lives in complete ignorance of love. Her face turned to the right as if blown by calm bay water, and she looked out the window where nothing was. Then she sniffed and sat up and was okay. It was like a magnet coming to life, nearer its opposite.

He dropped her off without fanfare at a stylish Victorian manse I had never noticed before, in a little neighborhood of bungalows, huts, and common houses built on the ground because not close to the sea. A light was on for her, up on the porch, by the door, and she climbed slowly toward it, like a tender fly hatched all over again. He waited until she was up there and had put her hand on the door and turned a quarter face towards the car, before quietly pulling away. Across the road, in the headlights, streamed a thousand cats (not a thousand, but a dozen like parti-colored troops in a trot), and Mr. Mingus slowed to let them pass without harm. I turned in the seat and saw them climb the stairs of the Victorian and weave in a writhing knot at the foot of the door.

Mr. Mingus flipped on the ceiling light and saw me clearly. The boss was sober as a judge and unafraid. Who would tell in his world? Who would concede that female beauty was a thing he hated? It's just that Big Stud went too far and needed too little. All he needed was that little thing. It would never take him home, but he was the Victor in knowing this. I didn't know shit from apple butter, then, but I had the thoughts and named them later.

"Please let me off at the Countess Eileen's," I said.

With the ceiling light still on, he parked alongside the Countess Eileen's, across from Fallen Apples, and told me to wait a minute, to "hold my horses." He took a large yellow envelope off the front seat and handed it back to me. He did not take off his sunglasses and did not appear afraid. The envelope was marked "Invoices."

"Give these to Lopez," he said.

"Thanks for the ride," I said, and got out.

He drove off and stopped and shifted into reverse and backed up. I was already walking toward him.

"Yours is in there," he said. "You can take it out."

Then he drove off toward Shotgun Lodge where he lived.

I had that old familiar feeling I always got of *How did I get here?* and looked into the Countess Eileen to see what she had there. In the daytime I couldn't press my hand against the window to see in. But at night Woodcock was like a sorry aquarium without water above the ankles, and any wanderer could look in any window. Who was going to bother you? The law?

I saw brass apples and Christmas samples, velvet rabbits and wooden roosters, a clothes rack full of hummy clothes, spin racks of postcards, hard-candy shelves of sticks in glossy boxes, and tin coffins of lemon bonbons. More shit than you could shake a stick at, to fill the hope chests of old maids and wholesome homosexuals longing to be Esme Only in dream-time horror as hidden away as the heart of a mockingbird.

A homosexual man worked for Chet's mother once, in her store. He was the kindest outward person I ever knew in my life. She fired him for cursing her husband's killing a cat with his slingshot. When he left the store, an old woman driving a Ford picked him up. The car was all dusty, like a desert Ford, and he sat up proud as a fine soldier. His name was Dusty, but not Dusty Ford, and he was a person deserving better. He was brave and stood up for cats. To tell the truth, and why not, he was my hero. I just felt sorry for him because I was absolutely ignorant of what dainty and rare and rich and beautiful things arranged in perfect order mean.

A mockingbird is this way. Hear it sing. That's the kind of thing Tung Hsi would say if he could talk away from the picture. Quaint shit personified by poetry, Chet would say if he'd ever gone to fucking college. Card-shop poetry. That's what I saw in the Countess Eileen.

CHAPTER TWENTY-TWO

I never told Chet I loved him, like old friends do. I had it in me, like a river underground, but not the knowledge to say. A river needs a hole to come up, a buried, worried river. A hole the size of an ocean.

CHAPTER TWENTY-THREE

Chet lit a short Camel off a stolen Zippo at dawn, Friday July first 1964, that he had stolen the night before when I was eating Norwegian sardines with Esmerelda Only in Big Stud's giant black Lincoln Continental. I did not ask how he had stolen it. He might have lied. He sat downwind of me in a lawn chair on the roof of THE CONSPICUOUS ABSENCE OF WISDOM OF ANY SORT bar across Beach Road from Shotgun Lodge, Woodcock, Texas, Gulf Coast, La Vaca Bay gun-barrel blue, average depth six feet, La Vaca Island six miles out. We had beaten Papa Lopez to the job and sat there waiting. We started getting paid at seven A.M. Chet gave me the cigarette and lit another off the stolen Zippo but it didn't smell as good. You put this smell into words as follows: a mixed green salad of tobacco and lighter fluid, grilled Caesar.

"Fuck it," Chet said. "He ain't showin' up. Let's go fishin'."

A few big trout wrenched their way between yachts in the basin beneath us. They knifed away in turns but stayed basically close. The boat hulls hung like slices of melon in the clear still water of the basin. I was standing up and could follow the fish a long way.

A car door shut behind us, and I peered over the storehouse roof to see an official El Camino (brown) with new dust parked in the gravel lot. It was not the sound of Papa's truck door shutting, so Chet never took his feet off the railing. I stared at the stairs leading up from the Cypress Bar, and two men ascended.

The sheriff of Refugio in uniform crisp as a cookie, and another man (white) (the sheriff himself was a white Mexican) without a uniform, dressed like a catalogue model for a coastal summer, smiling (he was), pulled up chairs around Chet and sat down.

They didn't talk. They just looked at my best friend who had not looked at them.

The sheriff got up and went downstairs to get a cup of coffee for himself, while the other man stayed there but got up, too, and crossed his legs and arms while leaning confidently against the railing not far from Chet's feet. He grinned at my best friend, and my best friend grinned at him. Fucking fearless and fif-fucking-teen.

The Model sniffed and smacked his lips to comfort himself, buffaloed without stint.

The sheriff resurfaced with a white cup of restaurant coffee on a saucer and offered it to Chet. Then like an urgent host at a slave's party for past masters, offered it to me. I took the coffee and held it.

"Murphy, traigame mas cafe," he said to Murphy. His accent was native.

Murphy obeyed quite coolly or smart-assedly, and came back with coffee for two. The sheriff's face beaded quickly in the sun; it was as still as it ever gets on the roof. The trout were still motivating, and Murphy noticed how fine they were. He sipped his coffee.

Chet got to his feet but the sheriff put a khaki leg and chocolate boot in his way. I put the cup and saucer on the top rail of the railing. This was instinct. Chet took the cigarette out of his mouth and let his hand hang close to the sheriff's hat, for the sheriff was bent over as if to grab Chet's ankle if he moved. With incredible courage which flows from a place I don't know, Chet just let that cigarette hang there.

The sheriff sat up as the Model moved forward and Chet stepped over the boot.

"Let's go fish, Will," he said.

God only knows why, but I said okay. Before we got to the bottom of the stairs, Murphy had leapt down there past us and barred our way like some kind of hoodlum.

"What do you know about a dead muleskinner on Dimple Road?"

He sounded northern, like an actor. He looked square at Chet without identity, like a real killer. Ready. Ready. Chet ducked under his arm and took a mighty step. The man grabbed him by the belt and Chet pulled away. The man took a handful of shirt and Chet spun half backward into a coffee urn that crashed to the floor, splattering the man's slacks and soaking Chet's jeans. Chet screamed something, halfway to his knees, and the man hauled him by the head, like a bull calf, back up the stairs, past me.

"Will! Call my fucking dad!"

I ran to the phone in the office and dialed Chet's home. No one was there. I dialed the Circle C, and a Mexican woman who couldn't talk answered and hung up. "Fucking bullshit!" I screamed at the phone. I tried to calm down instantaneously enough to just try to dial Fallen Apples. I could not! I could only see Chet's mother naked that day of the rosebud. Her right pink hard nipple. "JESUS CHRIST!" I screamed. I started to cry burning tears, gripping the phone like Lucifer's lucky snake in the fucked-up gardens of Eden, when a man put his hand on my back. I faded and God turned my face to see Stud Mingus steady as Peter behind me.

"Sir!" I pleaded. "They've got Chet Junior upstairs on the balcony and they're gonna fucking kill him! I heard him say it in P.A. last night!"

Or something like that, like a sick old lady without any strength, or a wormy little kitten mewing on her rib cage. Jonah's mother dying at the Mott. . .

"A fucking looter!" I kept saying to myself, and then aloud, with my eyes squeezed shut.

I looted a fucking sharecropper's house! . . .

"I looted a fucking sharecropper's house!" I said, and opened my eyes. Stud was facing me, gripping my shoulders. . .

Ghost bile from the honey I stole at Hutchins Mott volcanized my throat. Expressionless fear like a blind cat or faceless corpse groveling in dirt ate my heart that just stood still for it.

For it! *For it! For it!* I just kept moaning into the hole of myself where the worm had gone or which the worm had created or where the worm was born, not aware of what it was she who half made Jonah had that I needed so deafeningly much. . . Then the old woman in the valley of the sharecropper's bed became U-U, like a picture developing through soul over Time. . . I wanted to drown in her honey and smother in her legs glued around my ears like bees ambered in the moaning of a tree, her lips atop my live root and stinger. . . Angel, soul buddy. . .

"Fuck it!" I said. I cracked, and pulled away from Stud and walked outside, where Lopez was pulling up in his blue truck with U-U. I stood atop the ramp leading up to the Cypress Bar, and shook all over, even in my mouth, to not be a punk. A liar. A best fucking friend.

"U-U," I said.

She had on a white cotton sleeveless blouse and a simple blue skirt Jesus made for her.

"You look terrible. Someone has hurt you. What has happened?"

"Jonah's dead," I had to say.

"The Muleskinner?" she asked.

When that happened, when she said those very words, the world I half-ass knew stopped revolving, and it sighed; the liquid of her eyes assumed every depth of any sea on any planet; her burning tear was hot as any star. The bay tilted on the world's frozen axis and heaved out an oceanic whisper, though the lips of the sea spat out no translatable word. . . that meant what a picture means when it never moves. . . and there's nothing explainable on film anyway that's just one still picture after another still picture. No movie moving. Just a sound. An interruption. The Monotone Monologue of My Midget Life. But it was really nothing, just a sound the monks like Tung Hsi inhaled instantly as the world exhaled it. The oceanic sigh behind the fake shitty movie of my small life I had learned out of necessity to love. Genuine sound provided by the world's popping lung in the liquid track of the sea. Like Tonto leaping off a rock onto the Lone Ranger, the heave of their collision. All the individual pictures seeming to move together to cover up the unpictured soundless history and make up an alibi like Oswald at a movie, a mother in a bottle, a father in a working funk, a brother in a room when all the groaning's going on, the snap of little necks, the smothered brother's final gasp: my crime was my not telling, my convoluted weariness and the not knowing how to tell or to tell at all the little black man who was Jonah at the Blue Nickel, the little black lover, the big white beloved. . . The sad expressionless paragraph intending an impression where the original is lost from a mistake, pretends the sigh. . . For silly trite shit like this whole fucking tiredness fear alibi for failing the simple thing I loved, the ocean must have sighed. . . this thingless thing I loved: their tenderness.

"You should have seen them dancing, really a couple," I said to U-U. Or something. Not that or only that, but I couldn't talk well. My talk was swallowed by the speechless bay with the crabs sifting the remnants of its meaning, tender in their way, and old Neptune trying to lure back some titanic love sunk beneath his whiskers drifting into La Vaca Bay from the deeper Gulf where he had let them grow for millions of years like white seaweed, now, in mourning for his lost goddess. . . The whiskers Neptune grew because he couldn't really sing a lovesong under water.

"Oh, Willy," U-U said, and stroked my hair.

I shook all over with winter. . . summer.

"Will you cut my hair?" I pleaded.

My face in the shade of her head was in her hands. Her tight hair pulled her ears and eyes back foreignly, almondly.

Her cheeks and lips and ear bones shone silkily. Her thumbs worked my mouth over womanly.

"Do you have clippers?" she said, like a mother or aunt to a child.

"No."

"That's okay," she said.

I noticed a plastic baby barrette in her hair.

"Papa has some."

She hauled me by the hand to Papa's truck and I kept looking back to the green bleached-out door of the Cypress Bar entrance to THE CONSPICUOUS ABSENCE OF WISDOM OF ANY SORT bar, seeing nothing move except the sunshine burning against the door, whose temperature and brass knob I knew perfectly well.

Stud did not come out. No Chet.

Out to the truck we went and I stood like a zombie while U-U opened the door and helped me in. Just as I got in, the door to the Cypress Bar opened and out of the cold air-conditioned darkness stepped Darla Mingus carrying a martini, wearing a nightgown you could see through in the sun as she delicately descended the ramp to the white gravel of the lot.

She looked up at me but saw just a boy and lifted the martini glass slightly and smiled preciously hello.

We pulled out onto Beach Road, U-U driving. Like a toad or a frog that loses its tail in quick evolution, I turned without knowing how to turn in the front seat of Papa's blue truck and kept looking for someone else to emerge from the bar. Soon, a lone man emerged and watched Darla cross the road and climb the hill to the office at Shotgun Lodge. I automatically took the wheel and jerked it right, toward the bay. U-U hit the brakes and screamed. I don't know what she screamed. I kept looking in the rearview mirror, now, instead of being turned around in the seat. I just kept looking in the rearview mirror at Stud crossing the road, climbing the hill to where his wife sat upon the sleeping statuary fawn, and saw him place lightly both his hands upon her drunken, dreaming head.

CHAPTER TWENTY-FOUR

She took me in Papa Lopez's truck to her uncle's house in Dimple and parked in the sand amid cactus under a live oak tree. The cactus had long, sharp needles. It was big and old, grungy and spread out, and bits and pieces of things were snagged on it. She passed from the shade of the live oak into hot sunlight to the house and pulled the knot out of her hair as she stepped onto a concrete block to enter the house. Her hair had been newly dyed blonde and thickly waved, but in the devastation of Chet's arrest I hadn't noticed. I suddenly wished I knew some poems or something. I followed her into the house and we walked around it quietly looking for people and something good to eat. I suddenly thought that I had not washed my hands ever since leaving home two days before the previous morning, when I reached for a Hostess cupcake on top of the refrigerator and gave it to her. Her short fingernails looked eaten off and were painted a sparkling blue. The house was not air-conditioned fully but live oaks covered most of it and it was liveable. A little room in the back had been a beauty parlor, with a sink with a sprayer and a chair, but the beauty essentials and instruments you normally see there were gone. It hadn't been used in years, you could tell. You couldn't smell apples or lavender. She opened some hand-width-thick antique fucking Venetian goddamn vines that showed us a thick black rubber Halloween trick spider's web stuck by tape to the window and a rich gold bottle of Breck. The Breck Girl was the mother of angels and the Wife of Human God. U-U lit a cigarette of marijuana and set it in a tiny heavy thick clear crystal or cut glass ashtray and set the cradled document up on the sunny windowsill thick as cinderblock because the whole house was made of cinderblocks plastered and painted soft yellow.

Oh, Dear God, the feel of the spray on my hair! The Breck she reached for and warmly poured upon my hair! Jesus Christ, the stupidity of words like indictments to make known the hot touch of blind all-seeing Water, Tits, Tongue, and All Fingers, the Long of it, the Short of it, the unheard melody, the Song of it criminalized by God as quick as Kings fall in love or Dancing Girls tell truly how they feel. As Eustacia leaned over my head bent back in the sink, her naked cross dingled off the peerless apple of a holy God-given throat and without her seeing I darted my tongue out and touched it. My dad crisp and dry in his sports page never did that, I laughed, my eyes shut. Then blackening, ever briefer, a picture of Mom holding Merkel pretending to sleep in his monkey pajamas in the road at Nehi the day Trout died, but afterward, in the dusk of the day, cut my love experience with Holy Cross blondeena U-U like a card cut from a deck of fifty-two, and I let blondeena U-U drop away. The card-picture of Mom and Merkel expanded to include the dead Trout open eyed, standing with his arms down, sweaty in his rheumatic striped pajamas, in Nehi Road. The card flipped to show a fool in cap and bells and dropped away under the sheriff's boot heel in the Nehi roadbed of Time flat and still in my head with U-U's breast shaking in my face in Tio Leonito's yellow cinder-block house in Dimple. . . She dried off my hair with a towel from Heaven.

"How do you want it?"

"However you want it."

She had a pair of those ultralight haircutting scissors now in her nonmarijuana hand. The sunlight beaming through her curly hair enriched the Evil world we like so much and learn to Need, Tung Hsi would say (not I, Will Bell, at rest and just following fate to the beautician's chair). The fact of Papa's squeeze-clippers for cutting boys' hair was opted out before we even saw the sunflower at Esperanza, and she had taken the short road to Dimple, her uncle's house and the ultralights. It was like everything was decided for me and I liked it so much you could call it love. It was like a road had formed from the Hot Spring Spa to Nehi, Nehi to Hutchins Mott, Hutchins Mott to the Migrant Cemetery, the Migrant Cemetery to Earl's, Earl's to the Tarpon Inn, Tarpon Inn to Blue Nickel, Blue Nickel to Cotton Bale, Cotton Bale to Big Stud, Big Stud to Carbon City, Carbon City to Fallen Apples' sister shop the Countess Eileen, the Countess Eileen's to punch-in at Big Stud and Deer-Suckler Darla's roof over the wishing sea boning up to the boulder-reinforced Woodcock shore built of shattered rebar-hairy foundations and creosoted poles, and from the Shotgun roof to the Shotgun dining room where the Yankee actor-sounding model took Killer Chet's head. . . to the staircase. . . from the staircase to the leathery office pad where I called Chet's home and

Chet's mom and Chet's store and no one answered, like calling Bell Acres and Everyone Answers, all the Mexicans and my brothers at once. . . and every notch or hump in the road shaped the meaning of a new name for me: home, real home, not the house where Dad was, but heaven.

"You think Chet's dead?"

She laughed softly with teeth and kissed my forehead.

"Chet will never die," she said.

I reached up and pulled her head down and kissed her. She pulled away like it hurt and stepped to the window, turning away. That worm inside me flattened out like a tapeworm eating the road. I told her I was sorry; she was shaking all over. The cigarette was smoking in the window in its ashtray and she reached up and pressed it dead. Then with her face to the sun she stripped off her shirt so that the sun could flood her. Then she pulled off her skirt and backed toward me so that the star could flood her whole body, but it couldn't touch her feet. She kept flowing backwards to me till her thighs at the back touched the balls and toes of my feet which were filthy from the road. Yet I felt her with those feet.

That night we went to Refugio jail to see about Chet. She had convinced my insane blankness he wasn't dead. No way they kill a white person for maybe killing a black person, she said. It was the first time in my life I'd ever heard a negro person called black. The most respectful term for us was negro. But black wasn't respectful, it was just a color. Black is the color people turn when they blow up or shrivel and die, that some people are born believing in. Or black is the color of my true love's hair, the old song goes. The pure white and the pure black are the most mysterious, most rapt guardians of True Blue something or other. I laughed. Eustacia pulled the little Coke from between my legs and sipped it and held it up to my lips and I sipped it as she looked at the road to Refugio and at me and smiled. I remembered Natalie Wood telling Warren Beatty a poem, but not a blonde, so I lit a cigarette and offered it to U-U who refused it.

Someone, man or woman, at the jail told us Chet was being held for safekeeping until further notice or a judge decided otherwise.

"Where?" I asked, pissed.

This morphodite looked at me and had heavy mustache whiskers stubby under the skin.

"Here, of course."

"Why?" U-U asked.

The stranger was reading *Road & Track* or a magazine like it. "Do you have official business here?"

"Ma'am, I do. My best friend's locked up and I want to see about him."

She squinted at me and got up with keys on a big eternity ring, her chair sliding back to the wall. She put her biggest key in the Refugio jailhouse door and fished it around. The face on the brass lock was almost heart shaped and the ornate head of the key rhymed it like shoes to a dress. It spoke of the value of safety as part of the scheme of Forever. At the end of a row of six cells painted green was a large bold needlepoint framed in oak and hung from a screw on the wall, instead of any window. It said clearly, to be fathomed by prisoners, visitors, and keepers:

> Crows do often make
> the sounds of parrots.

I think there was a period at the end... She frisked us lightly and had U-U slip off her shoes. Her shoes were pastel or white sandals the Mexican and white girls always wore in summer. My feet were black up the toes from the road. The cells were dark but each lit by a little I swear to God brown bulb. The jailer waited. I put my hands on the bars to one cell and saw my best friend sitting on a steel cot bolted to the erect plane of the back wall. No chair nor nothing else there but a blanket under him. He didn't get up to greet us. The matron stood by, behind U-U five feet, her head cocked from practice. Football practice in her mind. I remember the magazine she was reading wasn't *Road & Track* but a *College Roundup*, a prognostication of prowess, freshman, sophomore, junior, senior, and redshirt greats of the Southwest Conference. She watched Venus put on her sandals like Festus Haggin wishing he were Jesus, and wiped sweat off her lip. U-U asked if we could be left alone with Chet, and she backed up slowly to the old door where it was darkest.

U-U put her hands on the bars, too, and Chet stood up. In one of the queerest things I ever saw in my fucked-up life, he wrapped the blanket about himself like a bedouin so that part of it covered his head. I laughed.

"Chet, man, what'd they do to you?"

He stepped to the bars where U-U's face was framed and kissed her gently. She hissed back through her teeth, stepped back a half step and covered her lips with her fingertips. She started crying immediately.

"Chet, man, I—"

He slid over and grabbed my shoulders through the bars and the blanket fell. He couldn't press his face into mine because it hurt too bad. I think he was crying, like a sad Man in the Moon.

The woman at the end of the hall sniffed.

"I resisted," he said.

He stood like a tree, then broke at the knees, squatted and picked up his wrap. U-U put her arm through the bars to help him rearrange it over his head.

"I thought Stud helped you," I said.

"It didn't take long," he said.

"You know," he said, "if I ever get out of here I'm gonna catch the biggest trout in the world and I'm gonna stuff it live up his ass, pull it out and make that Fucking Frito eat it."

I laughed in my chest and looked to see if U-U was offended.

I had never heard Chet be poetic or coin a word.

"Frito?" I said, and laughed.

He laughed and cried from hurt. He was crazy absolutely from pain. He never before cut down Mexicans, and he loved Papa Lopez like I did, like everybody did, without reason we knew of for anything else. We knew all kinds of Mexicans. He was crazy...

"Hey, Chet," I whispered. U-U turned to look at the deputy.

"When you getting out? Tomorrow?"

"No, man, I ain't ever gettin out."

He grimaced and touched his chest lightly, and blood filled his sacklike lips ballooning out like night crawlers.

"They think I killed that fuckin Muleskinner, man! I told em I had seen his mules in the pen, and all—"

He broke off, broke down, tears of sap dripping off his eyes, mouth, and jaws. I reached in and took his wrists before his rising hands could touch his face.

"It's okay, man. I swear to God."

U-U ran away towards the mongrel deputy and right through her, through Time itself, the steel door, like the Galloping Ghost. The door must have opened with the deputy an unconscious hinge. . .

"Man that chick's crazy man, I fuckin love her," he said. "She was with me by the dead soldiers at the settlement."

He meant Hutchins Mott was where they had been. Otherwise, the words *Huisache Mott* would have spun from him. The sunflowers were our young soldiers headless with seed-dropping heat at Hutchins Mott, Huisache Mott, Dimple, Nehi, up towards Carbon City, and all along the roads thereabouts we walked alongside each other sometimes before Chet was old enough to hot wire cars and see over the wheel. Since kids, we had talked of the sunflowers that way, a Wizard of Oz sort of thing but never mentioned that way, the asphalt and dirt roads and roads of sand our Yellow Brick Road going round and round our world we had to be studying and dreaming in, guarded by the sunflowers green and yellow, black and golden and gray and all we fucking had as living toy soldiers in our land called home that couldn't be home any more than Oz was to Dorothy. Our fathers didn't believe in toys, only history and sex. In Chet's battered, impersonal face, impersonal because it was like it was battered into someone else yawning and trying to be, I imagined the turtle wandering the Motts as Toto, gasping in heat instead of barking in frenzy, and grinned absently as Steelhead or Tung Hsi might have grinned in the face of suffering. . . Chet was spinning away into his world, in the cell. . .

"She had ahold of my. . . She had a hold of me when the lights rose up and—"

He stopped right there dead, and clammed his whole life shut right in front of me. Everything shut off, his tears, the serum, the wisdom, and he was not my friend. I put my hands in my pockets. I remembered Murphy cool on the deck, and I tried to stand like that. He spoke more urgently. His wirous fingers held the bars before me like the paws of a squirrel.

"You saw the mules, Jonah's mules?"

"No, man, it was Peter's and Paul's mules you dumb fucking shit!"

We both agreed in laughter.

The bulldog whistled.

"Man, Will, you gotta come back in the morning and you gotta tell my dad! Please!"

The freak began to walk toward us.

"As God is my witness," I said.

I put my hand over his fist gripping the pole and it stuck to his skin. I moved past her coming on and she said, "Satisfied?"

"Fuck you," I said safely.

She went to check Chet's cell door and I had to wait for her to return because the door our girl had literally flown through was locked. She had held it for U-U but locked it for me. She slid a partial pack of cigarettes under the cell door, squatting down, stood up and spread her feet kind of wide like she herself was being frisked, and took a book of matches from her shirt pocket and dropped them on the floor for him to reach for. Then she nudged them closer with her boot.

Chet's hand did not come out.

She nudged them closer.

Finally, he reached for the matches and she stomped on his fingers. Chet screamed. She walked back toward me with

Chet screaming obscenities, and a voice from the cell by the door spoke serenely.

"She's a rare piece, ain't she?"

I feared to look but did and it was Idiot Sperry standing with his clodhoppered feet crossed and his hands in his pockets under a gold-amber bulb on the ceiling. The bulb was caged in a fixture like a fencing helmet the size of a beekeeper's hat. The matron whistled past. He reached on tiptoe like a ballet dancer and cradled the fixture like Atlas a ball, then sprang like a spider to the door. He stank of vinegar or kerosene plus vinegar, and his antique wing tips were black-and-white boats of the same. They had been hardened and faded and knew fancy times.

"What whalers have dreamed of, sweet gondoliers know. Gondola'd in Venice the privateers go," he recited.

"What's that?" I asked.

"Give me my fuckin paycheck you piece of fuckin white trash motherfucker!" he fumed, "Mexican pussy eater!"

The matron paused.

"What paycheck?" she asked.

"I don't know," I said.

She could tell I was lying. He spat on me. She struck the bars near his face with a leather billy club and he stood back. She unlocked the door to the office and we went through. She looked at a clock on the wall and turned off the lights in the holding cells.

"Nigger lover! Giant pussy eater!" he yelled.

Sperry kept yelling through the old steel door. You could hear Chet praying aloud. The deputy sat at her desk and opened a personal cooler with lunch and two IBCs in it, and offered me one. I thanked her. Then she asked me to open hers for her. She opened a new pack of Camels and pulled one out. I lit it for her. I asked her why she had stepped on Chet's hand. She said it was a jailhouse trick they called the Refugio Rub for all the little bootlickers they got in there; then she rubbed the fingers of one hand lightly together, thumb to each finger's end, like she was rolling an invisible coin or feeling for powder or clean dryness on them. I noticed her fingernails were manicured short and perfect like Stud's. With her other hand she pulled at her crotch like a man whose pants were too tight, and exhaled smoke deep from her belly.

Visiting hours were over. U-U was gone.

"Bring his paycheck in the morning," she said, and locked the door.

CHAPTER TWENTY-FIVE

The Refugio jailhouse was an off-pink opaque stucco structure during the daylight hours, but at night from the solemn street it looked more like a welcoming hotel, with safety bars on the windows and bright lights in the office. The Dairy Queen was closed. I started walking towards Woodcock, probably instinctively because THE CONSPICUOUS ABSENCE OF WISDOM OF ANY SORT bar was there, at the sea-beaten heart of it, with work and food.

Since U-U was gone, had fled in the heat, I didn't see Papa's truck anywhere and didn't give a flip where she was. I knew Chet Evans loved her, and he was a hero now.

Refugio's a sleepy town, and it was nearly all asleep, black as a pearl, as I passed on through. The only light in town was provided by God behind the heavens without stars. The moon must have been somewhere, since it almost always has been, shining strong enough to project shadows.

The road south of Refugio bends west toward the ocean and takes you through egret-haunted swamps with rivers flowing through. Salt flats forget life to the left, like the old wet toes of Sperry's shoes, flats like maps of nothingness.

"I fucking love this," I said for history. No arguments, no reasons, no alibis, no birds, no fish, no frogs. I sort of half-assed wondered where my parents were but really didn't give a shit.

"The busted fuck life is," I said, and swigged the matron's gift of IBC.

I was happy, amid everything.

"Dad'll be glad I got a haircut," I said, the root beer hot.

The night hot. The sea hot. The road hot. That Chet might die in jail didn't seem bad or tragic, though I consciously figured out I loved him and would either drag his dad's sorry ass to the jail the next (next?) morning or have to kill him, marry Mrs. Evans, fuck her, and make her happy, whence I'd be Chet's dad but he'd be dead or in jail anyway.

"Boy oughta be a best friend's dad," I said.

You think about it. You think about the sleep you lost. On the cotton bale, years ago.

I heard a power whining back up the road and stuck out my thumb without facing it, facing Woodcock southwest, since coastal towns really have no bearing or direction of any kind. They just exist and the big ones have lights.

The truck blew past me and stopped on a bridge over a river. It had not skidded frighteningly or halted dangerously, like some maniac who'd want to stop and buttfuck me and decapitate me and feed me to the shrimp, but just like a curious person. He let me walk on toward him without backing up. His backup lights, the little white dots, did not come on. My knees and ankles felt banded together and moved more slowly by Necessity, like the legs of cranes looking for food or trying to stay hid while things pass by, or like the legs of cranes wired together by mean conservationists fed up with the system or fired.

I got up to the truck but didn't recognize it. The heat of the engine and royal red of the brake lights pushed against progress, my passing the truck and crossing the bridge, or stopping to say hello or get in, and it was like rubber bands were looped on my feet. I could feel my toes and the soles of my feet in the sand.

I chose not to pass the driver's window, that was rolled up, but to walk around the other side of the truck. Nothing was in the truck's bed. It was empty. An empty set of flat shining ribs without even scratches of work on it. As I passed the front bumper, he beeped and I ran in my mind but my body stopped. In my mind my foot was cut and I fell. He pulled forward, and the window at my shoulder came down.

"Want a ride?"

Cigar smoke and easy listening music drifted out. He turned on a light of some kind, or maybe he opened the door, and I looked in at the King of Darts. He was dressed crisp and ready for Friday night.

I got in and found the clock face on the dashboard and it said ten o'clock.

"Is that clock right?" I said, having already hitchhiked a lot.

He looked at it like a man checking the health of a farm animal, quite objectively, and tapped it with his finger. It didn't have a second hand.

"No," he said.

"Why ain't you wearing shoes? You step on a nail in the darkness and you're fucked. Infected."

I hadn't even thought of the darkness. I smelled sausage on a bun and he opened a sackful of hot links. He did not offer me one. He chewed the terrific bit of Texas, and looked at me. I didn't talk, but moved my head gradually to see out the window at my shoulder. Away.

"Why in the fuck is it, every time you look out the window you see some kind of lights. . . when there aren't any houses or anything human around?"

He reached and touched my leg with the sack of hot links.

I thought I had sounded real, adult.

"Go ahead. Eat one."

It was the first nourishment I'd had since Thursday morning. The time I'd raped the honey was another day. So Chet couldn't be in jail for joyriding the antique truck.

"Man, mister, this hot link tastes fucking good," I said.

"Circle C in Beeville," he said.

He wiped his hands on a towel he kept beside the seat.

"Where to?"

"Nehi."

"What the fuck's Nehi? Nehi's a kind of grape drink," he said, instantly laughing. He laughed like he had one in his hand. I laughed at the name of my home town. It wasn't a town. It was a cemetery. He reached behind the seat and pulled a beer out of a cooler. He opened it for himself, sipped it, belched, and laughed without hurting my feelings.

"Where's this?" he kidded. "Not far from Ankle Deep?"

Or he said something close to that, but it was funny.

"Nehi to a tall Indian?" he laughed.

"Dimple Road," I said.

He calmed quickly and tapped my leg with the last hot link in the bottom of the sack. I turned it down. He took the wrapper from my hand and rolled it in the sack and tossed it out. I hoped for a giant white bird to glide across our headlights. He took a toothpick from a toothpick holder that looked like a gunbelt for a miniature person, that was attached to the visor, and picked his teeth.

"Where you been?" he said.

The worm sank in me like an eel swallowed whole by a jewfish. The King knew who I was by first name, at least, and where I worked. He knew about U-U.

"Gone," I said.

It was too cool for a boy to a man. He sucked some meat from his teeth and rolled the toothpick. A moment came like a shark in the water and everybody cares. I looked out the landward window for whiteness but saw the flat black fucked up world jacking up.

"Where's gone?" he said.

I didn't answer and just decided to wait for death like everybody. This man fidgeted some and rebit his cigar he had placed in an ashtray. He wiggled and wobbled his head, neck, and shoulders with both hands on the wheel.

"I ain't going that far, but I'll take you home so as to get cleaned up. Stud'd kick your ass out of his place, dressed like that," he sounded harsh like a father.

He drove right to my house and let me out. I didn't know how he knew where it was. He knew a lot about me. He rubbed his face on the shoulder of the arm whose hand grasped the wheel, and looked out his personal window at the family graveyard.

"That used to be Mexican, didn't it?" he said.

"Uh-huh."

"Didn't your daddy teach you any manners, boy?"

I had not said yes, sir. With my hands on the door and my feet on the ground, I looked at him and wondered why they called him king. King of Darts.

"Thank you, sir."

"Well alright," he said, and drove off.

CHAPTER TWENTY-SIX

I'm trying to remember back on the empty IBC bottle of softdrink the matron gave me. What I did with it. I can't. I have been trying to remember back on it and can't. The King of Darts threw it out the window into a swamp.

When I escaped from his truck I went around behind my house to wash the hot link off my hands at the spigot. A turtle was drinking from the drops of water dripping and I squatted down close to speak to it.

"If ever I touched you with my hot-link hands a fox would eat you."

I washed my hands with soap and water at the spigot, first moving the turtle with my foot. It was light enough from somewhere to see the helmet of the turtle to begin with. With fresh clean hands I picked up the turtle and took him to Trout's and Merkel's graves to show it to them. I lay between their graves and held the turtle at arms' length heavenward and smiled back at the ancient who always smiled at me.

Who knows how long this took.

Who gives a busted fuck.

I put the blessed angel atop the crown of Merkel's grave and gave him every opportunity to move away. But he wouldn't move away or mourn or say a God-blessed thing. He was not so afraid. It was like his shell fit him perfectly and nothing could happen.

At that moment I heard something and looked between my feet to see a set of headlights rising up and coming home. They were not the lights of Mexicans coming to take back their land, their muertos ninitos infantissimos heaps, but Mom and Dad coming home up the driveway in their car. This was a '56 root beer-colored Rambler. It spoke of everything shitty and fucked up about their lives. Faded root beer in the sun. Our house had no garage. He refused to "milk the account" for one or use his own two hands to actually do the work himself to build one for my mother because he was insane.

They went inside the house and turned on lights.

I had been gone a long time but they probably thought I was at Chet's.

This was Friday night July first 1964.

I turned to look at the turtle to ask his advice but he was busy eating a cricket, some black thing small enough for his beak. He mawed it, crunch, crunch.

"You've made your decision," I told him, and picked him up at arms' full length. His narrow head dangled down to me. He was, you see, unafraid and a perfect commander, he had all his equipment, born with it all, plus confidence, plus real confidence and the disposition to act wisely. He swallowed.

I threw him off into the bushes where the live oak babies grew and a terrible commotion ensued. It was a family of javelinas that porked and screamed away out the sandy mouth of Bell Acres where my brothers Trout and Merkel were buried. The littlest one looked like a Mexican jumping bean running away with its worm half out, half hatched. Pitiful.

I found the turtle on his back against a chunk of gravestone, with his feet drawn in, like a helmet that just wouldn't do. So I picked him up and put him belly first on my head, like William Tell his apple boy. He panicked and began to swim up there, but his claws could not touch or reach my fingers. I had had years, millennia, of practice and would not bleed. I told him, "Good thing for you, King, with the open road and Merkel's stone nearby," but then he pissed down my back and I automatically dropped him. I heard a sad, explosive sigh. Oh Jesus, I thought, poor Merkel! He lay on his back in the sand, and I picked him up and blew him off; I even cleaned his feet.

I took the turtle inside to show Mom. She was in the kitchen with Dad. They were smoking together and their clothes were spattered all over, even slapped, it looked like, with pink paint. The clock on the wall with a wire said after ten o'clock. Some fucking time. Neither looked amazed or dismayed to see us. If anything, Dad looked happy, just plain happy, to see me bring the turtle into the kitchen. They must not have missed me. Sometimes in summer the days just roll into each other and vanish like changings of the tide or layers of cloud. . .

"Your mother's new rug, son," Dad said. Blood and urine leaked from the turtle's tail onto the braided rug you could throw in a washer and wash.

I took him back outdoors and placed him under the spigot.

Back inside, a horrible thing happened. Mom was eating old cottage cheese with a tablespoon. Dad was grinning stupidly at her. They had long had a bet that if he really quit the insurance business and got another job she would eat week-old cottage cheese with a spoon. She hated it when it was fresh as a daisy, clean and white. But this had that yellow line.

"You got a job, Dad?"

"Better than that, son," he jumped to his feet and grabbed my shoulders like a man with a nugget, a big gold nugget rock solid on the Klondike.

"We painted the spa! Pink on the inside, yellow on the outside! Your mom and I and Chester and Gloria Evans have gone into GODDAMN BUSINESS, Will!"

Mom kept eating. He turned, still holding my shoulders, and looked at her the way a Klondiker would look. He was a sourdough veteran of ice-worm mush and by God the worm had turned. He said as much as he dragged me down to his and her level at the table. We sat in metal chairs that didn't match or go with anything in the realm.

"Look," he said, and his head dropped to the table and banged it, his eyes had tears of glory in them, "I am so happy, Will. Someday, son, someday," he bit his lip, "you and Chet will run it. Then it'll be yours. All the free baths and the glorious romance a man can stand."

"What about a woman?" Mom said.

He tossed his head undaunted at her sucking a spoon and declared, "Of course a woman!" Still happy. Still very much alive. Still very much wired. The old clock of Time like a still picture ticked in Love.

"Love, son. We will furnish Love with all It needs."

Rooms, dildos, sheets, rubbers, Bibles of Portent, Gideons of Nonsense without the cookie.

"You mean, it'll be a motel?" I asked.

He shoved me back in my chair like he was having to push away a dream.

"Motel?" he amazed. I didn't stand. His head molded back into form like Jell-O opaque with dreams. Bibles. Hopes. Jobs. Checks. Mayday, mayday.

"This is a spa, son. This is a spa."

I wanted Moses. I needed Jesus. Mom threw the spoon into the sink and walked into the backyard and started the Rambler. He looked her over as she passed to the out-of-doors only as the insane look at people passing. Unflagged, unfogged, undaunted, peerless.

"And look at this," he said, never leaving my eyes. His eyes blue as March never leaving June. Blue not a color. With his foot he shoved something out from against the wall, under the table. A box. A box that was closed. Flapped and folded closed.

"What is it, Dad?"

"Open it. Please!"

In there was a puppy. A golden puppy. It had a little curved tail that wagged and pointed up over its back toward its head. I picked it up and held it.

"What's its name?" I said.

He reached forward and touched the dog's head, then he scruffed the top of mine.

"You name her, son. That'll be your decision."

"It's a girl dog?"

"Yes."

"Contessa," I said.

He looked eerily puzzled. Eerily eerily at us himself. Then he brushed her head with his fingertips the way you'd, anybody'd, wipe off the wisps of a sleeping infant.

"Contessa it is."
"I just love its little tail, how it does."
"Oh, it'll go. The tail will go," he said.

CHAPTER TWENTY-SEVEN

There was something beyond everything but I didn't know what it was. It was under the paper under the puppy, and under the box. The sky that night above Texas was like a great turtle shell full of stars, and Mom was out in the Rambler, roaming. It was her trait. And it was her rhyme with Dad. Like poems rhyme sometimes without sound, but pictures. A frozen woods, a snowy lake. A frozen lake, a snowy wood. I want a stickler for facts, a fucking driver.

Dad went in to shower and I followed him with a flashlight from a kitchen drawer without him knowing. He was singing in the rain in the shower as I looked at myself, not in the mirror, but in the picture-frame glass of Trout's and Merkel's picture Mom hung above the table of toiletries. The haircut was half-assed and stuck out all over. It was like she had waved the scissors over my head and waxed the old grown-out burr.

"Fuckin bitch. Fuckin Mexican slut," I said.

"What's that?" Dad said.

"I didn't know you were in here," he said, happily, the shower curtain under his chin, his face dripping water on the floor.

"I'm not," I said, flipped off the bathroom light, and walked out to the kitchen to eat a box of Little Debbies I knew were there. Dad laughed uproariously. It was our game. I wasn't being bad. I couldn't be bad. I was all that was left of the contents of the happy poem they had bled between them like spiders spinning yarns to catch and carry.

"Son!" he yelled from the shower. He took long showers.

"Gotta think of a name! Hot Springs Spa won't do anymore. That's the old world."

"Dildo Springs," I yelled.

"Nah," he shouted.

"Too many hard feelings against the Indians."

"We'll have to think about it."

He was scrubbing his head like a Nazi.

"Good name, though. Geronimo."

I grabbed a six of Shiner and the box of Debbies and split. In the back, I yelled at the dimpled bathroom window the name I had given the spa. Dad ran to the backdoor in a towel, flung it open, and with his fist in the stars shouted, "Geronimo!"

He didn't care. He might have had soap in his eyes.

Beer after beer I drank in the cemetery with Merkel and Trout, always giving them sips. I ate four Little Debbies and lined up four on each of their graves, like buttons. They got drunk easy, being dead. As Trout reached laughingly toward my can, I'd pull back like Dad used to in Trout's room. All for the good. Then, I'd let him sip my ice-cold beer.

"I wished I had salt to sprinkle on top, like Dad used to."

Secretly to sterilize the tin, Dad would salt down the top of the can, then thickly dab his tongue on it. It was an old-days custom, following the piff of the church key. It would taste good to him or anybody, to a woman, a boy, a turtle, an animal, a king, a countess, a toad. . .

Trout's head fell back on the pillow. His eyes floated up and out like stars full of air. He was asleep. He was dead again. Big burly rhyme. I made a smiling face between their graves with the empties and didn't give a shit if Santa Claus or Jesus found them.

"Come time."

When Trout and Merkel were dead Dad wrapped them in Texas flags except for their heads and placed suits of clothes atop them. Avoiding public scrutiny, he shut the dome-ish casket lids, having allowed only Mother and me to see. Then he clenched his fists atop the lids, one on each, and gnashed his teeth, humped over. He blubbered a prayer for all our forgiveness and Mother placed her leaf-shaped hand upon his back. He had fornicated, and they were born, in Beeville, he said. She put her leaf hands upon his face and told him Twins of Love, Herbert Bell, Twins of Love.

When the moon was halfway over and Mom had not come home, the house was dark and the cemetery still as a dime. Dad was asleep. Merk and Trout were resting. When you hope for raccoons, the whole world has gone to sleep. The worlds of knowledge and common sense. But me. I had a hard-on I could not explain. It made me laugh, and moved me, pretty hard, such that Merk and Trout woke up. Without anger, but dazed by Death, they rubbed their eyes and looked at it and asked, "What is it?" and "What's wrong?"

"Nothing, Brothers. Just a wand."

I tucked it back and started walking toward Woodcock proper, toward the sea, something about the thumby-thin dime of a black-backed diving moon more like a knothole in depth made me wish I had a seventh Shiner and that in real flesh and blood my older brothers could march with me. I hated not to turn around at the mouth of the cemetery to see what part of them had followed me. Some part of them had. I have seen this part of them and others, since. In feeling, the residue of the dead rhymes closely the nodding motion of a snail thinking it's unobserved, crawling at low speed in search of food. The feeling of being in contact or witnessing the residue of the dead you loved maybe without knowing you loved them has the same lucidity of air that hangs in the doghouse when the old beloved and partly ignored dog is dead, or the ample light left for nobody alive in a dead person's room, ample and independent of sun or moon or you because it's fucking spiritual. I let them tag along at their own pace because I had to, having awakened them, invalids who in life slept too much.

I took Dimple Road to look for my wife U-U at the yellow-block house of her uncle. "No. I really just need a trim off this fucked-up college-boy haircut you gave me." I laughed, empty as a can, and a cool breeze off a black field of cotton hit me from behind such that I felt it on my calves. I knew it was the dead calling my brothers back home; I shut my eyes and turned to wave good-bye but they were still there. I smelled the baby powder Mother dusted their corpses with. I opened my eyes and saw my brothers big as pillars, old men holding hands across the road. Six foot tall, silver dead sunflowers barely reached their knees. Now, though, they were real twins, identical twin giant old men. Their white beards and hair had the milk of kindness as mother and father should have exuding from the ghosts of their hair, true, unpainted, like the opaque ends of a rainbow where colors meet in a full circle past where you can see. . .

This happened a long time ago. I just stood as still as possible, having learned from them in the casket. But the moon must have moved. For the sunflowers parted, rattling, at my brothers' feet, and a woman big as God walked across Dimple Road beneath the arch formed by their arms. She was big as God and wore a without-Time, long peasant skirt that swept the tops of her giant bare feet. She had on a long-sleeve blousy blouse like a shirt made of table cloths buttoned at her wrists. Her hands hung relaxed, large like spade shovel blades and limp as partly folded catalpa leaves. Her hair was up and down in wonderful disarray the way prom girls' and old ladies' hair looks following the dream of a long sweaty honeysuckle dance or a moon dance or a rose-hot-orchid-nosegay-cold waltz for all the night at some lakelike time in youth and identically again or more lovely later in age in the oceanic night of remembering. In her own world, she looked, adrift on feet flat and big as pretty dories but plainly human off the field, walking, not floating. . . It was I who was mixed up, not the residue or she or they. . . But in her world, she was alone.

My brothers looked down at her passing under the bridge of their arms, then at me. Their white arms were white enough to opaque the stars and their happy eyes had witnessed whatever man can't write about or talk about or maybe even see until he becomes like them: dead to life, then bigger. . . She was gone past the sunflowers, into the shorter, dense, green-and-white world of cotton in the gigantic field toward the sea.

Then the white giants and I heard a moan like that of a woman who finds her own dead child flesh and face eaten down to the bone, far out in the field of cotton, many paces beyond the ranks of sunflowers. . . The cry shook off Time, and I was a spool-cribbed babe shook in my bed till Mother came running. A black thing in blackness like a big Tar Baby or a mountain with hands held me high and my head hit the ceiling, the top of the world. . . a gasping dead vacant bloody huff blew from me. . . a slam onto plastic I licked. . . mattress. . . my climbing, standing, gums on the railing. . . "Jenny Lind! You need a fucking goddamn Jenny Lind like you need another asshole. You need another asshole! You fucking whore! Mother of my sons, you fucking whore! You come here!"

My mother knelt and picked me up, my lungs like an empty stomach. We twirled. She blessed me with kisses and licked the blood off my mouth. . . her naked as born, and Herbert my father had a little shoe in his hand.

Just my memory. Just my fucked-up memory.

"The Giant Contessa had beautiful hands and the love of a man called Jonah. The Giant Contessa had beautiful hands and the love of a man called Jonah. We live in a blue house on Mockingbird Lane some other place someday we will paint. We live in a blue house on Mockingbird Lane some other place someday we will paint," she kept saying against my head, against her face and breast I could have lived within if buried in an iceberg, so warm and good and right, goddamn it: The Giant Contessa had beautiful hands and the love of a man called Jonah. She bent and sheltered me in a corner, her head jammed in the corner. It's funny her head wasn't pointed. The rocking. The noiselessness except for the creaking of knee joints, the gentle flipping of her breasts across my face. Her gentle, almost glovelike sleepy fingers cradling my back. My father's feet as in pain she turned me over and I saw them on the floor, bare and bony, the

feet of the Devil. My stiff baby neck. His curling toes and sinful gasp. The pool of his withdrawal.

Then silence like a velvet curtain fold, and turning back toward the Jenny Lind:

"Merkel goes," he said.

"He is draining Trout of all his energy."

He put the shoe down in the pool of sperm and went away to lie down on his bed. He had to be alone, he said. . . "Long drive to Beeville."... He would shower in a motel and had plenty of shirts still left in his closet where he went to be alone in his and my Mother's room.

"Someday!" he shouted from in there. "Someday I'll have work. . . Work!—and not just a job! I'll cut out all the travel. . . and wasted money on gas!"

He was jolly.

Mother and I showered and bathed until dawn, when he drove away to Beeville. Mother recited her jingle. She rocked me on her lap in the steamy grave of the shower smelling of Ivory.

The Giant Contessa had beautiful hands and the love of a man called Jonah. . .

Somebody started shooting fireworks off the top of Irrigation Ridge, to my right as I faced toward Nehi that I couldn't see with my back to Dimple that I couldn't see either. Of course, my eyes had shut on the baby vision or memory caused by Little Debbies and Shiner, and the fireworks being tested three days early dimly lit the insides of my eyes like the smooth glass bellies of Tiffany shades or the undersides of parachutes. The cotton field lit up like No-Man's-Land in a battlefield as the big soft white stars boomed. I looked down at my feet for security, and saw their original form black with toes on the asphalt. In the cotton field you saw no soldiers, no giant forms, no people, just a blotch expansive of thick green bushes dotted white.

Irrigation Ridge ribbed the Texas coast from Corpus north to Refugio. The pipeline atop it carried water to thirsty maize, sorghum, cotton, and corn. The corn was for hogs and fodder, and gardens for vegetables were watered by hand. . . Atop Irrigation Ridge north of Dimple Road where I stood high and sick on Little Debbies and Shiner, three people stood testing rockets off a launcher like a tripod tilted toward Woodcock. The shush and boom woke some folks in cinder-block Dimple, and they came out. A few walked into the field, toward Irrigation Ridge, like they were still asleep.

One of the people, a boy in pajamas, climbed the ridge and stood a distance from the experimenters blasting off rockets. It was over quickly. They didn't want to waste all their rockets. And the people walked back to their houses. I had watched the fields and seen no one big. When the boy in pajamas came down, I asked him to describe the people by the launcher, but he didn't speak English.

"El gente alla. Grande?"

"The people there. Big?"

He smiled hugely, a big, even gigantic rubbery smile. My gutful of memories quaked. . . the wavy thickness of my brother's lips.

"Merkel?" I said.

His eyes settled back some, but he smiled.

"Hermano?"

His mother called him in. He lived in a little cinder-block house like Tio Genaro's, but much smaller. As his mother held the door open for him and he ran to it excited by the rockets and life, I saw past her stern ugly face to the neatness of everything in the cube: bright white lightbulbs, a yellow-painted pictureless nail like a railroad spike high on a bare red wall, a portrait of Christ by the ceiling. I could not remember how to say good night in any language. She slammed the *fucking* door, and locked it. She threw her *legs* into the slamming. It was *her* idea. Her *whole* self. She *hated* me. Through the cinder-block wall, the boy who looked like Merkel sobbed and shrieked a child's prayer in Mexican.

I turned from the house. The people on the ridge, manning the rockets, went down the other side, to Pentecost Road.

Gun smoke clouds covered the cantaloupe moon. Cantaloupe, paper plate, thumb-thin dime, silver knothole, white of the eye in black ribbon, all the moon that very night at different hours. I tried to see the smokestack at Carbon City but couldn't see it.

"Find me a muskmelon! Cut that motherfucker! Find me a cantaloupe! Eat that bitch!" I exhorted the cotton. "Why in the fuck would anybody want to be a shrimper. The smell of that shit on your hands night and day."

I started to cry. My hands came up to my mouth like Little Debbie and Shiner were still there, though nothing was. A tiny cool breeze like a thimbleful of ice water hit the back of my neck, and I collapsed inside while standing straight, not falling to the sandy ground, but just dissolving inside, no integrity left, like a horse electrocuted in a slaughterhouse. . . I feared facing Merkel's cold-breathing ghost behind me on the stilts Dad gave him to practice being taller on when I was a baby. . . I fell out like a witness overcome. Into the church-tent stillness of Dimple's night I spun. My face slanted to the right as in the condition the doctors call Bell's palsy. My chin slacked downward as if ready for a blow

I couldn't withstand. . . Then Eustacia's soft voice spoke my name, "Willie Bell". . . She put her hands on the balls of my shoulders, and stopped me, and kissed the back of my neck such that I swallowed Merkel's stilts and smile and all his sorrow and Trout's original well-wishes not reported here and Dad's dildo'd pool and Mother's wonderful why-ning, and I spun hole-tongue to whole tongue open and a perfect match like sweet clean worm to sweet clean worm meeting in the perfect earth. . . Then it was us. . . and U-U laughed for glory, for she had found me. She had found me in the night when I had been looking for her, there in the confines of Dimple sprayed by cotton-ball warm-up pre-Fourth of July fireworks, both of us wandering around like it was New York City or Dallas and we'd never been there, or some phantasmagoric wilderness not the Woodcock precinct we knew, me always, her that summer. . .

A light like a big hand-held spotlight swam across the road from a house in Dimple. It wriggled like an eel through puffs of gun smoke drifting off the ridge. It didn't see us and wasn't advancing.

I pulled her blouse up and off and right there in the asphalt road finished my haircut, her laughing and licking the top of my head like a mama cat milkless but laughing, laughing, laughing, laughing, and I was lapping, lapping, lapping the salt not of woman but of the sea and God where she'd come from, off her shoulders and everywhere, I swear it: "Will—Willie. . ." Then a belly crunch, gurgle, and the gusher came in, Old Number One, Old Spindletop, soprano jolt and tenor quiver. . . a door slammed in Dimple, a Spanish female screeched, spume fumed out my nose and U-U swam. . . Her lost, the link. . . me lost, the silk eyes. . . us lost. . . the world pinked outward not a color, the unworried incantation of come, the misspelled uses and misguided memories and murder even then, the strain the muscles knew. . .

"Willie. Willie. I love you."

"I love you," I said. Her swimming had stopped. The ocean rested. The atmosphere was silver over the road and cotton. Her inner thigh made a saddle for my head as I rode for just a second the everlasting firmament and studied the immobile firework of the stars. . . The heels of my hands had pebbled under my weight. They were still hot with asphalt. I touched them to her. I smelled the heels of my hands, searching for hot life, which I formed and held, harvested and wasted, in the half shells of my hands, immediately after diving to the bottom of the sea.

"Good for us this road is old," she said. Her newborn eyes, her mouth unchanged since the beginning of time.

We laughed about this together. The oldness of the road and young love's rolly-polly rhyme with it. Once among the deer at Shotgun Lodge she had said how she and Chet knew they were still young, but I didn't. The light that had swum toward us, before, had withdrawn and swum away.

"Did that light come from your house?"

"My uncle's house. The barber. My house is far away."

She said it like we had never been there. She looked like she was sitting on a swing, but she was sitting on the asphalt, in the road.

I helped her to her feet and to her house, her uncle Tio Genaro's house. The house of the barber. He was already snoring. She let herself in. I stood on the porch of steps and put my lips next to her fingers on the screen. She moved away her hand and put her lips there. I told her to put her breast there. She did. I went blind kissing it. Him snoring. No sound. The wheeze of a seesaw whiffing out the wick of time. The nick. The shit. The sweet. The cloth. The rag. The Good Night Get Lost Guts of Gone Nuts Time. The good bad barefootedness, the drop there. The curly hair. The God-made curly hair. The air kiss. The standing droop. The shut-eye decay of yes love no word needed good-bye Willie. The flat hollow cheap-shit door painted a color. The backing down stairs. Cicadas rattle. Hutchins Mott. Mules. Hands. Smell. Back kitchen window slides open where the drive goes live oaky to Dimple's Road, and U-U says, "Psst! Come here!" and hands me a big brown envelope. Forget. Smell. U. Her.

Almost quick as the window shut I doubled back and tapped it. I didn't care how big her uncle was. She slid it back and was in a robe that tied at the neck like Darla Mingus's.

"What's this?"

The envelope was sixteen times the size of a playing card. But it felt brown.

"I searched all over for you for it!"

"When?"

"After Refugio!"

Chet came back to me, where I had lost him in love a few heartbeats back. Fuck this shit. Fuck life, I thought. My bag of love was filling on its own like the ocean never stops moving, throbbing, even in the fucking Arctic at either end. Icebergs groaning.

"Willie!"

Her rabbity hand shot out and grabbed my chin.

"Look at the pictures! The info!" she said.

"You need a shave," she said, and smiled like Gidget with children.

I grabbed her wrist. The window shut. I heard no Mexican talk inside. I looked up on the roof and saw no animals. No children. No moon. No view. No weathervane. I held the envelope up to the sky like a king a joker or a fucking jester a wild card. It had a pale company name printed across it in big, childlike letters made of hollow connected dots faked by an adult or machine. I couldn't tell. You could write other information, like customers' names, in ink over the company name that was set in the paper. I ran out into a field to gather light and spooked a family of animals that scampered furiously down rows, and slanted the envelope, looked:

Brundetti.

My feet in the sand felt like big shoes that fit me.

Brundetti.

I stared and stared at the name. A squinter. A squire six hundred years late. Dotty, holographic, shuttering: *Brundetti Brundetti*. The name over the name's ghost. Light bubble chains under already light bubble chains. Like film of film. Shadow of shadow. Father of child. Baby of brother. Feckless then, a feature now: Brundetti.

CHAPTER TWENTY-EIGHT

On automatic mind past Huisache Mott up the sandy road I went on to Hutchins Mott and found a farm light shining tall on a modern pole like it didn't belong to the rustic gray-ribbed quartet of slaves-turned-sharecroppers quarters and Jonah's early home I'd raided for wild onion honey and meaning. Farm light a too-bright, expensive rhyme-in-the-body for the rolly-polly moon hid behind it, the moon like a rolling albino bug head separate from the bug's body; farm light separate from the Woodcock world where the incandescence belonged, not the holy family quarters where you but need a lantern, I said to myself, and shook and laughed. . . I was trying to relax for the envelope: impossible to explain except stealing scared moments of time in spots of darkness down the sandy roads from Dimple all around till the farm light drew me to it like a dumb cicada at night jumbled up with love and only a buzzing song to lead it somewhere a few days after thirteen years of sleep at the roots of a tree.

Stood against the light pole and took a breath. Thorax shook like a green cicada. Tried to relax for the envelope breathing like a flat brown lung in my hands. Farm light burnt like Dad's pole lamp illuminating the ghost of his chair. . . The ghost of Jonah's boyhood, gray. . . The decap moon man grinning. . .

"Happy moon," I said.

Stood in the flaming evanescent cape of the farm light, against the pole, my foot against it, relaxed somewhat, and watched the quarters for ghosts. Laughed. Cried.

"Fuck it!" whispered.

Opened the envelope and pulled out big slick color picture of a pants-off crotchless black-legged corpse lying on its back on corn-stubbled ground, holding up its own shirt tails, with its knees veed up and its crotch a gaping hole maybe hacked with an ax. . . gentle relaxed black hands held up a hem-gathered blue plaid shirt. . . hazy rim of an old beaver Stetson, leather belt and new blue work britches under his elbows. . . Next photograph: side of this small man's shoulder in same plaid shirt, ground level, camera on the ground, must have been: small man lying down flat on his back with no ear and no face anymore of skin or features dear God, scalp pulled back over top of head like tight sock hat. . . Next picture, other-side shoulder, ground-level shot of same head's meat-red cheek of skull scalp ripped and foggy bulge of scalp itself thick red corpuscled. . . "Jonah, Baby, Jonah, Baby" I urged softly as a resonant whisper come out of me helpless automatic as that of lady-mama shouting dying whose honey I needed. . . again, "Jonah, Baby, Jonah, Baby". . . the flap of Jonah's now-holy face was drawn over his head, the upper lip, nose, eye holsters and forehead like a heavy mask of latex administered over years by the knight of respectability known by two squires as quiet, cool, knowledgeable and just the Muleskinner: him: once-pulled mighty by a strong evil hand back over his head that had loved her milky mountain in the shack where we saw her sleeping, we squires saw her sleeping after love, holy moment the mules bawled, remember, now his No-Man's face like a true knight's fatty glove thrown down in torture. . . mix of my mind. . . scalp visor for gauntlet. Didn't weep. On instinct, automatic. Objectively, without much feeling, hoped he was dead when they ripped off his face.

". . . Jonah, Honey, Baby, Baby. . ." I actually spoke, objective as a record with all its feelings in a groove, dull, black, and plastic.

And no sharp dog tooth hanging down, no white, gold, or black rotten dog tooth, like the gold sleeve he'd hang on his dog teeth was stolen by the torturers, white men at war with their blackness. Spifffft!—sound of my spitting. Spat out a big fuckin chunka soul. . .

"Just none, teeth knocked out I guess. . ."

And hazy past the ground-level profile of butchered Jonah stood suave in beach couture the deputy Murphy. I swear to God I had to spit out another chunk of disgusted soul, drained off my head already snotty with clots of failure. . .

"Posing cocksucker."

Next picture was Misty Lorraine George, Earl's assistant, smoking a cigarette, Orphan Annie haired, drunk in a black dress on a green couch at home, red-pearl sex-haggard eyes iridescently expressionless. . .

Next picture was a dead woman hung by the neck off the side of a yacht called *Your Serene Highness* or *Your Sweet Highazz*, couldn't read it. . .

"Maybe Misty."

Then pulled out a glossy publicity-type head shot of Martin Luther King with goats' horns penned in blue Bic over his head and "Son of Cain" scrawled across his forehead.

Other pictures. None of mules. None of Mexicans. Just colors and slickness poorly developed in the farm-lit frames of butchered Jonah glossy like the eyeballs of God seeing this and maybe the lynched Misty George.

I turned over the sure picture of Misty George. On the back was penned "Nigger lover" in same Bic blue discernible under the farm light. I put my face up toward the light on the pole and could feel its presence like the Holy Ghost raining down in particles of particulate clear matter that is colorless and fills all spectrums I know about, dazzling and hot in the unclouded carcass-quiet stillness of night I did not report, before the big reflective moon it could not rhyme. Stupid. I was thinking or spinning like a tired cicada in old worlds and using old words I had never used or maybe even heard before, like "oft" in the silent raging poem of my mind buzzing under the jellyfish tone of the light. But my body was selfish, working independent of stupidity.

I knew what I saw.

I leaned against the light pole and crossed my feet like I would reading *Outdoor Life* at Earl's against a window or seated, in a chair. I used to wait for my haircut, with Dad in the twirling chair and Earl talking man talk to him, and Dad listening during his summer haircut with me, the one tradition. I'd be hoping down deep in my dick for someday to lay my face on Misty's belly covered with the cool, almost chilly sheath of her pleated skirt that was probably just a sleeveless dress cut in half by a belt that came sewed on it, and then, instinctive as a mule or bug or a dolphin, nudge my ignorant pleading face down below, for she'd be sitting there dull and curly and shining in wreathes of cigarette smoke, reading *Playboy* glossy eyed like now in her picture in the manilla envelope in my hands...

I stood still and shook all over. Everything was clear. Everything meant nothing or something meant worse. Stupid. I could be wrong about it all. Something I ate on U-U. I could taste my wife in my mouth. I strained up at the farm light to find a moth. I quaked so hard the pictures rattled and I laughed a little Merkel laugh aloud. It scared me. Dancing perverted at night across the barnyard opening like a country lane between the dismal quarters and where I stood laughing under the pole that lit another building I'll never describe because didn't see, came a hornet carrying half a caterpillar so heavy the devil dragged the ground. My brothers were dead and my wife U-U wasn't with me. The farm light buzzed above me like a burning angel saying Ah, and the moon had moved away. Whenever I squeezed my eyes shut and slapped shut my ears and then opened all four, the farm light was still saying Ah nasally through teeth... Every picture had had something dead in it... The woman hung there was white... I looked back at the photo of the yacht named *Your Sweet Highness* and tried to see the shadow of curly hair against the prow... It was there. She had on a simple white dress that clung like a shadow to her form. Her limp arms and legs I used to worship in the barbershop sort of poem-ed her lank strapless dress wet with ocean...

"Maybe she was dragged," I said. I laughed again.

"Keelhauled." Stupid. I was thinking like Steelhead.

I breathed a deep sigh of night air and curled the envelope with the pictures in it into a firm stick and drummed my leg like Chet would have. *Chet gave her the pictures...*

The headlights of a car turned up the road into the Mott and I ran like hell down the lane of barnyard to the barn. I ran in the glory of death already present, across the barnyard sloping in the pounded-flat fluorescence of a century, to the dirt lane where the hem of the farm light frayed, between cool ghosts of dead slaves I could feel come round like when you wade out deep into water. My head turned naturally like a camera toward the last verge of the shack where Jonah grew up and the square-mouthed barn where he must have played. I ran through the barn because the far doors were open like a perfect rhyme but blacker onto a field of cotton, and there were houses on either side. The square black door almost sucked me through it because maybe a few thousand black ghosts were waiting in surprise, unused to this.

Straw blew at my feet digging the dirt where men and mules had died. In the less-than-one breath it took me to beat through the entirety of the barn, I found the mules, Jonah's children, not stinking yet, perhaps never worried but just been run into cotton and shot. They had fallen across two rows of cotton. I put my hands on their faces in the dirt, on my knees... hard skulls and dusty precious hair, the dead children of Jonah... for the moment it takes to fall, a boy, a monument, a mule. Their fogged dismal eyes were open and their powerful cheeks still round and firm, thick as trout or wheels of cheese. I petted Smokey and Whiskey together and prayed Oh Jesus God Christ One And Only, Oh Jesus Christ God One And Only, a born catholic in the dirt, born just then, and saw light from the headlights of the boatlike car back behind me shine on the cataracts of their eyes like sadness scabbed over still clear enough and fresh to see through.

I glanced back. The car was in the barn. There lay on the earth before its headlights a little mule, donkey, or hump of something covered entirely with gray cloths like a knotted layering of rags. The mountain of rags had a red dot in the headlights. A patch of red. A man in a dark suit got out with a camera, carefully, I would say delicately pushed aside some of the covering, and flashed five pictures, squatting this side, that, shooting the muzzle and rear. The fifth photo he took from astride the animal's head, for he had tried to stand atop the creature, but could not maintain his balance on its shoulder.

Down in the cotton row, I clinched a dead mule's halter in each of my hands, hoping the children might drag me off to Heaven where Jonah really was, waiting for the Contessa. . .

The man with the camera went back to the driver of the vehicle. They talked. I could not hear the big engine of the big car running in the night chiming with cicadas now. It was an older car from the early fifties, and dark. The driver got out, did not shut his door, and both men rolled the animal onto its back. Its legs did not jut up and I wondered why. . . Maybe cut off, I thought. . . Under the blanket of rags that rolled with it, the torso was like that of a jenny, perhaps a child's pony or petite jack. It had something female about it I can't explain as a smell because on the little puff of wind that funneled through the barn off the engine of the car and crossed the rags came a whiff of gasoline. This feminine thing exudes from the form and exists in the eyes of a sexless jenny. . . From under the mountain of rags flopped out a queer dark mane.

Each man took a leg and dragged the creature into the darkness behind the car. They cursed, futilely trying to lift it.

They sounded like northerners or ultrasophisticated Mexicans who knew English. It amazed me, even among the dead mules. . . The trunk lid slammed. The men got back into the car and pulled out of the barn, accelerated, fishtailing. They cut a hard, jerking left toward an opening where a broken gate hung open. The great Goliath beetle of a car lurched through the hole as the carcass wrapped in rags slid sideways across the loose dirt of the corral. Dragged by a rope around its feet, the carcass torqued across the corral like a skier on his back. I felt the breeze and smelled the gasoline off its wrappings. It hit a rise toward the vale of cotton where my foot lay, and a dreamy woman's face turned out from the pillow of her white arm toward me. . . She shuddered, rolled sideways. . . rolled over. . . onto her face like Shirley Temple's. . . Black hair fluttered like a veil across the sleepy arms of the Giant Contessa.

I lay with the mules for a while. The stars got bigger. The night got so calm for awhile, with the cicadas and insects resting after love, that you could feel the stars burning on the skin and shining in the eyes of the mules. I ate a tongueful of dirt because the earth was holy where Jonah had walked as a boy and Smokey had fallen. I put my tongue to earth where Smokey had fallen to his knees when shot. I screamed at heaven the way stars do, with nothing coming out.

    I lay back down flat on my back, tongue out, still crying that nothing, ripped my shirt and rattled backward in cotton like my king turtle on his back, fallen to earth from Heaven, onto its round shell. . . Insane like my father and every snake crossing the road, I groveled. The wishful thinking of invalids waving good-bye in their pajamas, entered my mind. Merkel's love and Merkel, entered my mind. *Trout was hooked on rheumatic fever, rheumatic rummy, and Dad should have killed him before,* I thought, insane. . . I could smell baby powder in the green cotton, and packed my mouth with early fibers.

You can only pray and cry so long. Crickets and cicadas and whippoorwills sexed up again and blew the night into a galaxy of insect and animal music grand regardless of death or tragedy. I rose to my knees and felt enough wind cross my face to make me think the world was really still alive. But I was really so scared that no thought fully entered my mind, then. . . Only now do thoughts come alive after years of helpless wonder about facts plowed under and buried, about why people do what they do. . .

Then, I don't know when, but still at night, still in the field with the mules, I saw the headlights of a car re-enter Hutchins Mott road and rifle up the lane between the barn and the quarters so poorly described before. I slid to my face like a skin diver would diving from his knees to the surface of water. The car barreled through the barn and skidded across the time-flattened dirt of the corral opening. It fishtailed to a halt and the man in the suit got out and picked up a rag that had fallen from the Contessa's head as she had spun toward me before. He smelled the rag and took out a cigarette lighter and set it afire. He held the rag till he was sure it would all burn, then dropped it in the dirt, raced back to the car, got in, and the car took off in a donuting rush.

I crawled over to the burning rag from the cotton. I could not rise to my feet. I wonder why, now.

I watched the rag as it changed to ash and read the name Sperry stitched in scarlet along the hem.

I crawled back to my place between Smokey and Whiskey, with the ashes of the rag in my hand. I placed the ashes inside the envelope with the pictures...

Time threw a blanket over me. I rested my head on the neck of a mule for a while. Awakened by a Mexican voice, I scooted off the neck of the mule and lay flat as a flounder in the soil.

"Quien esta?" he yelled.

A light beam swam over the cotton. Flat as a flounder, I listened.

"Quien esta?" he yelled, then "Usted!"... It could have been Tio Genaro, or the sheriff from Refugio or a caretaker hired by Jonah for his mom before they butchered him.

I rose to my knees and bolted for life across the cotton. Death came rumbling up behind me in the sound of a man's feet and pants rustling across the field. I could hear his loose pants flap against his legs like flags. I ran with the smell of pussy all over me and pictures of the lynched in my hand. I hurdled the cotton rows and laughed to outrun him barefoot, prob'ly shorter than me, when I heard no one coming. Laughter hoovered up in me like my soul with all its sick lint blasted out. The lint-sprinkled floor of Big Stud's office at the lodge came to mind because I liked to sweep it... Chet's tough arms came to mind: veiny from nicotine like the King of Darts'... Eustacia's ankle I had sucked...

Came to a dry ravine cutting a flat of dead unpicked cotton leading to nowhere except maybe the Gulf of Mexico. Thought in the dying night I could see the sparkling blue of the Gulf, but the bay and the island were between me and it...

Came to a fence of barbed wire I tried to jump and cut my testicle.

Right then there was a blacktop road. It was blacktop Dimple Road shining like a silver ribbon in the moonlight and nobody on it. I had to stand still in my bare feet on the road to feel its exact pebbleness just a moment, to know it was in fact Dimple Road.

I looked back across the section of cotton I'd run across and saw the farm light burning at Hutchins Mott.

It was on towards dawn, right then, but dusky.

I started walking toward Woodcock, maybe because of Stud's protection I dreamed of even then when I didn't know I was dreaming. Maybe Darla Mingus I pitied and wanted to fuck. Maybe Chet's mother I secretly worshipped and wanted to marry and father children with. . . The impossible. . . Could've been the few stores like Fallen Apples or even the Circle C where life stalked in women who shopped sexy and I'd wanted to feel them a million times. . . Men think about women when they get really scared, desperate. . . I walked toward Woodcock and I don't know why. . . Darts. Hot links. Hopes. . . I walked along the road's shoulder, near the mostly headless sunflowers. Their armorlike, spiny stalks brushed my arm.

Then car lights rounded a corner ahead and I stopped dead in my tracks like a criminal who had been captured. He flashed his brights and blew past me. It was the Goliath beetle car.

"Roll on, sir. Please roll on," I begged.

The sunflowers were headless, dead, never living like me and Jonah. It got quiet again in the world of the roads and the fields. Maize and cotton covered the dirt like pictures of sleeping doves. Then the car came back. From behind me this time. Brights on, windows up, it rolled alongside me. I felt the heat off the engine tremendous as a sun. I tried to walk faster than the car, without seeming to speed up out of fear, like I did with the King of Darts, not looking in, but the passenger door swung open and stopped me in my tracks. The edge of the door literally entered the ranks of the sunflowers. I could smell the paneling or the cushioning of the door, the elbow rest, saturated with cigarette smoke.

A curly haired man resembling Brundetti in a suit looked at me. His feet wiggled in polished shoes. His white-cuffed, gold cuff-linked hands were folded in his lap. Heat churning off the engine burnt the tops of my feet. He looked at my feet. Cold air gushed from the car.

"You in trouble, son?"

A yankee or midwestern voice.

"No, sir."

"You William Herbert Bell, Jr.?"

I saw the camera with its silver dome come into his hands from his left, from the driver. Fast as a gunman, he flashed my picture. It blinded me like I'd been shot, and I fell back into the sunflowers. They were my comrades catching me. I crossed my arms over my face, preparing for death or a picture. The Brundetti twin stepped out of the car and picked the envelope of pictures from my hand and got back in the car. I had not thought of the pictures since seeing the Giant Contessa dragged across the corral. With his car door open, Brundetti's twin talked to the driver for a minute. I did not want to see the driver. He spoke quietly. My arms still covered my face in an X.

I heard a pop. An ejected bulb landed in the dirt beside my ear. My right eye opened instantly, automatically, and I saw the wasted flashbulb had landed by a snail. Dawn pinked the snail's swirling shell as it glided peacefully along the sand under the sunflowers.

He flashed another picture and shut his door.

CHAPTER TWENTY-NINE

Rain woke me gently and crows cawed atop telephone poles along Dimple Road. I had run a mile. A red-wing blackbird bobbed and sang upon a living sunflower close to me. "The devil's whippin' his wife," I said, because it was sunny above and around all the turbulence. The raindrops felt so good, with feeling. A few fire ants bit my feet and I let them for a while. In the back pocket of my jeans the checks Stud gave me were still dry. Everything was so clear because it had no meaning, but I didn't think of that then. I drank a little rain licking a puddle on the road that was moist and picked up the shot bulb the man ejected. What an invention, its filaments, its darkness, its proof. I walked quite a ways but the rain stopped and left no rainbow. I pissed beer in the road, like Chet, you could see down for miles of black fresh asphalt, enjoying the miracle. I tramped in the weeds for a while with a little armadillo, and gave him some orders, some authority, the way I did when I was much littler, and a young mockingbird stretching its boomerang wings flew-hopped from fence post to fence post after us. Would he have done so without me there, just the armadillo?

I took the checks out and looked at them and saw mine was right. Something sicker or prouder than nightmares and maybe death in me wanted to go back up the road to Hutchins Mott where the honey jar was, but I lacked whatever it took to make that turn, willpower or bravery, and chose the main route back to Woodcock.

It must have still been early. Because it was Saturday July second, the carbon plant was closed and there weren't any shrimpers. On the other hand, if it was past six o'clock, and it had to be, you wouldn't see any conscientious shrimpers anyway. They'd be plowing the bays.

The Countess Eileen was closed till ten and locked. (I even looked in the window!) Across the street I went to Fallen Apples to tell Chet's mom he was in jail. It wasn't open, but a novelty clock I could see said nine o'clock. A speechless Mexican woman was working the Circle C. While I was there, the phone rang and she picked it up and just listened. The person I could hear on the other end needed something. She looked worried and handed me the phone and went about her work making coffee when the pot was still full and fresh. She set the fresh pot atop the coffeemaker and put an empty pot on the burner. It wasn't rinsed; you could smell the soap and see the cloud burning in it.

"Hello. This is Chester Evans' Circle C. Can I help you?"

I would say it different, now. A woman's voice said something alluring and then a male Yankee took the phone.

"This Evans?"

The speechless woman was wiping down the face of the Brewmeister with a cloth. She looked sleepy.

"Evans," he said. The woman behind him laughed. "We've got something for you," he said, and couldn't contain himself. "Listen to this." The woman with him shrieked and silenced and there wasn't any sound.

"Hear that?" he said.

"That's the sound of your wife's pussy with a phone in it."

Every muscle and minuscule of personhood in my gut bunched, and I set down the receiver. I watched the mute woman work.

"EVANS!" the person yelled.

The Mexican woman came to the counter and gently hung it up. She pointed at her mouth and shrugged. Then she lifted her hands as if to say, "Who knows?"

I couldn't speak. I was thinking of nothing.

"Quien sabe?" I said.

She shrugged her shoulders and lifted her hands again. Every dead saint rose up in anger.

"Hombres malos. Hombres muchisimos malos," I said. But it made no sense to her because she didn't know English.

I went over to Fallen Apples and waited there till ten o'clock. When she showed, she smelled good, and her hair was wet from the shower. She invited me in for a cup of spice tea with her, Apple Mull. I declined and she asked me what was wrong. She could tell some big thing was. Her simple dress moved when she stood still with her hand on the key in the door, questioning me, because a breeze pressed it down and back and in.

"Chet's in jail," I told her. All I told her.

She looked shocked.

"My Chet?"

"Chet Junior."

She put her hand to her chest and her breasts showed whole and small under the fabric. . .

I got in her car to go to Refugio jail with her to finally spring Chet after his one whole day behind bars. It had only been one whole day behind bars. The bitter matron, Sperry's jokes, boot heels and slogans, the sheriff's starch, all would frighten her. Her son would be learning. She drove like a bat out of hell. She wasn't crying. She got increasingly so mad I thought she'd crack the wheel. She squeezed it. Its color changed deep inside the molecular fabric of the plastic. My helpless eyes were Jesus locked on her like a study from fucked up Eternity now gutting out one Perfect Form called love. Her determination made her veiny jaw spring out and every good or necessary idgit of every good or goddamn thing in the whole Moby Dick world possible. Her fingers were thin and red. It made me know things. She uttered things in anger you could not hear, nor make out. So she was perfect: Unavoidable hope ensnared in impossible love eating its leg off in a trap of family. The deep-freeze Eskimos moiling in snow and the dead cannibals of yesteryear Woodcock who fought bullets used to feel it: That was the last sunshine or moonshine in the eye of Smokey looking at Whiskey; and bam: That was the last look of a lobster boiled alive at Shotgun Lodge with some memory of some sweet hole or a crab aghast in the lobster pot of the sea just six feet down but might as well be a mile, good as dead, still waving: The light film of slime in the oyster's smile: That was the unattainable Beyond you cannot touch, if true, here, boy to woman, old to young: That was the instantaneous thing no sentinel protects, the unutterable syllable in human shape you just have to watch float away. . . I caved, I withered like a thin twisted orchid in the windy heat of the car seat next to her. I bawled out rhythmic but drowned-out noiseless on watch in the Beach Road rush with the hoping of waves alongside it, like Merkel must have howled silent in Mom's bedroom watching with his horror the sick opposite—for her, for Glory Techumpspieh Tuscaloosa Tennessee Texas Evans— for the flying corpse of the Giant Contessa covered with rags and Jonah's children at last totally still like they always wanted to be in the corral at night, flying white Shirley Temple but grown woman arms with black hair flashing still alive even if dead. . . they say. . . for no more ashes in the restole envelope Chet stole first and U gave me and the maybe dead Brundetti's maybe dead twin brother took, brothers in photography in New fucking York, hating rainbows; no more envelope now. . . for the wavings of Eileen's hair come back years late, like everything else, thirty years trimming trees like everything else. . . dry and brown like sepia breath exhaled from a no-smell generation-old douche bag or the white crypt of an angel, I cried to fucking show. . . I bawled and looked a little sideways like a quiet mule stepping out, proud, horrible, on show, stupid, or the mule's daddy a simple Tennessee walking horse you see on TV when its rider says "Show!" and the poor horse stretches out fore and aft, all legs and four, pitiful and goddamn perfect, shaped like a mule, a mule is an animal with long funny ears, a tufty tail, shaped like a horse and kicks up at anything it hears, like a camera flash. . .

When Mrs. Evans squeezed that wheel I thought of nothing, not of the wheel as my dick, not of the wheel as the only rose in Esperanza—if any rose was ever there—not of the Lopez sunflower whose sun-bleached plastic I could see now rhymed in color and substance the steering wheel turning also on a silver stick. . . xactamente, la misma. . . Jesus! the giving, clear, and uncolored wheel wrap like a snake skin Chet wound so patiently and tightly around his mother's pinkish wheel I saw there on July second 1964 unravel in her hands, bruise as she pounded, throb with hope its pinkish crushed-out juice God through Ford and Color put there: I saw, even grimacing to be quiet myself, only a little hope unraveling. . . "He's sixteen!" she shouted. . . No. . . Never. . . Not their love unraveling, just the hope over the wheel. . . But the misshapen word "shit" came out of my mouth silenced by the rushing road. . . And the sea was waves hoping, hoping, hoping like a girl in a china closet or a mule in a barn or an old woman in her bed or a boy in a quiet vertical chest full of memories pinned up like butterflies and moths on a slave's closet wall. . . to show, to show. . .

Without turning her head to see where I was she reached and put her hand upon my face. I kissed it. She put her finger on my lip and I kissed it.

"It's alright. It will be alright."

But I was crying so hard the waves of the bay increased in depth just absorbing all the hints of life to come.

CHAPTER THIRTY

The sun came out strong in Refugio. The matron I was cruel in describing wasn't there. She worked at night. For some reason I want to tell you everything in the jail office was clean and slammed against the walls, cabinets bolted on, so that movement was easy through the office and the only furniture off the walls the desk and rolling chair. The sheriff was sitting in it when we got there.

"Welcome," he said. He had something in a square ring box that comes with a ring, that he set on his desk and put in a drawer after he unlocked the drawer.

"I've come to see my son," she said.

"You cannot."

He was cool. He searched up and down her with clear eyes. Chet's mom stiffened. She wisely did not scream.

"Where is he, sir, and why can't I?"

"Don't you wish to know why he was held?"

He smirked and his lips bubbled out. He folded his fingers woven together loosely and her fist came down hard on the table.

"Where is he and I want to see him now!"

He was cool and fully physically alive. Latin.

Her thumbnail had lightly or almost touched his hand.

His hands unwove themselves and he took a pair of handcuffs out of a drawer, unlocked them and put them on the desk. He looked at them. We looked at them. He stood and took the handcuffs with him over to the cell-block door. By moving his head he told her to come over there. By staring at me for a billionth of an hour he told me to stay. Without telling her anything he stood behind her and took her wrists back behind her back and she didn't fight it.

"Sir, what are you doing this for, handcuffing me?"

She sounded experienced beyond him, and she was younger than he was. The look on her face was limber, and her neck was limber.

"It is this or a frisk," he said.

"And we would have to wait for the matron."

He unlocked the door to the cells and they went in. I moved somewhat towards the door but he shut and locked it. I heard laughter. Only his big male laughter like a deck of cards being cut and shuffled. Murphy came in through the door from the street, the only door, and walked to the door to the cells. He pounded on it.

"Nice suit," the sheriff said.

It was a blue seersucker.

"Very light."

Mrs. Evans passed around them with her wrists free and out through front door of the jailhouse. I followed her out. I felt like I was getting away from something, I mean with something. They were mumbling. Every tire on the old Ford was punctured. Flat. Mrs. Evans stood beside the car with her hand on her forehead, thinking, and I wondered where Mr. Evans was. I had forgotten about my best friend. I hadn't heard him calling, or anything, and his mother had left. I pushed on a flat tire with my bare foot by now black as the tire.

"Mexicans," the blonde-haired sheriff said.

"Niggers," said Murphy.

"They're everywhere you look. Black as a Bell telephone."

The sheriff actually laughed, but Murphy didn't.

I saw a large family of black folks walking home together from the grocery store. Then I heard a whistle and looked across the street to a ramshackle, dark garage where Sperry stood smiling big and waving. There were stacks of tires inside.

"Got my pay?" he yelled.

She had no idea what he was talking about. I went over there to give Sperry his paycheck and looked at a calendar nailed to concrete. It was pristinely fresh and clean and the year was correct. 1964. All you saw were dates, till you picked it up and saw an insatiable woman. I thought the wind picked it up, but it was my hand. Sperry did not look at me, and took his pay. He had a big spud wrench or heavy-duty tire tool in his hand, and he looked at an old tire half on one of those machines that spin slowly and allow a worker to pry a tire off a rim, with a mag wheel on it, and he absentmindedly dropped the wrench that rang on the ground and bounced onto my little toe, the sharp end of it.

"You've cut your foot."

He looked down at my filthy bleeding toe. He looked like an ugly god.

"Mistah Hutchin!" he shouted.

A black man wandered in from the sunshine out back. He had been burnt all over at some time and all his features except his fingers and feet were erased. He had on heavy black work boots of a western style.

"Get this man some Mercurochrome. He's cut his foot."

The man turned and as he turned, without pausing in time, looked at my feet. When he came back inside from the oceanic sun he glanced up at me, I mean at my eyes, with eyelids that worked.

"Pour that shit on his foot."

It was in a quart bottle. I had not screamed. I winced, then.

The Mercurachrome puddled my feet and the man took a clean handkerchief from his back pocket and wiped them off. The skin had tiny hairs. Excess blood and medicine dribbled down a hole. I thanked him. Sperry had lit a cigarette and he looked pained as I said thank you, like words were electric, and he went over to the calendar and flipped through it. He called me over.

"Looka this."

He carefully showed me each picture. With each picture, he looked at me.

"Know what they all have in common?"

"No sir."

He had that electrical look again.

"They all bleed. And they all bleed white."

He was serious. He was as serious as the sun and the sea and all the stillness that surrounds.

Mister Hutchin was sitting on a small chair beside the back door. He had his hands on his knees. Sperry called out to him to go on to the picnic.

Sperry took out a picture from his wallet and handed it to me. It was of a black woman in a movie, dressed as a nun.

"Can you even fucking believe," he said. It sounded in his throat like he had swallowed his cigarette. He rolled it over in his lips. "A monkey nun?" With his eyes and then his cheeks and then his jaws and then his mouth, he built a grin. His thumb and finger had never completely abandoned the picture, and shaking his head with incredibly quiet laughter, he put it back in its place in his wallet. . . A racing tire was set to go on the mag rim aboard the tire changer; he jammed his big wrench in. The rubber popped and the wheel exploded with a percussive sound you could never get used to if you heard it.

"Whee-oo doggie!" he exclaimed, much relieved at the wheel of his work.

We got four new tires for the Ford. Sperry gave her a list of estimates in a fluorescent hand on plain white paper: "One Dollar Per Mile Towing, Personal Transfer to Woodcock Free, Fifty Dollars Per Tire Balanced and Aligned." These were double the normal; he had the only show in town. The personal transfer meant him driving Mrs. Evans back with him in the front seat alone with her in his absolutely filthy barely running tow truck. It would be extra for me, fifty cents a mile. I had my paycheck but nowhere to cash it. Saturday in Refugio. I had the five dollars the old folks gave me (I had told them I was trying to surprise my dad with a haircut; five dollars in 1964 bought ten boys haircuts till age sixteen) and the petrified rosebud that rhymed Glory Evans' nipples, in my jeans. These things stayed dry and matured in the rain. I watched Sperry put on the tires and each time he loosened a rusty nut or jacked her up a little or down a little I thought things I don't really remember. That is because souvenirs prevent remembering. People buy souvenirs to take home to children who will never know where their parents have gone. Just like tires exactly. Perfect rhymes rotting in fields, housing toads and turtles, burning in junkyards. Piles of fossil donuts black as sin. Wedding rings of rubber painted gold suspended and sinking slowly in the gray waters of Dad's new wonderland. Where he and Mom stood in pink new rooms smelling like bubble gum. The outside of the ranch house was hot moon jaundice yellow, but on the can said Texas Victorian Yellow. The nuts creaked, rusted on. The old Ford Chet Junior loved. Put her in reverse, put her in forward, put her in neutral, Son, said Dad Evans with me and my best friend in the front seat at a family cookout long ago. We were in school, but young. The thrill of the tilted wheel gripped so permanent with finger valleys factory made you could fly ahead, back, left or right without walking or money or time or kids or house fucking payments. Spit. Dad Bell spat to show he was real as anybody Beeville ever put out. "Where you from, Chet?" he said over the top of the car. From the driver's side, outside, all cleaned up, not smoky yet from the charcoal fiercely flaming all by itself stacked in a big black kettle: "Poetry." "Poetry?" "Poetry Texas." "Where's Poetry?" Then the car started. Chet Junior had turned the key with transmission in neutral. The car shook alive. Instinctively, my best friend goosed it. He had to reach with his foot because he was shorter than his mother. It was by then his mother's car to Fallen Apples. His father by then had a truck to pick up dead things in, mostly inorganic or Organic Antique (skeletons, furs, teeth, horns, twisted, bent, balding, thrashed, burnt, confiscated, absorbed, greased, nailed, ripped, feared, voodood, holed, haired, stiff, coon, cat, mouse, dilla, o-poss, buck, jackrabbit his first skeletal item from a family trip to a greyhound farm in Nederwald), nothing that smelled. A set of yellow teeth older than plastic, piano perfect, that a human being had tried to use. But to be fair, his treasures were mostly metal, wood, or stone. His truck at times so full it struggled on its axle. "Oh, Chet! Come in, Darling! Come fetch the patties! Salad's ready!" She yelled. In a sort of imprisoned, happy daze, Mr. Evans turned off the engine by reaching through his son's arms and turning the key. The tag a blue apple. Then Glory came out. She wore flip-flop fancy sandals for the party of six and kicked them off in the grass. The St. Augustine. Her calves brown and smooth as butterscotch. I could not smell her from the car. I wanted with my eyes to smell her all, but this is knowledge. Timeless. Timeless as nakedness. God Almighty, the balls of her shoulders. Turn around. The trim of her dress. No word fits the diligence of sex but the plumb line of a dress. All worlds constructed on the collarbone. No one put a phone there. You blink because it hurts and it's just wrong, you know. The tongueless know. The languageless diligent know, who act. But you hate to blink when you're in love. Don't you. A question mark by itself is the shape of a dress on a woman stripped naked by a boy. His wheel mind. The shape of things. The unburnt prefix of burnt generation or mildewed clothing the luckiest man in the world hung on his treasure house wall prefabricated by Sears. Instead of punching it out, the prefix unfixed fixity a black hole poured to, through, out, and every Mary forever loved has One. Blink. Too hard to love. There. Here. Now. Always. Not an eye nor a tire nor a vagina but a rhyme. Sperry had a display tire in the window, wrapped in gold. Pirelli in Refugio. The only. Had he pride he was proud of it. It had magazines fanning within it, stacked on end in a tight circle like a jet engine inside. I put my fingers on the magazines, and he put down his wrench and came to the office and turned off the light. He had Venetian blinds he shut. He looked at her and me. She seated on a cracked leather chair by a Ford gum machine and a Tom's peanut machine. One cent. One cent. He half shut the door back to the garage off the office, of course. My heart. My hunger. My pennies in the peanuts. She had no purse. No law knew. I bought her five hundred handfuls of peanuts and thirty-two hundred handfuls of Ford gum in my loving mind, but all my pennies were gone.

On the windowsill in the daylight under the Venetian blind he had lowered was an Indian-head penny. One cent. An antique belonging to someone. Sperry probably. Mister Hutchin no. I pried up the old penny and reached for the slot on the Ford machine, when Sperry burst into the office and slapped my hand. Mrs. Evans fetched the penny.

He was chewing tobacco, now, and smoking.

"Gum'll rot your teeth, Mister Bell," he said, wiping his hands on a rag, smiling.

He tugged at his crotch. A tuft of hair at the base of his throat filled out as he swallowed, and his eyes balled out.

"You chew, Mister Willie?"

"I do not."

He pulled a plug from his back pocket and freshened it with his fingers, squeezed and rolled it with personal style, and held it out to me.

"Take all you want. Try it. Do. You're welcome. Just smell it then."

It was right on my nose, then my lips. Mrs. Evans arose to go and walked out behind him. He disgustedly withdrew the plug.

"White trash pussy nigger lover. Bet you chew mule cock."

It's even hard to pronounce in line, in audible sentences, the things he said to my face.

He walked out. In the garage he told Mrs. Evans he expected his money in cash come 4:30, it was 12:30 now, or he'd be forced to tell on her to the sheriff. She had his note and he had her promise.

She said nothing, had committed to nothing, but had his note in her hand on the big Ford wheel when she finally lifted her face to look at him.

CHAPTER THIRTY-ONE

You just want to feel secure and not afraid. You do not speak the vulgar things that cross your mind. But you are like a sea horse in Brundetti's ear, armless to prevent it coming near, curling and uncurling in the sea man always there, turning your head and body stiff with remembrance the rhyme of little time, speaking the whole truth and nothing but a grain or smidgen of sand in the memory-shaped hourglass figure of human time. You failed to love or forgot to love, the same, la misma, Español and English, a perfect peerless feature-free rhyme with real solid flesh-and-blood faces and fingers and toes of those Those you loved. The unremittent unrepentant irrefutable clearly visible smellable feelable impossibility of life to take on lies and turn them into arms is what holds evil at bay. The sea horse has no arms, nor do the fishes or dolphins or whales. See how they glean and wander in school, alone, in pods, at play. And if they sleep, they rock. Rock but don't notice. Rock but don't jar. Deep in the valley the whale that ate Jonah's proof is asleep. Behemoth, what do you dream, and how big is it? A mountain cloud of krill in iceberg blue. A black harpoon with a shark-fin barb. Boat bobbing the faces of men first seen where the plunge holds and the rope of earth ties the bind between you, them, blood in the water which is air and salt in the blood of Jonah red in black, blood water ocean night? Yes, I think so. One Jonah, one whale. The sea horse in the net. The sea horse looking through the bowl back at you. The failure to live eternally in secret flesh is the truth life could not take on and lie about. Lasso a sea horse and make it dance. Not at all. It dances on its own a beautiful delicate dance to the end, when the sea dances it.

Out of your cradle endlessly rocking, out of your bellicose foretime, out of your fishbowl, Beautiful Dreamer, wake unto me. Out of your books, out of your clothing, out of your shoes. Wake unto me. Beautiful Dreamer. Wake unto me. Dead goldfish in the Woolworth bowl, still bent like living. The dead erection Death forgot. The hanged man's honeymoon. The target of time the honey hole. The lost book, the lost story, the lost plot. The twins' graves. The owl and swallow of dawn. The beginning of dusk each day. The unreturnable bottle of Coke you're scared to open. The shape. The beautiful female shape of the armless, legless bottle Stud hands you, the matron hands you not. She had iced the cylinder of an IBC root beer can. The inarticulate birds, gulls, thrushes, sparrows, crows, parrots, and mockingbirds and swallows with one song only varied by distress. Crows and parrots taught to talk, not sing. Please teach this bird to sing. Please teach my sea horse to whinny. Jonah's children talked with rolling eyes. They sang hee-haws we loved, motherfucker, fathered out. Stud a father mothered out. Because when he made love to Darla it was just fucking, making him a strong motherfucker. Poor drunk and crazy Darla with her duplicate son not part of this lovesong! Could she saddle up a sea horse and dance away she would. I would. Brundetti did. Big mule of a man. The birds of the air swim on wings their medium; the armless and legless bottles of perfume, beer, whiskey, and else drink in time that never saturates; the fish fly on fins the waters, armless, legless but for freaks in mud holes, completely surrounded, at death entering other media; the fur bearing with arms and legs mostly walk and grasp in love or need, la misma, inarticulate till all's forgot and nothing forgave, till like now and then you get wild and wooly enough you spill the beans, as the old saying goes, you spill the precious jar of oil the animals gave you to carry, and there it is, it is, your father bending over Trout all his weight on a pillow and the sealike silence of the room. Merkel screaming out in his room next door, a normal scream in a miniature man. Your mom not home at all, babe, but exploring Death with Chester Evans. There it is. There's the spring at the spa. I guess. The delirium. The rheumatic soul of it which bars melody and brooks no apology. The lovesong spine without sound or tone. Just bone and meat make water move at touch make dirt like whales the little dolphin fingertips make no sound till bit like the sea till moved. Just bone. Just like the sea electric and dark, a lovesong without sound or tone till lit or moved. Whale spine in the iceberg. Tink upon it, Merkel's fingers. Just bone and ice where the whale had love and children, frozen sea jewelry. A squeaking song signifying something. Moby Dick's lovesong for Moby Jane Ahab witnessed and moved him, My Moby Jane. Marriage of whales, marriage of Dove, marriage of monkeys. Just bone humping bone: the cartilage of song unrecorded unadvisable under the sea. Ahab waving. Ditty with ye. The sea a battery with isotopes of bone. The mermaids singing each to each are in the bars. The whale of a woman peters out and her catalpa hand droops off the table like a ham. How beautiful. The gold-tooth man sucks it like a bull calf dolphin whale porpoisely crying. The guitarist shivers a

Spanish serenade. Jonah's tooth of gold. (For he smiles back crying, sucking her sleepy finger drunk on music and love her only chance, her normal mother left only money and love, a memory dark and rich as a retina, the black marble soul of the deep blue sea, and he knows they're gonna kill him for his tooth. They said. Stinky gone already. "Where, Contessa? Where?" I heard him utter when the guitar rested.) A whaling man spruced up for love. Her big box-ankle feet in boats of shoes lean live-oak inward to the dark navy of her infinite dress below her knee he sits upon, holding her like Trout used to Mom in the lap of afternoon when they had personal Mother-Son Jesus talks. I on the floor, my cheek upon linoleum, happy. Trout's little arms around his mother's neck, his white Bible in his hand, his skin a purple glow of gray intensity swollen where his blue head sunk into her neck from off her face where it slid and landed heavy, too heavy, she sighed and smacked him, and he woke up quoting Jesus with glue eyes, happy, smiling, wailing weakly, "The meek! The meek!" Aw Jesus God Christ Buddha Hindu Logic Sea Horse Pentax Ansel Adams Alfred Stieglitz Georgia Pollock O'Keeffe Picasso why in the Van Gogh did Dad do it? Church of God, One Star, Real Father, No Mother, Just Love, Just Mary U-U Glory Her Son Called Gloria And Killed Me Who Loved Her: why did Dad have to nibble off my brother's fingertips? Who'd know? Was he smothered, Lord? Tell me I'm just dreaming. From the crypt of serendipity the twin screams out Daddy...

The Giant Contessa had beautiful hands and the love of a man called Jonah. Sing it. The Giant Contessa had beautiful hands and the love of a man called Jonah. Melody. The Giant Contessa had beautiful hands and the love of a man called Jonah. Time. The Giant Contessa Had Beautiful Hands and the Love of a Man Called JONAH. Conviction.

THE GIANT CONTESSA HAD BEAUTIFUL HANDS AND THE LOVE OF A MAN CALLED JONAH. Belief. Solitude. Vacancy. Hoovered. Love. A normal mother who taught school in Corpus Christi and got in trouble and had to quit had beautiful hands, too. Merkel said. Ten years old. Just before he came home and showed Dad with little casts on his legs and arms he could walk like a man. Dad cried. Mom cried. Dad took him to his room and put him in the old crib, mine last. Mom said. Years and decades later. The sea along Beach Road in Woodcock full of promise and musical song hardly changed, years later. We had a big family cookout, the four of us, that night of reunion. Merk home from the hospital. Trout and him together, both kind and loving children. Oh, love, let us be true, even if it means drowning together in love, let us, regardless of abnormalcy, regardless of size, regardless of job, regardless of failure, regardless of the fear side saying something else. Listen. The sea. The normal Plain Jane sea. Contents unclear. Irrefutably indefatigably whatever that means, accepting Brundetti.

CHAPTER THIRTY-TWO

Gallons of fish heads and shrimp trash fell gushing into the sea out of two rubber buckets Chet had hoisted to the railing at the end of the yacht basin dock behind THE CONSPICUOUS ABSENCE OF WISDOM OF ANY SORT bar where his mother had let me off about one o'clock in the afternoon, Saturday, July second, 1964. He was not supposed to do this, but he did it. He did so defiantly.

"I'm sixteen today," he said.

In the cloud of seafood remnants from the kitchen at the restaurant run tight as a ship, catfish moiled, fish I couldn't see cut through, minnows. Almost invisible white lips.

"Man, I didn't know you were sixteen today. Happy Birthday."

"I am sixteen," he said.

I started to say my birthday wasn't anywhere near, but I didn't expect him to get me anything for it, we never got each other presents, but I didn't because I looked at his face. It had gotten darker overnight.

"Who sprung you, Chet?"

"Stud."

"Why call me Chet? I'm standing right here."

His face looked fully Oriental. The damage. I figured he would hit me to get it over with because I had lied about bringing his father to the jail, but he didn't. He was sixteen, now. As soon as the buckets were dripped empty off the pier, Chet turned away from me and stepped toward the restaurant.

"Man, I tried!"

He spun with the buckets like a windmill at me.

"You didn't do shit!"

"I—"

He looked away north up the shore two miles at least to where the unmet-yet Big Man's eternally incomplete dream construction site was, where he said he saw Contessa naked with her paramour, some colored man, he'd said so excited that night last week, Fire Engine Tradition Night, a Friday, where we'd snuck up in the live oaks and spied. He wailed up a big hawker of bloody lung and blew it into the sea.

"I will never forgive you."

I let him go. He carried my lungs in the buckets. I looked back and down at the shrimp heads with their attendant spears. The minnows that mocked them. I sat down on the dock and put my feet in the water. They were black as teak with asphalt soot and dust kilned in the sun. Minnows nibbled my toes that didn't change color. Kind of like black on a black person's...

I just had to lay back and shut my eyes for a little while in the sun.

A sweet smell wafted over me like exhaled air from a pocket of stillness. Then a cloud. And I looked up and saw U-U in a flowing pink dress standing there. Looking down at me. She had on older-woman's earrings and her hair had been cut to above her shoulder. She shoved it behind her ear and it hung there. She was smiling as she almost always did, like that first night on the donkey.

"Why you so dressed up?" I asked her. It was Saturday afternoon and I could see no reason for it.

"My father died thirteen years ago today. I wear a dress to honor him."

She lit a cigarette like an older woman.

"Korea."

She looked beautifully out over the bay.

"I love you," I told her. "I still love you. I will forever and ever love you."

She knelt down and kissed me.

She stood back up and dragged her cigarette and released one of those deep breaths that kills something momentarily. She sat down beside me on the dock. A light aircraft flew over and she craned her neck back to look at it. I kissed her neck. Looked at her.

"I didn't hear you creep up. You must have crept up on little cat's feet."

She held up a pair of golden sandals.

"What's that perfume?"

"White Shoulders."

I had never smelled it. Chet's dad had perfume at the store. Evening in Paris.

"Where'd you get it?"

"Chet stole it for me."

"Where from?"

She looked at her cigarette. So did I. They didn't have White Shoulders at the store. She took a drag off her cigarette and let out a rich flume of smoke that poured away. It looked like a head scarf made of ectoplasm flipping from her mouth. Half drawn by a ghost.

"Did he say?"

She tossed her cigarette loosely into the water and immediately a tiny fish bumped it.

"He said he stole it at Frosts in Corpus Christi but I know he's lying. That lesbian deputy had it in her desk."

She looked disgusted. Sexy-old. A fancy speed boat worked hard across the bay a long way out.

"I wonder if that's Stud."

"Who gives a shit if it's Stud."

I took a cigarette from her pretty dress pocket, lit it, and gave it to her; she puffed it and put it back in my fingers.

"Put it in my lips," she said.

She put her hand on my wrist to stop me, then took a red lipstick from her other pocket and put some on.

"Now."

She held back her hair and I put the cigarette in. It hurt to smoke, and she was young. I told her Stud sprung Chet and where would we be without him. She asked me if I had looked at the pictures. I said I had.

"That blonde whore," she said, "Misty, she cut my hair, these are her earrings."

I laughed quietly like a fish. A smashed clam. A jellyfish floated up in wonder. I got up and walked back down the dock to THE CONSPICUOUS ABSENCE OF WISDOM OF ANY SORT bar and she ran after me barefoot, she caught my arm in hers and pulled back towards the sea. I started to tell her I loved her but she threw her sandals into the sea and I dove after them. . .

A bunch of Boy Scouts on a bus pulled into Shotgun Lodge that evening, to camp there. The people of Grassy Plain on Goose Island would not let them camp there for some kind of graduation ritual into Eagle. On Goose Island there's a magic oak dating back to Christ, a haunted chapel built by Catholics before the Revolution, and the ruins of a cannibal Indian village the Boy Scouts from Beeville, Corpus, and Sinton traditionally cleaned of debris three times a year, once each. This fascinated me and Chet because we could never be Boy Scouts; the closest troop was too far away to walk to when I was at the right age to begin earning my Tenderfoot, and when I told my mother about it she told me to talk to my father because it was a man thing. This was right about the time Merkel was learning to walk on stilts with brown shoes on them and Dad would go to Scottish Rite to see him. . . Scottish Rite Hospital for Burned and Crippled Children, Corpus Christi. . . The short stilts were like long legs that bent, creaked, and flipped out. The hospital was run by Masons with money and Stud was one of them. I saw Merk take two steps on them once before falling and remember his babylike arms and the snaily smile on his face as he cried and the big nurse picked him up with tears in her foggy eyes after all those years. Jesus. One night Dad came home dismayed about Merkel's progress, but, excited as I was to show him the old Boy Scout manual I had found and to talk it over with him, I ignored the Merkel Report and got down to brass tacks. I asked if he'd take me to the meetings. "Where?" he said. "A.P. I think."

"It's impossible. With Merkel and Trout and the debit, it's impossible."

Mother went to the kitchen. Trout cried out from his bedroom.

"It's not impossible, Dad!" and then he coughed. A rich popping of phlegm.

Dad looked at me. That pale, shitty shine on his dumbfuck insane face like the glimmer of a nickel. A smirk like Jefferson's.

"See?" he said silently.

"We've got our own troop here," he said, turning to the sports pages.

"Troop Number One, Nehi."

Then Trout's fit resurfaced and recommenced with a vengeance and Dad told me to be a good Scout and go in and see about my brother earning his "Life badge" and about to get it. His cowboy pajamas were soaked in sweat and his hair long as a girl's but shiny clean. He had a striped pair and a cowboy pair Mom changed every other day. They were thin as facial tissue and tore easily. Even moving in bed, he had to be careful not to tear them, or suffer demerits in Dad's mind. He grabbed my shirt and with peaked strength pulled me down to him and said with that same rubber mouth of the Bells that Merkel had: "Ma Ma, get Ma Ma!"

I pulled off his hands and let him down gently and went back into the livingroom where Mom stood bent over beside Dad's lazyboy. Dad was in the chair with the paper folded on his lap and his hands on her wrists. Gripping them but she wasn't fighting. He looked surprised.

"Trout says he wants Mom."

He let her go and she went in there. I had my eyes on him and he went back to his reading. I don't know how old

I was, or if it happened exactly this way, but I was old enough for Webelos...

The Scouts arrived in an old white school bus. Stud told them to camp in the clearing above the lodge and before the highway. This was a quarter mile from Beach Road. They couldn't see the ocean from there. Even the tallest. If you walked out the Cypress Bar in front of THE CONSPICUOUS ABSENCE OF WISDOM OF ANY SORT bar, and down the ramp to the gravel lot, and headed straight inland like an arrow toward Beeville, and crossed Beach Road, mounting the driveway past the family of deer Darla planted on the motel hill the day of U-U's and my first date, and kept walking, winding past the swimming pool clean and chlorinated, you'd reach the seaward edge of the clearing where the Boy Scouts camped in approximately four hundred and fifty-eight steps or three hundred and eight giant steps. An old hobo cowboy sign up at the highway, underneath the new Shotgun Lodge sign shaped like a blunderbuss or huge teardroplike shotgun, said "Rag-A-Tag Campgrounds FREE, No Amenities, City of Woodcock, Welcome." Stud had bought all that property plus the lodge. With his absolutely clean perfectionism, I don't know why he kept the old amateur sign for the campground up, leaning like a drunk cowboy trying to draw his gun. But he did ask me to tear it down that Saturday, July second, nineteen hundred and sixty-four. The Boy Scouts had pulled in and asked if they could camp there, rejected at Grassy Plain on Goose Island. I pointed with my hammer down the hill to the lodge office. From where the scoutmaster sat at the wheel of the bus, he could see the bay. I told him to check and see at the office. Where he'd see a lady in a negligee, drunk, ask her. A young Boy Scout listening in wondered if I was on a chain gang, doing County work. An older Scout, who looked too old to be a Scout, poked his head out and looked at me and said, "Heck no, Heck! He's earning his Webelo!" and everybody I could hear laughed. The scoutmaster thanked me and pulled on down the hill. At the very tailend of the bus, off to one side because you couldn't sit by the emergency door, I saw a young black face staring straight at me. Had his face been a gun, it would have gone off. It was coal black, chilly, still, and defiantly hopeless or just plain strong in a way nobody can ever describe. But they've seen it, without love and all fucked up in a world pulling away. It's the face of Good-bye. He was looking at the sign. I should say that I saw a sad black face like a deepening portrait of somebody cut from hot ice burning straight through me at the cowboy sign. . . glaring straight through me Good-bye at the sign. . . Then suddenly white boys' faces surrounded it like gleeful flowers on a wall, and they pointed down at his head, mouthing "Tenderfoot! Tenderfoot!" He wore no rightful uniform, but a yellow neckerchief, anyway. . . I turned and whipped the sign with the hammer. The first blow to the head smashed right through it (painted 3/8" plywood). The hammer hung. I wobbled and wobbled and ripped it out. The next two blows went to the ankles of pine rotted from weather. They blew apart with succeeding whacks, and the cowboy fell without my ever laying a finger on him.

U-U worked in the office with Darla Mingus, at first, then some as a maid or housekeeper. She's the one who told me that when Stud saw the white bus come over the hill to the office he ran, physically "ran" to the office from across the road in the parking lot, by the bait stand, and screamed at

Darla to put on some clothes. Darla withered and U-U helped her into a day office and shut the door. Stud handled it.

My feet were beginning to change shape severely, from lack of care and no shoes. They had suffered abrasions. As said. Stud had offered some old camp moccasins, some Clark's Wallabees, high-top, and a pair of work boots from his old days to wear, but I couldn't talk right about it, I couldn't take them. I kept what-abouting the mules in my head with my hands full of shoes. He had a pair of queer clogs he called mules he passed over when he showed me his closet full of fine things.

Since I wouldn't put on shoes or change clothes, he took me to Papa who gave me the hammer to tear down the sign.

When quitting time came I could feel it and I laid the Rag-A-Tag welcome sign down beside the road. The Boy Scouts were gone on some kind of hike but their trustworthy tents and the white bus were there waiting for their return. I marched over the hill of the clearing to the lodge office and looked in the window to see if U-U was in there, where it was air-conditioned and she said she would wait for me. She wasn't visibly there, through the window, but Mrs. Mingus saw me and excitedly waved me inside. The room was chill. I had been outdoors forever.

"Eustacia!" then she blanked and looked away. It was like she had a stroke or seizure. But she had only forgotten. She brightened and told me the rest.

"Ella esta en el carro," she said.

"Que carro?"

"El carro de su tio, Papa," she said well and proudly.

"Donde esta el carro, Senora?"

"Acerca de la cafe," she said.

I looked at the hotel pot of hot coffee they always kept going all day into the night for the guests. She looked at it, too.

"No, no!"

"A la restaurante, alla," she said, and pointed across the road, triumphant.

I was freezing without a shirt on in the room. It was very pleasantly decorated and welcoming. A deer rack, a stuffed duck flying across the chimney, austere trophies. A tall vase of feathers.

"Hasta luego, Senora Mingus," I said and nodded thanks. Smiling big. Then something dawned on her. She held up her hand. "Alto! Espera te! Hombrecito!" and she reached under the desk of the motel. There was a small refrigerator there that I discovered then, when she opened it and took out a bouquet of orchids. She held them sweetly to her breast, below her chin, and with both hands steady offered them to me.

"Para ti, Guillermo. Para tu amo."

She said it all right. Almost as well as a teacher. I took the flowers and headed down the hill past the deer to the road, across it trafficless to the restaurant and couldn't find Eustacia, mi amo. Papa was through with work, at the bar with the new female bartender, drinking a beer. I asked him where Eustacia was, in English because he never talked with me in Spanish when I tried, and he said he did not know. Look behind the bait house. I wondered why my love would be waiting for me there, but I went there quick with the precious orchids and found her sitting in a fancy red Corvette with the top down, staring out at the sea. I had not even known there was a place big enough to park a car there. I crept up to the car like a timid cat would, and put my hand on the hood hot with shade being cast by the shack.

"Jesus Christ, U, where'd you get this? Whose is it?"

"Ours for the night of July second nineteen sixty-four."

"Saturday," I said.

"Saturday."

She said it all in "Saturday." As I got in the car from the passenger side and carefully shut the door, changing hands with the flowers, I felt the gut-level knowledge of pleasure kings live with. I loved her, but I didn't really care. I had a whole fucking kingdom to worry about and wallow in.

Two joints of marijuana lay on the console between us. She lit them both and handed one to me. "Indies." I refused it. "Don't need it." I offered her the flowers, she looked away and flipped one of the joints into the bay. It reached the water. She took the flowers and furiously threw them toward the water but they fanned away and didn't make it. "They're from Hawaii, U-U." She pulled back her hair and put it in a bun and got out of the car and picked up the flowers and angrily gave them back to me. They had been broken, in part. She got back into the car, behind the wheel, and cranked the engine that roared in place like a personal animal daring the sea. Come on. Come on. She floored the engine right there loud and hard and it scared me. With the car in park, it could still freak into gear and scream into the sea backward. Whoever had parked the Corvette there had pulled in backward. I pulled back on the gearshift lever to hold that baby in place and screamed at her to stop it. She would not. She kept pressing. She laughed and threw back her head like someone in the bait house had a string on it.

"Flowers for debutantes. Orchids for the dead," she said.

She pried my fingers loose off the gearshift and furiously shifted into reverse. The Corvette plowed back through a thousand years of sand under a decade of gravel and lurched toward the sea. She laughed and hit the brakes. She had all the Stop and Go in her legs and arms and belly and face and head to accomplish anything, crack kingdoms. Shit, U-U! The car lurched forward off the shoulder of the sea and we were on our way in a tailspin hitch right around the bait house fucking Gone.

CHAPTER THIRTY-THREE

Hard to explain. Trajectory. The feeling. Stillness rushing night wind motionless swaddling clothes lying in a manger of red Corvette sinful and glad and kind of in love and who gives a busted ball about dead brother fantasies when (turning my head on the seat back to look at her) you got a Red Queen driving, taking you God Knows Where at speeds approaching Time up Beach Road Woodcock Texas... *if Perry Mason or Paul Drake or Lieutenant Tragg sniffin out Nancy Drew's long-legged blonde best friend from upstate college (freshman English major headed to med school and a fine career as a haunting novelist marrying rich long after children an organic possibility extenuating dumb perfect self in God-man woman fuck it Merkel, Trout, he didn't have to kill you or have you, he coulda kept it tucked in his pants, a Korean veteran with experience with basket whores in Seoul, he said to Mom who taught me the meaning of Love Is Where You Find It in Chet's Treasure Hut, but dead in love was Nancy Drew's best long-legged friend with her Uranian Ambassador) tries to cross the road they're fucking dead...* I laughed but wasn't high. I was balmy. Low in the pasty-thick wind a convertible traps behind its front window off the bay. La Vaca. I looked at her. She had the joint on the wheel in her fingers like Mom and Mrs. Evans drive smoking. In prison, Chet said his sweet mama smoked marijuana, too. She offered me the joint again because she was stupid. I loved her. I told Chet later I'd kill him if he didn't believe me. But I never told him she was my wife because that was her holy meaning. I think I was meaningfully sober and meaninglessly filthy in the Corvette. She was meaninglessly innocent and stupidly fearless, a girl on a donkey, good as Queen Elizabeth, then or ever. "I'd fuck her in a minute," Chet said of Queen E on TV. Who wouldn't? What king?

I've lost myself. . .

We went to the ruins and fucked where the Boy Scouts had put logs of green live oak cut with hatchets in a square around a circular hole six feet wide. Grass had been there, soft long green grass God loved, and loves, and U-U and I naked piled the soft long grass cuttings pulled out by their roots back into the sandy black fire hole the Boy Scouts had dug before being evicted, for their campfire. The butt ends of the logs had no discernible smell and bled bright water sweet and clean.

"Don't you wish you had a camera to photograph me?"

My gut ground down a physical meaning of light and darkness on film without color. We had made love in the fire hole, my third time. (I laugh now, thirty years later, without moving my face, without color. Pallid, bullshit, dried-up, old fart laughter.)

"You're dumb as a fuckin log, you know that?"

Her eyes changed. Her hair settled into a shape. She covered her breasts with her hands and ran to the Vette. I picked up her clothes like an old nanny and chased her.

"I hate you! I hate you!" she just kept crying.

I wondered, beaten, what I had done and why. This wonder is a physical fact and the same old fucking story. You never regret how naked beauty looks and moves in moonlight running. You can forgive yourself because God can or you have to to go on, but you never regret how naked beauty looks running in moonlight. It's worth all of Time and all of Shakespeare and half of Life to receive the Mass of One-Tenth of One Shoulder or One-Tenth of One Buttock or One Flicker of One Heel. Look ahead or aside or askance through the trees... But do this in no one's name for no one has a name. She's gone. The one who had a name. In the soft green hole her head bouncing. The live oak pillow. Green unforgiving blood sweet on the deuce lick. Gone in her fiery red chariot.

"What a fucking idiot!" I swore to myself about myself.

Because I was an animal, I didn't cry. I just saw that mound of rock they call the ruin. I had no philosophy you could call a philosophy of life, still don't, nor many meanings sounded out or soundable in words. I laughed like a jittering idiot, a sputtering fool, a jester set out on his ear by the Queen who fucked him. Not yet or then or now ever a man. You. You. You. I said. I danced in the fire hole and bounced like a mountebank out of it. "Jackinape! Jackinape! Jackinape!" I grimaced grape eyed at the black-halfed moon.

This all naked, I found the giant oak and climbed it till I found a branch I could hold. And I lay down dick solid upon the branch and said my full name a dozen times or more, with my mouth wide open, to let it drip and cleanse it, till drool hit the earth ten feet below, and a shadow hopped. I stood on the limb and peed on the shadow, figuring, after consideration, nothing would eat the toad then.

"I wish for Trout he could have been a Boy Scout."

That was said. I squatted down and felt my feet where the sandy earth had stuck to blood and formed a coating like over a sugar cookie. No surprises. Long toenail sharp as a clam shell. Should be this way. All blood inside the same. Sand of every land the same. Toenails on every man the same. Pygmy, white, Mexican.

I descended from the tree and still naked searched out a settlement house to wash down my cuts, calling this hunt a raid in my mind. I called it a raid in my mind because of my burglary of the Mott, where my whole existence changed, when I started labeling things intentionally and differently and privately till now in my mind. I found a small dark settlement house made of wood that was neatly sided and painted with "Hittite Family, Rose, Mary, and Joe" calligraphied unprofessionally in moony white letters on the mailbox, and washed my cuts off with their stiff old garden hose.

The Hittite house was all dark. With their windows open and screened, they could have heard the running water. I can't say that they did. A fatherlike shape who must have been Joe Hittite came to the back door, opened it. The wood squeaked below his feet, and the door to the outside of their world groaned. The worm of knowledge living in me climbed up my leg to my crotch. The tip of my penis itched where the worm was searching. The man stepped forward into the brighter night as if his stocking feet had simply slid off the threshold bottom of the door. A metal strip across the door shone in moonlight behind his calves. He was balding and big. His face was heavy like a beer drinker's. Both his arms dangled relaxed, though he saw me, until he raised a hand and reached back inside to flip on a switch too high up the wall. They had run short of wire in their serious effort to build their own house. But no light came on, thank God.

"What you want?"

He looked doggish at the hose running and saw my form.

"Just water."

He lifted his other hand. A red dot from a roll-your-own glowed strong as a lightning bug in his cupped hand. He stepped up backward and quietly shut the door.

CHAPTER THIRTY-FOUR

Sometimes a song gets buried in you like a peach pit that begins to grow. The tree becomes heavy with peaches even a child could pick if the child could find it. . . I have told you lies and inconsistencies because I let them hang too long, fearing worms. Sometimes the notes and notelike words of the unuttered song hang too long, droop, swing, and fall to the ground where ant, slug, sly monkey, and quiet possum revel in their juggling melt. The hot body of the overripe peach melts in the palm of the monkey or the man, softens the belly of the slug under the hole of skin, sticks in the pincers of the goopy ant. But even if you pick the song in time, perfectly, just in time, before the peaches fall, and eat each one like a note attracting bees to your mouth, words fail the melody always. Talking of love is like singing to a bee.

I remember Jonah walking in a used sport coat that fit him. It felt relaxed. Not to spoil it for you, I must tell you it was gray corduroy. It was winter in Woodcock, and cool. The palm trees and live oaks rhymed green flashing in the sun. Modulation was the air of every thing.

"Chet, he's going to call on Eileen," I said.

"I know," Chet said.

Anointed with peaches we had smashed on our heads from a basket of culls at our feet, juice and flesh on our faces, chins and feet bare in the sand where drunk bees hovered, we dove into Jonah's and Eileen's real tender love like bees into wounded peaches previously softened by others—animal thumbs, fingers, beaks, or the tentacles of Time—as the Muleskinner stepped up into the Countess Eileen. Between me and Chet, only inside *me* was she called the Giant Contessa...

Upon the branch of the giant oak I licked the wounds of my feet, chewed the swallowed sand, and pissed on the toad to keep it from harm. A custom.

The Giant Contessa had beautiful hands and the love of a man called Jonah, brothers.

The Giant Contessa had beautiful hands and the love of a man called Jonah, sisters.

The Giant Contessa had beautiful hands and the love of a man called Jonah, mother. Father. Child.

Without a name or fingers yet, Eileen was an egg in her mother.

These would be peaches.

These fallen peaches.

CHAPTER THIRTY-FIVE

Who knows what time I arrived at the Giant Contessa's cabin built under the live oaks by the old man's dream, the vast construction site, a ruin of newness, that would not be finished for fifteen years, then painted blue? I had no fucking idea. After the Hittite raid I swam in the bay with my clothes on and walked from Goose Island back across the bridge to the outer limits of Woodcock where the cabin was still among the trees. The trashy trees trashed by construction workers' trash. Plastic bags, empty nail boxes, conical paper cups crumpled, trampled, and whole. A sorry fucking mess. I had no life anymore, without U-U.

"If I had only had a camera," I said in the middle of the bridge with a horde of porpoise flying landward, then seaward, then landward, hopscotching the waters under it.

"I could have taken her picture."

It was late at night, July second, I know.

My father was at home masturbating and washing his hands.

On the posts of the bridge I kept seeing a little bird hopping along I called Hop-a-long Cassady without knowledge. Only imaginary. I had read a poem by Matthew Arnold in an at-home leather-bound anthology that I alone read, about his need, but I couldn't remember it past the first line or two. In the wind off the bay, the strong, steady motionless wind soft as cotton candy, I could smell life and fish and tried to pick up the scent of dung off La Vaca Island way out there, but I could not. In the salty tasteless cotton-candy wind, I tongued out hard and opened wide and faced the Gulf and tried to gulp it down like water at the Hittite hose. I strode sideways like a ghost crab and heard my footsteps chopping like waves against a rock or pier, as if the giant bridge were rocking under my stupidity, when it hardly shimmied under the full weight of a dozen trucks loaded with sand. I kept up the steady gait the full length of the long bridge from Goose Island, where the whooping cranes get ugly, all the way south-southwest to the outskirts of Woodcock where the Giant Contessa's cabin was. It was a fast march. Steady. I could only hear my feet when I tried to outsmart the wind. I'd duck, go sideways, speed up some and slow down some. But steady. I'd hammer at a pillar to hear the heels of my hands. But moving, like a cannibal drummer from days of yore when the last Indians lived here. Like I was beating the life out of a death march as penance for killing a dead cannibal drummer a hundred years ago. Just plain fucking stupid, weightless thoughts, weightless as a ghost crab. . . The water was way down there and shallow as a grave; three genuine giants, eight feet tall, standing upon each other's shoulders could touch the bottom of the bridge. . . At the south end of the bridge, in the quarter mile of wilderness before the construction site, a speeding car headed at me, chased me off the road, Beach Road, where I was walking down it in the middle. The horn blew. I did not know the horn. It almost almost almost hit me. I was chicken, and jumped away first. Laughter's thing. I smelled nothing unusually guilty in the wake of the car. It was a car. I knew where a deer crossing was and I waited. I heard footsteps and spoke but saw nothing. I went on, in case the animal really needed to cross the road.

The cicadas rang so loud it blocked a prayer that blew off my lips solid enough you could bite it off word for word like taffy—black, white, and red shanks of saltwater taffy flat as a fucking road and thick as blacktop. . .

Maybe Dad'll commit suicide and help us all out, I thought.

At the cabin door everything was still. Back under the live oaks a whining car passed up Beach Road and I looked back to see if the animal had followed me. Hoped to see its eyes. Nope.

The door was locked at the handle. I walked around back to the open window where Chet and I had peeked in. Him first. I looked in and saw nothing. I quietly gripped the window I figured to be frozen but it jiggled and slid up. You could have put the whole moon in my heart right then. I climbed in as easily as gum or candy or peanuts falling from the mouth of a round machine.

I took the rosebud from my pocket and placed it on her pillow. Then I placed it off the pillow and searched for a better or the best place to leave it, when I heard a noise in another room like a swallowed snicker or a smothered grunt. It was not as dark, now, gauzy. Uh, Uh, Uh, Uh, Uh, Uh, Uh, Uh. Slam. Something fell. Quiet in the agony of wood that moonlight becomes like sunlight does. The door opened like a leaf swinging on a tree and I saw Chet with U-U.

It was him did it. Opened the door.

He charged me like a bull and I dropped the rosebud. I felt for it frantically as he kicked me with shoes on.

"You motherfucker! You double-crossing lying motherfucker!"

I felt the rosebud finally under the bed, and stayed there.

"Stay there!" he screamed at me.

I saw the tranquil nothingness of a well-trimmed corner where the walls met the floor under the bed. They put their clothes on hurriedly without a word between them, and left. The borrowed car was parked a distance off but it started and roared.

I pushed out from under the bed and found Mrs. Mingus's Hawaiian orchids not all crushed in the other room and placed them like a nest on a table for two which had toppled over when Chet bulldozed me, then placed the petrified rosebud at the center of the nest.

With freedom intact I walked out to the roadside and pivoting toward Woodcock saw a red horizon. Not a red horizon like an edge the sun makes, but like a burning coin. It was worth studying. Like a Roman or Greek coin of reddish gold still hot from the forge of funny old Festus Haggin.

It's worth laughing, just to hear some fucking noise sometimes.

"It's burning," I said. "It sure as fuck is on fire."

I looked back quickly at the Contessa's cabin, to see if some light had come on. Like a strobe of silent camera light shot from the trees, a picture of the veil of Eileen's hair backflowing between her white arms at the slave corral popped me like a towel Chet stung me with after gym class; it lit the air, and lit the cabin, just like that, snap, and so softly, and I thought I saw a flicker. With alarm, I remembered a child's candelabra Chet and U-U had lit in the spare room, and returned to extinguish it. It was a big dollhouse candelabra like a little girl might get for Christmas in July. But when I returned it was gone.

"Smell of sea horses on her ten salty fingers: eyes shut, tongue out" came to me like Tung Hsi dipping his net and shaking it out on the table. . . "Sixteen," I said, meaning syllables, meaning years. . . I saw the table with the flowers guarding the gift. I put the two chairs that belonged to the table upright and took a seat. "Welcome," I spoke. I thought by chance Brundetti might come if I waited serenely. Or Tung Hsi, Trout, Merkel, or Matthew Arnold. But, no. Not even to the window. I dared not even think in audible words all the names I'm using here. Only years later did those peaches fall. . . When the cicadas churned up diamond hard in their hysterical circle, I moved on.

CHAPTER THIRTY-SIX

I have left something out because I am stupid and afraid. Still, after all these years, with everybody dead, I fear things. That night on the bridge from Goose Island to the mainland, after the ritual bath at the Hittite Settlement (for by then bathing under a hose had begun to mark my way: good enough for a turtle king, good enough for me), my mother drove by in her car with Chet's dad in the front seat. She was crying more and greater tears than I could ever have dreamed produceable from two eyes. Her dress front was soaked and she had wiped them back into her frizzled hair. Her nose poured and Chester Evans sat stone rigid as a wooden Indian in the passenger seat. Yet he glared at something alive down the road in the headlights. She had rolled down Chet's window, or it was already down.

"Mom?" I said.

"Is it Dad?"

She shook her head. The mixture of hair and tears, her excruciated eyes walling toward me, her bloodhound mouth with teeth in it wretching out words of no earthly order or harmony should have moved him.

"Where have you been?"

She flexed like a crawfish shrivelling under a huge magnifying glass intensifying sunlight, and Mr. Evans laughed, looked at the animal up the road, tilted his head.

"Did you see these?"

He held up a crop of photographs showing me and U-U and his son and U-U and him and Mom in various poses.

"And this?"

He shuffled out from under the stack a picture hard to make out. He handed me the picture and turned on the ceiling light by cracking open the door.

"Shut it!" Mom screamed.

He shut his door and, wincing like someone having a baby, Mother turned on the dome light by taking her left hand off the Rambler wheel and twisting the headlamp's knob to the left and holding it.

"Quickly, Bill! Quickly! Oh Lord!"

Mother had never called me Bill in my life. It was always the simple Will or my whole name if she was beside herself, as in her period once when she slapped me twenty times across the face and shoulders for calling Merk a hopeless invalid bearing the burden of Dad's ambition. I tried hard to study it clearly before making a decision, but Mom let go of the knob. I took the picture out of the car and studied it by available light. The moon lit things like a spotlight through black Swiss cheese.

"Recognize her?" Evans said, and reached out for the photo. I pulled it back with two hands framing eternity. Not where proof belongs but what it is. Pictures. Fucked-up pictures everywhere. Picture this.

"Recognize who?"

"Glory."

Grinning like a dead cat or dog he was. The smile sharpened his beautiful eyes that his son inherited with the tendency to roll slowly.

"No. I don't see it."

He pointed with his finger at a white face looking upward. The black hump of a person blocked the rest of the white face's body except for two legs veeing up like a broken vee. With shoes on. You couldn't tell.

"You don't see it?" he seemed hurt, or wronged.

"I guess not."

"Did you take these?" Mom said.

"We want to know who took these."

"Nobody took these, Mom. They have to be doctored."

Mother choked and balked and actually snickered and wiped her nose with a thumb.

"You're not owning up? You think my son did this?"

My best friend himself was in one picture.

"No, sir."

"Then who?"

My mouth flooded with spit, and I swallowed.

"Brundetti," I said, changing the world.

He burst into laughter.

"The corpse! Janet, the corpse took these pictures!"

"Not each one," I said not knowing what I said.

He stopped laughing and I took the photograph of the black hump and white face and legs from his fingers and threw it off the bridge. He started to get out but Janet grabbed him. Enraged, he said, "And these? What of these?" and fanned the photographs at me in the window like a hand of poker. I grabbed a fistful of pictures and pulled one away. He sputtered something as empty as a fishhead in the sun that you kick over and the gulls and cats won't peck or sniff at, and they drove away.

I thought Father had killed himself for the insurance "investment" in his holy "whole life" policy to valiantly make her happy after smothering my brothers, and they had come to tell me after searching a long time, but I was wrong.

The photograph I had taken I stuck in my back pocket like a little gun to shoot myself with someday.

The black veil of invisible night felt lovely fluttering over the bridge off the gigantic bay beneath and almost all around it with nobody there.

This was about a mile from the Giant Contessa's, and mine an average gait. No red fire yet visible in Woodcock. The moon we have up there may as well be black all over for its good as a timepiece. You have to know the season and the place. The most interesting treasures have no date or place. Old bottles. Old locks. Old feathers from a crypt. A pharaoh's wan, attentive smile. A hank of hair and a piece of bone and a walkin' talkin' honeycomb. To suck, to love, to feel and store. To not lie or forget. "To be yourself," Dad said to Trout one day when he was conscious. His hot globe eyeballs. His eyelids like a lizard's drawn slowly, adequately like the faded capes of two bullfighters unfurling Trout's passionate dream. Mom rushed to pick up his hand and his eyes moved toward her eyes as she said, "Yes, Darling, Daddy's right! Just be yourself, just always be yourself!" She shook her head and his eyes shut.

"It's time," Daddy said. "It is time."

He looked at Mom and she and I hankied away to another room. God, the force of someone striving to just be himself, the tears of his mother, the strength of his father. Under a pillow, he thrashed and tore Dad's shirt, which was an old one. Merkel had awoken and called out in his funny voice, "Daddy! Daddee!" And after a glass of water, Dad went to Merkel, lectured him over his excitement to just keep dreaming, keep trying to grow in his dreams, and then in his way said good-bye.

CHAPTER THIRTY-SEVEN

After I left the cabin I saw the mock sunrise or burning star down by Woodcock town itself and decided to avoid it. As a matter of reality I was already becoming an artist at avoiding pain. I have failed repeatedly to show you why. Armed with the picture derringer in my back pocket, William the Kid, I wandered new roads with no settlements on them between the Giant Contessa's cabin and THE CONSPICUOUS ABSENCE OF WISDOM OF ANY SORT bar, about a two-mile distance, the sea on your left walking south, the roads about which I am speaking on your right, climbing little rises to a shelf of sand fifty miles long and twelve feet deep toward Beeville. Fuck it. I needed... I needed someone new I never knew, something new I never had, somewhere new I never saw, but not a pair of shoes. Not a pair of matching shoes. Wing tips, mules, Wallabees, boots. For my feet had developed soles of their own. I remember praying a constant stream of noises.

On the roads of which I speak were uninhabited lands where animals lived and maybe no house had ever been built.

Scrub oak and pod bearers worshipped the world having never grown tall. . . enough to see the sea. I ate grass. "God," I said. God, I said you are. Not knowing shit from apple butter and not being able to remember Dover Beach. The Matthew Arnold love poem. But then Merkel's face and shoulders and living arms, tucked in his bed at the Scottish Rite Hospital for Burned and Crippled Children in Corpus Christi Texas came back to me, burgeoning from the hospital twilight of his gray room: "The sea is calm tonight. . . The moon lies fair upon the straits. . . Across the channel a green light glitters and is gone. . . Come to the window. . . Sweet is the night air. . . Listen!. . . The ceaseless grate and roar of pebbles the moon drags back and the waves whip. . . vast ceaseless grating roar Socrates called human mystery. . . The Sea of Faith. . ."—and his eyes glittered—". . . Ah, Love, Let us be true," and then he started to cough. No one came in to rescue him. I was there in everyone's place. He pulled his little fists away from his buckled mouth to hold me.

About dawn where it gets gray I came across one of those holiness signs the invisible people hammer into the roadside and it said "MAKE DO." It had the feeling of holiness or scripture around it, and balancing on one foot I reached up with my other foot and traced the red letters with my big toe. I was lost. I could not have been more than five miles as the crow flies from Nehi but I was anemic by nature or birth in the soul. Be-jesus I heard a bell, a soft electronic bell like a doorbell melody tiny and soft, and a priest rode up behind me on a bicycle with a battery-driven bell he had rung to warn me and to say hello, and he passed me at his old rate of speed without speeding up around me, and he pulled into a chapel hidden a little ways off the road among some pines artificially introduced to the area. I wanted to be sure, and I strained to see for sure if he wore a gray robe, a mousy color, and he did. He was getting things ready for the day.

The cicadas had been quiet a long time around me, but with the suddenness of broad hot daylight they were back, stirred and mad like a tribe of bumblebees with brooding drums. Mexican Catholics drove by in their cars for church in the chapel behind me. *Las familias de los viviendos, yo lo creo que si. The families of the living, I believe it is so. Y otros atras de mio, sin muerte, sin religiones, sin casas, sin dolorosos tu puedes llamar la Vida, Life. And others behind me, without death, without religions, without houses, without pains you could call Life.* I said these words, in essence, as a sermon to the Invisibles and the settlers to come, who had inspired me to Make Do. Instantly Merkel smiled and Trout turned in his bed the way he used to to kiss me good morning every day when I toddled in there.

A green Ford Galaxy full of Mexicans going to church drove on a busted frame cockeyed on a slant toward me, and as I lifted my hand to greet them a red dot drenched in sunlight that I perfectly knew was the Corvette blew around them and snugly passed them. The precious Godly children dressed beautifully in the Galaxy were startled and near Death mouthing O. The Sweet Father, his hands on the green plastic wheel never moving, held steady for the love of life, and the Mother, the Holy Mother reading, pressed against the far door. Jesus if U-U didn't fucking cut them off and almost wreck just to reach the effect of a one-eighty spin out in the road that slung her into a ditch of dead soldiers, the silvered sunflowers without heads. The Galaxy did not beep or brake hard, and the father made no gesture. Just went around. He was a Champion above everything. His car was slanted, a crippled horse. He looked back slightly to see she was okay, and she was: her muddy hair a mass of love and wind and salt. The Corvette filthy. Chet gone.

"Willie, you can't go back! You have to go! I have been all over the Peninsula looking, searching for you! There's a dead Boy Scout! They think you did it because you made faces!"

"Faces?"

She shook her head yes but she wasn't crying. She was way past crying.

"They say you rolled your lips back and rolled your eyes. Or something. You angered the scoutmaster with your greeting!"

Those were not her exact words, but they're close. You curled your lips and rolled your eyes, you offended the scoutmaster with your greeting. I told her all I told them was where to camp. I was innocent. I hadn't hurt anybody.

"I know that. I know, honey," she said.

I jumped into the Corvette and felt her legs and breasts to my heart's content till we found a secluded place and made love there.

CHAPTER THIRTY-EIGHT

She sat up under the big cottonwood at Cibolo Creek and buttoned her blouse. The heart-shaped leaves of the tree clapped insanely their little hands to the music of the creek I couldn't hear. I looked up past her cheek and love-saturated face into the tree. Crows called from the cottonwood, across the creek to a huisache tree, to a small, lime green mesquite all by itself in a fallow field, and then back across the creek to a patch of corn behind us. The patch of corn, already burnt to a crisp by the sun, was probably for cattle fodder. I wasn't a farmer and didn't know. A crow perched on a stalk of corn blared harshly behind us, up the slight embankment like a crumbling shoulder, scaring U-U. She had buttoned the first two white buttons at the waist of her blouse, and when she quaked at the crow, with her fingers on the next button, she turned to see it, and her skin glimmered.

"I dreamed I was singing a folksong in German but I don't know any German."

"Cuando?"

She tied back her hair with a ribbon.

"Last night."

"Estaba cantando un canto del gente anoche, pero yo no se Aleman."

"There was an old grandma with me and I was a baby-woman like happens in a dream."

She looked at me for confirmation.

"Estabas teniendo un fucking nightmare my beautiful Spanish bitch."

U-U looked away softly at the sick little creek starving and stranding amid rocky plates becoming sand.

"Why do you say things like that to me? Why do you treat me like a whore?"

I had no answer. Anymore than birds have an answer. Just reasons. Thoughts. Kindness. Unkindness. Likeness and unlikeness. Fucking history. A photograph. So I didn't answer. It was a beginning. She stood up and a bullfrog jumped.

"Got any food?"

She walked to the car parked in the parched corn. There had been rain earlier in the summer, and the corn was as tall as she was. She wore only her blouse and the sandals. She took her purse from behind the driver's seat and carried it to a low limb of the cottonwood that hung out over the creek. She put her purse on that limb and lit a cigarette. I thought about somebody smelling the smoke and coming after us, but we were too far from town. I went up to the car to look for food and found a bag of old popcorn under the front seat and ate it hoggishly, even the old maids unchewed, and shook-popped the salt down to my mouth. A snake entered the creek from somewhere, and I pretended my hand was a pistol and shot at it. It wriggled languidly downstream to where it paused in the weak almost nonexistent current under the elbow of the limb that stuck out over the stream. U-U flipped her cigarette at it accurately, but short, and the snake swam over to the floating Winston.

"You don't know shit about love."

She shook her head, staring at the creek.

"You say you love me. But you don't know shit about love."

My parents knew about love. . . The nurse that taught Merk the poem. . . Fuck yes. . . Chet's dad buttfucking my mom in the picture. I raised my hands to U-U's shoulders and pulled back from the fire. I talked.

"Yeah. I'll learn from you."

She knew exactly instantly what I meant and she had known exactly instantly what I meant and she still knows exactly instantly what I meant but I may never know.

She reached up and wiped salt from my mouth and applied it vaginally. She fell back against the limb.

"God U-U!"

She kept rubbing herself and I threw her into the water.

"You don't love me! Chet loves me! Chet knows my heart!"

The creek rose and panted. I waded out to her and held her the way people do who can't make love anymore.

She sank to her knees and pulled me down. I floated down. The sandy mud felt like something our knees and toes needed. Then I lay down in the water with her and we kept rolling in it and she kept crying, adding to the creek, and I thought we would roll in the creek until we became linked skeletons with the meat rubbed off. But it wasn't a thought or words. It was a spine. Her closed, quiet eyes meant more than her open, talking eyes. The water deepened and we twirled cheek to cheek. I opened my eyes all I could. Her twilit smile took everything. A bubble, tiny, peeped. . .

I let her go and surfaced, but she did not. Insanely, I searched the creekbanks for my love who was dead. I turned in a circle. This took TIME but not even two seconds. Then I dove in from where I stood and swung across the bottom with my arms and fingers and legs and feet like a blinded starfish as wide as I could. No answer. No ringing. No crows. No music. I screamed her name Eustacia under the water and thrust out my face. Something like a fingertip poked my eye lightly and I shot to the surface with a snake the color of honey riding my shoulder. I slung it away and saw the heel of U-U's sandal protrude above the water. To this I swam like God intended and dragged her lifeless body to the shore. I breathed in and pounded her. I stood and held her by the heels and shook her and dragged her lolling head over to the cottonwood tree and held her heels up to the limb and got up on the limb and the cicadas went crazy, the crows flew over together five in a rugged vee, and I pulled her legs up high on the limb where I stood humped over her dead body till her neck left the ground and her head lolled. Gripping her ankles with all my strength I lifted her free of the earth by squatting on the limb and standing, never letting go, till I just couldn't do it anymore and dropped her.

The creek was totally calm, in and of itself again. Suffered no loss.

I squatted there for a second and looked at the Corvette shining blindingly like a cherry in the cornfield. She gurgled, and I looked down at her. Perfectly clean, pure water trickled from her mouth. She just looked dead asleep. I cannot tell what it took out of me. I leapt down and lifted her hand and it was creek temperature. I thought maybe the snake had bitten her while we danced but I couldn't find fang marks or any marks on her anywhere. On her buttocks or head or neck or feet. I checked all over her scalp. Not even a mole. I began to sort of weep, like a bird trying to sing. The early bird. "Shit," I said, laughing. Then I noticed blood in a little lightning streak between her legs. It was barely enough to trickle over her thigh to the ground. Her face was white and fresh. Blue with milk. Summoning strength, I pulled apart her legs and found the source, a leech, and plucked it off. It had found a loving sore. On U-U's face a dawn crept up, and her eyes opened and she smiled.

She was never dead. Just pretending. Or maybe death was pretending.

I lay down beside her with my head on her arm, and she pushed away my hair here and there.

"What was that thing?"

"A leech."

The creek and trees and fields became as still as a teething ring.

"I wonder where the crows went."

"I don't know."

A brushing sound like a dog in the corn came from above us, behind the tree. All the little hearts in the leaves were still.

"Look and see what it is."

I rolled onto my stomach and saw the corn moving, separating, like a toad separating grass. I rolled back close to her ear and whispered as quietly as possible, "Someone's here!"

Her eyes flashed backwards up over her head with her neck bent just enough to see the blackened stalks and nothing there.

I knew I had seen things.

We settled into a nap until it was almost dusk and woke up. I didn't know you could lie in someone's arms on plain earth that long and really sleep.

"Did you have your dream?"

"No," she said, and laughed.

We told each other we loved each other and went up to the car. Halfway there she remembered her purse on the limb and ran back to get it. The seats of the car were burning hot from the top being off in the field, even at that late moment. U-U ran back to the car and handed me the keys. She was smoking a cigarette. I did not know how to drive and handed her back the keys. She thought nothing of it and got in with just her blouse on and started the engine. She had hissed when she sat on the leather. It must have been the hottest day in July. Terrifically hot. I got in gingerly and smelled something vague.

"Turn off the engine," I said.

"You smell something?"

She looked sweetly at me and said she did not. She restarted the engine and backed up a little into the path we had made through the corn. Then, we definitely smelled some sickeningly sweet thing. You could feel it back in your mouth.

She backed up a little bit more quite carefully and looked at me whimsically. U-U looked just like she looked on her cousin's donkey that night when she laid eyes on me at the utmost very first.

I got out of the car and looked around it in the corn and a ways up the broken corn. I walked pushingly into it on one side, the part of the field that was behind the tree, and back to the car. U-U reached back behind my seat for her party skirt she had borrowed from Misty. Beneath the skirt was a paper sack rolled shut about the size of a football. It had incredible weight and feel like a thick spongy itch. I picked it up and carried it by the wadded handle into the field and heaved it into the corn as far as I could. The wind blew over the corn and it clattered. Millions of little ears and leafy hands.

She had put on her skirt. I stared at her skirt unbelievably.

"What was it?"

"I think it was a dead parrot or an old hat."

I had not looked in the sack or squeezed it hard. I had let it swing in my hand.

U-U shifted into drive and turned into the corn to intersect the path I had made.

"No! goddamn it U-U!"

She would find it. She would see into its itch. I feebly grabbed the wheel and pulled it toward the path we had plowed to get to the tree and the stream but it whipped back in position under her hands. It was like a baby tugging at the world. She screamed above the crashing cornstalks, "Where'd you put it?"

"No!"

The car lurched and shot forward and stalled. You could reach out and touch the ground. The sand was hot. It wasn't even close to fucking dusk.

She stood up on the console or the door and stepped across the windshield onto the hood of the car. The hot wind lifted her hair and the blue sky burnt away every miserable thing uttered or done bad or scary.

I climbed up there with her and we gazed out over the corn. You could not see the road or the path or the top of the cottonwood. We had landed in a place you could never know was there until you were there. A little valley. The car was suspended somewhat nose down but you'd never notice it until you stood up and got your bearings on the hood. The sweep downward of the land was so subtle.

"Goddamn, U-U. Whose car is this?"

"Esme Only."

"Man, we're ass deep in sand. We'll never get out of here."

"You want to burn the field?" she said. It was crazy and meant nothing. It was a bad place to hide. Come harvest time, they'd find us. I was so fucking fucked-up hungry I picked an ear of parched hard corn and tried to gnaw it. U-U laughed and smoked. Back in the car we sat till dark really started to come. She had started the car and I had, too, many times, but all the armored horses could not pull their weight out of the sand.

It got dark. Almost completely dark, and there was not a cloud in the sky. We had found several packs of gum in the glove compartment and ate them just to see what would happen to us. It was calm and stiflingly hot, like the Corvette was planted in a huge terrarium. A little tiny whiffle of air blew down the hill with a vibrantly wonderful ammonia smell on it and I turned in the seat to see on the black horizon a blacker shape. "Hey!" I yelled, and whistled. The vagrant shape dawdled towards us through the sea of stalks parting sideways for the floating newcomer to our valley. I stood up on the back of the car to greet him. U-U touched my calf.

"Who are you?" I yelled at the shape. I had not realized he was right upon me because of the height of the crop and the darkness of the figure bobbing.

"Joseph," he said.

The animal he was on was blacker than he was. You could hear he was a little black boy with a cold.

"This your picnic?" he said, and reached down a sack to me. "What's your mule's name?"

"He's not a mule, he's a horse!"

The side of the animal's face and its shoulder were apparent, but not its ears. I reached out and stroked its neck and smelled my hand.

"He smells like a horse," I said, stupid and foolish.

"He smell good," the little boy said.

"Darn right he does," I said.

I gave him the five dollars the old folks gave me, wet from my pocket. Wet from sweat. Not knowing what it was at first, he held it up and waved it and gave it back.

"Good-bye," he said, and pulled his animal away with a cluck. I stepped free of the car onto the sand as quickly as I could to smell the wake of the animal. The fragrance of roses will tell their color, but not to me.

It got lighter as it got darker, with stars and the moon. I wondered if the boy would go to the fireworks in Woodcock next night or if he could see them where he lived.

We got sick of being there and jumped off the hood and walked down the gentle valley to the creek where it was even brighter without the corn absorbing light. Unexplainably, U-U had not tried to look in the sack or take it from me.

A sandbar ribbed up in the creek and I waded the shallows out to it and set the bag on the sand. Facing downstream, I took a deep breath and squatted and rolled open the sack. It was too dark to see and I stood up and turned away and took another breath. U-U backed off up the bank to run from the smell that a breeze had caught, and asked me what it was. I had no idea, and my head was light with hunger. She shouted downhill, "Goddamn it! What is it?"

Kneeling down, I ripped down the side of the sack and saw hair piled in a beehive shape but more whirled up like a Dairy Queen ice-cream cone: a lady giant's mane, twirled into the sack like a mooring rope on the AP ferry, or the long tufted hairs of a sweet mule's tail?

U-U ran into the water. She reached down and picked up the hair that unravelled like a long ponytail with a knot on the end of it and threw it into the air. She wasn't aiming, I don't think, at anything, but it landed in the water. She had the dead seriousness of a doctor or policeman on her face as she peered into the sack again and stepped backward into the water, turned away and walked up the hill. Taking the edges of the sack I flipped it over and a person's nose and lips and ears fell out. I wasn't sure of this until I got a stick and arranged them into a face. Dead, you couldn't tell their color. Unattached, they were sexless. They did not stink as badly as one might imagine. I flicked them with the stick into the water. Threw the stick in. Looked at the sand where they had lain.

Up at the car U-U worked furiously to dig out. On her hands and knees around the car she dug better and more efficiently than any animal I have ever seen. I got down on my knees and helped her. We used ears of corn as shovels and pulled the earth back. The soft sandy loam. We worked hard, side by side. The heat of the engine and tail pipes was still there, preserved in sand and kept warm. In the thin breach of air beneath the car you could smell the White Shoulders Chet had sprinkled in her hair.

CHAPTER THIRTY-NINE

We dug out successfully and started the car and let it roll in first gear under the pressure of its own magnificence down the swale to the creek where the ranchers of the past had graveled a ford. We shook across the creek with fear of being swallowed but made it to another height of swaling bank and a field of treelike bally weeds all burnt from the sun and dead but high as the windshield. Keeping it in first we tangoed here and sutured there till U-U hit a tractor road along a fence that led to Dimple Road the mile between Hutchins Mott and Huisache Mott, which brought back the black boy and his basically full name *he told me:* Joseph Hutchins. I got a chill because the whole fucking thing was a fantasy. The horse-mule, the rubber lips, the way you go, Necessity.

"What are you laughing about?"

"I just got a chill. . . remembering the leech."

I looked at her how sweaty she was and all life. Her fragrance just love. I bent down and kissed her between the curtain of style. She hung sharp left into someplace and had to stop. I did not lift up. She pressed everything about her down and up and away until what was essential flew. A thousand sparrows. I sat up and saw the shot-out yard light under which I'd stood looking at Brundetti's pictures. But now it was shot out like a broken silver space helmet. U-U shut her eyes and let her head fall back. I have doggedly tried but can't remember headrests, just a seat. She adjusted the seat as far back as it would go and went to a kind of sleep. I opened the door and stood up on the old farm ground. Impacted by years of wheels, it was hard and solid.

"Damn, this shit feels good."

"Where you going, Willie? Please don't go."

I bet she could not tell you what she had said because she was so asleep. Her need for me not to leave had surfaced from her sleep in such a way that word bubbles had burst across her lips. A maiden slickness coated her open lips like lipstick. She was so full of water, her teeth glistened like the eyes of the birds that flew away. I congratulated God for her beauty and rubbed my hands on my face.

"Were you African, I could understand you," I said, sleeptalking like her, somnambulistically stupid like her. But she was like that more than me, all the time, even excited. I remember her the first time I ever saw her with her cousin on the donkey and her blue toenails. Sleepy. . . It could not have meant anything. . . Her arms raised up her hands. Beautifully dull. I went over to her side of the Corvette and smelled this woman's face.

O Jesus, religion's a funny thing.

Up at the house where I had seen Jonah's mother cradled in the bed of his wagon, junked off by him tenderly wrapped in quilts like the treasure of everything. . . I murdered a box of crackers and the rest of the honey in the jar. I marched right to them like a person raiding at will his own kitchen. I needed more and found a string light in a narrow closet I could pull on. This I pulled and saw at once the photograph-lined innards of the closet, its walls a virtual path of still moments of joy. Everybody was smiling. All black folks. Unintentional wonder at the reality of happiness. At some time. . . I sighed and my heart beat deeply, thudding organ. I felt guilty and shut the door except about the width of my foot. To hide. To be in there. Alone with the pictures, I smiled but suddenly in Time thought of Father, Herbert alone at home with his pictures, and I backed out of the closet, leaving the light on so that I could still see the nimbus around the door and navigate by it. There was no more food and on the bed just a valley. I tried to smell Jonah's mother there, but failed, and then lay down like an old widower to feel her touch, but felt the cleanliness next to dust as dead as clean where you know life is abandoned.

It gave me the creeps, after everything, and I went outside to U-U who hadn't moved. I held the open honey jar under her nose. She didn't move. Sound asleep. I smelled the jar again, its wild oniony garlic, and placed it under her nose. Her nostrils didn't move. I backed away and went to the barn where there was nothing, not a rag, not an ash, not a remnant of anything. The corral had been swept clean or always was. The gap where the Goliath car had dragged Contessa out and her fingers lilted like a still baby's too-long fingers drawn across a harp. . . that fence hole was a bright, sunny spot in a mule-trodden, board-warped fence. Into the cotton rows, I found no mules. No Smokey. No Whiskey. Where I had finally gotten to touch them together truly simultaneously as long as I wanted and hold them by their halters, I got down on my knees and tried to smell where their bodies had been. I thought I could. I looked closely at the dirt where Smokey's left eye and Whiskey's right must have peered in death, touched the soil with my eyelashes, but how many grains would be removed glued to an eyeball?—and how could they be counted, subtracted from the other grains of dirt, rolly-polly shit and grounds of the master's coffee? The sides of their heads had crushed cotton, but so had my body wallowing and hiding and creeping. . . I could not find any blood or any ash in the cotton or corral. . . I started to wonder if U-U was dead, not just asleep. . . I walked back into the barn. A look up at the top of the barn put a big dust mote in my eye. A fleck of straw shaken off a roosting bird. It felt refreshing to see the bird rustle, expand, and resettle. Rubbing my eye, I felt hungry, and licked all I could from the jar. "Damn, wish I had some Picosos." Soft as heat lightning, and brushing by, a dove flew out of the barn and a big owl followed. Their wings touched the crown of my head, and their fragrance like the smell of rain or a skyful of mice masked my face as I sank to my knees, calling U-U. . . On my back I opened my eyes and saw the peak of the barn as a star. Perhaps it was noon. Not a whole sound was being made in the earshot world. I felt so sleepy. Turning onto my side like we used to go to sleep, my brothers and I without our blankets, Merk and I and Trout without our blankees in one free night when Dad must have been on the road, I saw a long black hair in the burnt orange dirt of the barn. . . I slept awhile, saw in my sleep a normal-sized woman riding a mule slowly across the corral and into the cotton. . . "Her mother was a regular, beautiful woman, who got into trouble and had to quit teaching school," Mother said.

In the peaceful sound of grasshoppers, U-U woke me. You could say my love stirred me off the barn floor and I jumped up like a sleepy toy. The Fourth of July was dawning. I pointed out to the cotton where I had lain.

U-U had thought I was crazy, smelling the earth.

"That's where the Muleskinner's children were, U."

She had never looked at the pictures.

The honey jar lay in the barn floor dirt with the black hair stuck to its neck, long and wavy.

I plucked off the hair and drew it across my tongue. It tasted of garlic.

U-U, smoking, took the jar from me after it was clean and licked it...

We drove to Esme Only's house and parked in a one-car shed that was really tight.

In broad daylight we went inside through the backdoor for breakfast of bacon and eggs with the eggs mountained up and scrambled in bacon grease. White toast and jelly. A beautiful young teenage black girl with beads in her long bush of black hair wistfully cooked it. Wistfully served it. Wistfully went away.

I drank coffee for the first time in my life. The day they had nailed Chet at THE CONSPICUOUS ABSENCE OF WISDOM OF ANY SORT bar I had just held it. I loved the taste and was immediately hooked.

"It's like pussy or joy," this black man said, cleaning up behind me. He had a broom and a pot of coffee in his great hands like he couldn't know what to do but you knew he did. He wore suspenders and a bow tie.

"You just love it."

"Coffee."

He laughed on his own time.

"Doggies!" he stated, glancing down at U-U. She had her elbows on the table and ate voraciously, absentmindedly, jelly, toast, sausage he had put there on a special white plate. Her fingers were slick. She swallowed hard. Her arms were golden from the sun. He studied her arms from behind her, pleasantly dazed. U-U excused herself and went away, leaving me alone with him. He dragged his sandy feet and cleaned up the kitchen mess with the most lonely kind of slowness you can dream up.

"I'd greatly appreciate your not flirting with her," I said.

He had been gazing out the bright, brilliant back kitchen window over the sink with his hands at work. When I warned him about U-U, he became slackly solemn and turned arthritically and slung fingers of soap suds at me.

"You kill that Scout?"

I had a sud on my lip.

"Shit, man, I was at the Big Oak when that happened."

"I knew that," he said so serenely, looking at his dishes.

"Soon as I saw you with that little girl."

In the adjacent room I heard voices, the light voices of women. These were new. French doors, tall, that divided the hallway in half and hung on valuable hinges that hid springs under colored brass, hung in half and shut off that world from this one.

"Go in there," the caretaker said.

"Go on!"

I got up from my chair and touched the gaily painted Parisian doors with their old scenes of luxury and valor. Their whispers weren't really quiet. The caretaker watched, urging. Really friendly. I pressed open the doors a crack when he swung through around me with a silver plate of sweet rolls for the women and as he put it solemnly on the massive dark table covered with breakfast trash and spoons and cigarettes out in ashtrays, one of them said, "There's the Kid. The Shakespeare fucking Kid!" and laughed with a smokey laugh silly and harmless.

Esme Only slouchingly disapproved of her friend's words and mockery, but Esme was smart. She just had no pretense. She was smoking a Lucky Strike then. They all were smoking Lucky Strikes.

It was impossible not to look at them and not want them and fear them.

"You sixteen?" a brunette asked coldly.

"No."

They all laughed except the Queen. It wasn't mean. Just flat, silly whore laughter. I laughed, too. Then Esme looked at the ceiling and shushed the table as a big blonde pulled me under it. Men walked across the floor above the table and down the stairs as I adored the fat of her titties. She patted and stroked my hair. "Margie," she said. "I'm Margie." She elastically arched down her neck and kissed me tenderly with flavored lips. She moistened my sunburnt face with the tip of her tongue and I had never seen her before in my life. Her large head was covered with tight blonde curls. "I'll protect you!" she said. Her eyes shone with liquid life, small, blue, urgent, and undeniable. I drank her breath as the front door slammed and Esme and Julia hauled me out. When they saw my lusty need, all of them laughed. But my Protectress got to her feet with the help of the table and a chair and pulled me to her preciously and sternly with power that has sex in it and rushed me up to her room.

CHAPTER FORTY

The rich quick transparency reaches you, and that is the way to go. Brought on quickly by Margie up in her room, that was the way to go. A whole oceanful of transparencies floated in her hot pink belly. A harmless stingray entering a giant jellyfish without any stingers, an oceanic sex picture within the frame of her legs or on the film of her transparent glistening belly. O. . . Outside Margie's window Mexican palms fanned sharp and perfect. A fly landed on her calf and I watched it. Her fingers fanned on her pillow like somebody treading water through the belly of the world, or the tail fin of a resting fish. Her face was shiny. . . "O Jesus, O Jesus. Thank you," I said dead alive in the net of love but Margie was asleep. She belched breakfast and I sucked it through my gills and kissed it up. All I could. She smiled but then her face bubbled up into true sleep. I said no more prayer because I had met the oversized sheath of Destiny and it fit the Shakespeare Kid.

I was so fucking tired I fell asleep, too, and dreamed a great dream of the Giant Contessa riding a whitened Whiskey now called Soda. Someone had safely painted Jonah's resurrected child a white color. Upon Soda she rode at a steady, peaceful clop through Woodcock, my black-haired Lady Godiva. The street was empty. Then the street turned the mule like a little green chameleon, and she silently clopped up to me. Silence in dreams, quiet in life. I never saw myself there, till now at a white table looking back. On love I waited, a boy. The smell of the mule was of itself. Through the paint reality had made it.

At three o'clock the black Juliette came in with lunch on a tray and put it down on a bigger tray that sat on a folding support beside the window. A cicada had smacked against the window and the thud awakened me, not Juliette. She wore an apron over a simple gray dress that I bet she made. I wondered if I would ever have her, the way you sometimes wonder when you're hiding and you don't know that, really, you're being hidden by the mercy of God you begged for long ago in tears the woman doesn't see because no one could in your stupefied face. Stupeficent.

Margie smelled the food and woke up wide awake like she had never slept and never known me. Vigorous and whole, this blonde attacker of food. She had fed me so much I can't even describe her invaluable Name. Margie was the opposite of a dungeon. Until I said that to you, I could not remember the food on the platter as big as the tray, the plate a light yellow oval and the tray a dark red rectangle. They had fixed her a bushel of barbecued ribs without the basket. As Margie plowed into them (and them alone, there was nothing else), Juliette returned with a silver pitcher tarnished on the sweat-bespeckled chilly outside. God, I was dying of thirst. I reached from the bed for the pitcher, and Margie gently slapped my wrist.

"Juliette, bring the Kid a proper glass, please. A water glass."

She pulled a starched white napkin off a little shallow stack of these on a bookshelf, flipped it out, wiped her lips and chin and fingers, and then took the hand she'd slapped and licked the sauce off the wrist. With the bone back in both hands, she lifted her shoulders in the opposite meaning of a shrug, and sighed. She went back to work on the bone while gazing out the window. Juliette returned with a heavy crystal glass and filled it for me and gave it to me, without a word but smiling. Margie glanced at her and licked her lips and moaned at the bone and Juliette left. It was jealousy, or ownership. It was her room: how I might have felt had I been a real customer, what Esme called a guest. The house did not yet have a name, and there were no recognized members. Some renovation was not yet complete, for instance the molding.

"You feel like you're dying but you're not, right?" Margie said, and grinned at me. She looked as stupid as any woman I have ever seen in my life I can remember, and she was right.

"You killed that colored gentleman and that Eagle Scout, didn't you?"

"Eagle Scout?"

"He was getting his badge."

I knew exactly what she was talking about. He had looked like a Tenderfoot through the back window of the bus.

"He was getting his merit badge when the school bus blew up on the hill and he ran up there to rescue his cat," she said, all saucy and bald as a fucking tape recorder. Her eating blue eyes were black in the middle and the only color blue they could ever be. I might as well have been paralyzed.

"You know about it?" I said.

"What?"

"Badges."

She became confused or mired down for just a moment. It was like a seizure, but she just had gas.

"Badges? I was there, Willie Boy."

A chord struck in me like a bell in a bottomless ship.

"What'd you see?"

She swallowed and really belched bug-eyed.

"Excuse you," she said. She smiled like a pixie.

"Truly, Margie. What'd you see?"

When I said her name, she looked out the window.

"Him."

I got off the end of the bed and looked out the window. Sperry or his look-alike was walking down the street. A little boy barely the age to pedal a tricycle, making a motor sound with his lips and speeding toward him, had to go into the street. Walnut Street, which becomes Pentecost Road way down. The tyke's mother, standing on her porch, saw this and ran into the street and scooped up her boy, trike and all. You could almost hear the little streamers on the bars.

"That is endearing," Margie said.

After Sperry was out of sight I sat back down on the edge of her bed and watched her eat. A camera with feelings was how I was. I had no merit badges. She looked at my feet and called Juliette.

"Wash his feet."

She looked back down with genuine interest at my feet. Juliette excitedly signalled toward the hallway with her thumb.

"Hm? Hm?" she sounded with her lips closed: *here, here?* She couldn't talk. She still had her thumb in the air. It was delicate and the color of it was beautiful.

"No. Right here. Bring a pan."

Juliette brought a huge pan of hot water I stood in. I marvelled. It must have weighed fifty pounds. Margie lit a cigarette and laughed.

"No, silly! Take your pants off!"

I took off my pants without getting out of the pan, and Juliette washed my feet and legs with soap and water. She might have been washing a dog. She looked at Margie, and Margie nodded and burped, watching closely. Juliette washed my privates and buttocks. Her bushy long hair came close to my parts she was washing. She finished. Margie waved her off, nodding vehemently. Juliette came back with a second huge pan and rinsed me off. Margie smiled. She approved. Juliette cleaned up the thimbleful of splashes she made on the floor with her apron. Never once did Juliette look in my eyes.

"Go 'way! Go 'way! Go on!" Margie ordered. It wasn't cruel. Margie looked sternly at me. A flat, business fact.

"They cut her tongue out."

"An inch from the tip," she winked, "but it was thick."

She offered me a Lucky. I couldn't pick it out. She picked it out, lit it, and put it in my mouth.

"Juliette! Come here!" she yelled. The mother across and down the street could have heard her, but it wasn't intended that way.

"Juliette, honey, show him your mouth."

Like a two-year-old child, she shook her head. Her tremendous hair moved like an African jester's hat made of all the jungles. Margie smiled and stroked the girl's cheek. She pulled her near. Her great bosom bulged out and Juliette opened her lips a little bit like a sweet little fish or bubbling baby.

"Aw, now," Margie said.

With her mouth open like that, Margie told me to kiss her and brought me by the shoulder nearer. Juliette closed her eyes and I kissed her. Juliette looked at me ever so briefly and then up at Margie. Margie placed her hands behind our heads and pressed our faces together.

"With tongue."

Her mouth opened like a warm mineral spring and our tongues touched and she cried.

"Not like that!"

Margie pulled our faces apart and kissed the girl herself. "Like that!" she said.

We kissed without her hands on us at all, and Juliette shook all over. I couldn't tell a difference in her tongue and U-U's, the only other tongue I knew. Chet's mother had kissed me so tenderly. The rosebud day.

Margie could tell nothing registered, and pulled us apart. She ordered the girl to open up. She wouldn't. Margie slapped her. "God, Margie, come on. . ." Juliette straightened with a shiver tall and opened her mouth widely and looked away with her eyes. Her teeth were perfect.

"Look at those pearls. Look at that tongue."

She sounded like a doctor vulgar with his unconscious patient, solemn glory.

Juliette's pink tongue jerked back in her mouth like a bitten-off worm. Margie shook and smacked her.

"Stick it out!"

She stuck it out as far as it could go, and it was like a little calf's tongue with a jagged end. The piece that could reach the tail was gone. She tried to hold it still by clenching her fists. Involuntarily swallowed.

"Did it with pliers."

Calmly, she wiped the girl's tears with her thumbs and softly told her not to tell Miss Esme that we had lost our tempers a little bit, not even by one of her little notes, either, and gently pecked her on the lips and shook her by the chin and told her to go away. I tried to put on my pants and follow but Margie barred the door. Esme's orders. But Esme doesn't even know me, I said. She looked amazed. Utterly. Well, you shared a meal with her one time, she said, and became her old self again.

CHAPTER FORTY-ONE

Margie lay under a blue towel beside me. Juliette had quietly come in and covered her breasts and belly and hips with the freshly laundered towel after the gyrating world had stopped rolling under, around, and over me with me on it like a dog walking in its sleep upon the moon. You know that old phrase you hardly ever hear anymore; I didn't know whether I was coming or going. Sex strips you of time. A white girl came in about midway and placed her lily hand upon the small of Margie's back while Margie nudged the bleached pouch of her charms around my knees.

After all the years of wakefulness and ending and re-ending and unending, I can feel the clear hot berry of juice burst with a pulse off the hanging loose bell of her lower lip. . .

Her big useful hands were clean and white and her short nails delicate pink, painted that way. We were not touching at all now, and dusk came over Woodcock, Texas. Dusk on the Day of Our Birth. The Union. The Nation. You could almost hear dusk falling, the shadow of a blanket Daddy waves over you. Juliette came with a towel, a Cannon Royal

Velvet wash cloth, and wiped my eyes. It had been resting in a china-white bowl of hot water. Margie was not awake. She snored very gently, like a clock under a pillow, a young emphysema ticking that did not make her cough. As Juliette touched my eyes with the rag I could venture backwards. Stripped of time, the veil lifted, not the animal veil of transparent earthy dusk you see and which dims your sight, but the translucent flesh of filthy loving fucking life that drops and rises and flattens out like the sea of things, and I saw Merkel happy with simple miniature little-boy joy as Mama touched his bulging eyelids with a washrag in the tub. Before he went to Scottish Rite to learn to walk in Corpus Christi Texas in June of 1952, Mom or Dad would see to all his needs, every staple of good or ill, the bath, the food, the prayer, the way to the toilet, the way back to bed or his toys. (Jesus, how old was I? Two or four. Years like extra fingers or hair on your back. Who needs it.) One of those needs was the certain cleanliness of private parts Dad had to watch Mom do. The bald smoothing of their homeless features was one meaning of Time. "Cut back on the suds," Dad would say. "They are clearly irritating my son." The area between Herbert's eyes had expanded during the procedure like a drawbridge of skin closing down, and evil ships of fate and sick hope, with colorful sails of dreamtime made, were passing inland from the sea into him. Little Herbert Bell. He shared with my mother by the tub with Merkel in it the fact that Violet Louise, his own mother, had washed him clean in a steel wash tub till he was old enough and had guts enough to do so himself. "Could you sit down in the wash tub, Daddy?" "No, Merkel, son. By that time I was standing.". . . "Oo, doggie." He looked at Janet. Merkel shrieked with burning soap in his penis and rubbed himself in the tub (a bathtub universally white, normal for then). Dad: "For God's sake, Janet, serve the boy! Don't let him touch himself! He'll infect!" And Janet splashed soap suds into Merkel's eyes and he cried, shrieking, oo-oo-oo-oo, Mom fumbled like a broken doll mechanized within (23 years of age!), a palsied frothing epileptic clock of fucked up sex bathroom gutmonkey reality in the tiny Billy Bell house, and Dad emergencied a fresh hot rag from the boys' bassinet always handy, soaked it in steaming rushing hot water under the sink faucet (not the bath faucet, for fear of scalding Merk, his decision still a year off), and slapped the hot rag over my brother's whole face and told crying Janet mechanically crying already at the age most women are happy, to rub it off. "Rub off all the soap, Mama!" he excruciated. . .

The room was silent except for the wheeze of Margie's clock when Juliette lifted the rag off my face and smiled quietly at me or for me without looking at my eyes. She had rifled through her jungle of viny hair, marshalled it, or maybe Esme had, and she swung it to one side of her head by just tilting it and letting it drop with ribbons red in the inner dusk. I pulled her head down halfway to mine and we kissed. When I opened my eyes, her eyes were still idling on my cheeks and I tried to trick her into seeing into my eyes, but she would not. But she did not laugh at me or at herself. She had some kind of genetic bravery or blood bravery nobody could ever slap out of her. She went away and left the door ajar. I had seen down her blouse her white caramel chest and raisinette nipples inedible by the angels who would always follow her.

Little bells began to go off on the second floor of Esme's house and I heard running feet. Margie stirred awake and reached for her little gold bell in a drawer of her bedside table. I put myself against her huge whiteness perfect as a whale. She lit a Salem or a Lucky and pulled the satin-trimmed bedspread or blanket up over us. I lay beneath it completely hidden and sucked on the cruel beating heart milky with stupidity. "Fit for kings," she said, and tapped my head through the covers. She reached with a surging movement for a light switch on her table lamp which had little pink balls on it that danced, and I rolled along with her like a boy on a dolphin.

"Look," she said. "I want to show you something."

I arose or withdrew with a racing heart from beneath the covers and the shield of her and saw on the covers, resting on her chest, a gilded cage with a toad inside it. This cage was square, with convex mansard roofs coming to a rooster. A tiny finch could just barely fly around the bottom room. I took the cage and smelled it and rattled the hollow toad lacquered and painted gray and green and gold and black under the finish.

"My first kind husband was a taxidermist," she said, smoking. The sexual Everything seeped out of Margie like satin paint. A semigloss sea saturating the Whale of Everything. To talk of it is tantamount to putting your arms around the sea. To think of it generates the silent ticking of life. The striving, driving buzz saw of cicadas wheeling over Woodcock weltered on cue, arisen after seven or thirteen years of tribal isolation in the soil around the roots of live oaks.

"You look like him."

The world has to turn.

"He smelled things, too."

The globe of fish and starfish and sea horses and sunflowers and tiny gardenias was turning away, in, on, under, around, between, and through.

"He liked to smell things he had used... All done."

Never all done are the three words God taught things to say without so much as a sound. I think it is in the air every wheel cut through. I think it is in the water fin split and healing constantly. Loving. Not loving. Cruel and beautiful. It is the ribbons in Juliette I remember. The rags holding to form the wine hall, the castle, the traveling homeward of hair.

"He loved perfumes. He would go to Frost's and purchase them and keep them in his car and little blue boat. But for him at home it was only the fully marinated smell of me," she confided. All done. All ached out. Turning to face me, her blue undrained beauty lighting the pivot of a soul's axle... "And it was only me on the little boat, too."

Never all done. Never done at all? The blubber, the Eskimo Pie of sandwiching life. The Earl of Sandwich rode a pecan sandy mare into the mane of the king's white stallion of the sea Jonah laughing happy with Eileen houseful of kids. Sleep music. Dinghy of no tone. Dumbshit Fourth of July happy first time out "You sixteen?" Mrs. Evans still in love Ah U-U, Chet, the mule-faced man Brundetti no dreamer now no love affair no buttfuck either no filth or filthy talk just a out-n-out Snicker in the freezer Mom Merkel want one Get it for him Trout. A void of white frozenness on a chair, her face feeling the freezer compartment dusk, a little North Pole Eskimo hamlet unlike anything in Texas, my Mom. The Snicker is out. Dad unwraps it and breaks it in half for the twins. Janet, bring me a towel, please. Dasn't lick it off, as Grandma says.

To this day, I see my breath in the freezer and think of Mother. I feel she saw the Northern Lights in the hills and valleys and skies of mogulled frost in the precious, previously owned, unfrostfree Frigidaire. Don't you? She would dare to take that little household vacation with Herbert in the living room oo-doggied for his nap. It was when I was older and no longer needed a chair to fish out a Snicker from the freezer for Merkel that Mother started to smoke and learned to drive the Nash and go for spins on her own that she gained some measure of independence and life was more than just a labor of love with liberty to snatch at here and there.

CHAPTER FORTY-TWO

It is hard to make plain a vision of Destiny. I have tried for many moons to muster... the common sense to put down in words what the moon saw, the dried toad saw, the dead saw, the sea saw. This is not it. No images. Stillness like a pocketful of photographs picked up off the road of what happened to me and Chet and U-U and Jonah and "Brundetti"... Pictures of an ungone, untidy world. Because when you're forty-five years old the moon is still the same world it was thirty summers ago. The sun is the same star, just as unbearably perfect, with firestorms instead of pockmarks, round singular passion instead of a smile. One sun, one moon. My saying.

Powderpuffs of white fireworks boomed and popped over Dimple. They were all there, active, and real. They shot from Irrigation Ridge over Pentecost Road. I bet the Boy Scout wasn't buried yet. He had burned to death in the sea, running to get there with his kitten, said an article in the weekly called *The Bend*; said he was getting his Eagle that night (July 3, Sunday), and had come all the way by bus alone from

Waxahachie. "Valiant to the end, a true Eagle," the scoutmaster said. But I didn't know that, then. Then, I was imprisoned under Margie's weight. She sat astraddle my much smaller pelvis, her sweaty breasts flaunted and still, her face blanched by light from somewhere outside the window where I saw the cottonball fireworks, or from light from under the door. Her face and tight curls were lost in a vacant misery of vacuous light with every poem of love converted into skin. I reached up and touched her face and she gasped and flashed and dipped and swallowed my face. Personal records are set without pity.

Of course, the inevitable happens. The fireworks stopped, and Margie rolled down beside me. It smelled so good. Where Time comes from smells so good. . .

It must have been nine-thirty or ten o'clock at night, because they started the fireworks at just past dusk and they lasted, I'd say, an hour. . . Silent, Esme Only's house was solidly, solidly, solidly empty of women and men, girls and boys, except for us in Margie's room on the second floor. I longed for water, and felt for a tiny perfume bottle she had rubbed on herself and shaken out and I sucked the honor of roses, put the cap back on the bottle and placed it in Margie's sleeping hand. She was fully asleep. Her fingers folded around it like a scallop shell.

Mother's old saying came to me. It spurred me on. To seek water and life where everything was lost, shot, exploded. The belly of a whore. Bible knowledge. Knot tying. Water water everywhere, all around Woodcock.

"I wonder what the old priest is doing?" I said as I descended to the kitchen for water. There might have been a glass in the second-floor bathroom I could wash and drink out of but it never dawned on me. I would go out the way I came in, sleepless through the back kitchen door, after water and food I could steal.

On the kitchen table was a note: "Margie, we are at the ruins picnic. Remember?" It was signed E. In the corner of my eye I saw the black caretaker standing at the window above the sink. Outside. His stolid face a cluster of hatred and blossom of knowledge. About to act, to move, he stood there. I would not or could not move. This made water from the tap out of the question, so in the refrigerator I found a bottle of ice-cold vodka and a container of mashed strawberries which I mixed in a big white mixing bowl with two whole strawberries in it from the bottom shelf, mixed it on the table with my hands, figuring to fool the caretaker into seeing I was innocent and on a household lark. I had not reached for a spoon, for searching for a spoon would require an approach to the sink, a false shifting of head and eyes downward instead of at the window.

I heard a bolting sound, like somebody latching a bolt on a door, really slamming it, and my eyes looked to the window as my hands lifted the bowl to my lips, and there I saw the caretaker still as a statue of hatred angrily staring outside the window. I smiled at him and held out the bowl. I thought I saw his head shake. Water trickled from his nostrils. I saw his hands on the windowsill, stepped toward him, and he fell away. He fell away. He fell but I heard nothing. I cannot remember his real name.

"Give me some of that," a man said, and it was the King of Darts, behind me. He took the bowl and smelled it.

"Where's the whores?" he said.

"At a picnic. At the ruins."

"Where's Juliette?"

"I figure she's with them."

He peered at me like he knew enough to be a Knight, a Knight of Solitary Darkness, blue eyed, but not a king. It was stabbing. He had knowledge. Fear's old helmet was in his belly. I can't explain. I'm sorry. He conjured fear exactly suddenly equal his size and weight, including his clothes and hair, his hat and boots, and he wasn't any bigger than I was. A freckle twinkled as he lifted the bowl to his mouth.

"You sure?"

"I'm the only one here."

"Liar."

He laughed and gave me back the bowl and told me to drink it. I took it from his hands, his freckled hands, and our fingers touched. O Jesus I felt sick.

"Drink," he said calmly, like a priest.

I couldn't.

"You mixed it," he said, and forced me to drink some, then dumped the bowl on my head. He left the bowl on my head and hit it down with the heel of his hand.

"There it is," he said, and put his hand over my face and shoved me backwards into the refrigerator. I kicked at his heels and watched him walk out through the front door of the house. I think the front door was left open, so that anybody on the street, any child, lingering in the street after the fireworks, could have seen. You could see down the hallway to the kitchen. The French doors were jalousied, tied back to hooks with sashes.

I lay on the floor and cried, I cried for my puppy. I hoped Father hadn't cut off its tail. My precious Contessa. The old song. I would bury her in a hat box from Fallen Apples, between Trout and Merkel. It was inevitable though the Inevitable must still Yet Be. I got onto my stomach and scooped a dozen cockroaches into the bowl and put it back into the refrigerator. It had not broken when he pushed me back, for the bowl was of some white milky ringing true space-age substance. Holding the refrigerator handle, I sighed to think twice, and took the bowl of cockroach carcasses like little tin soldiers hollow with night and bronze with power and glory, and dumped them into the trash. . . No, I dumped them into the sink and down the garbage disposal, with plenty of water, and washed the bowl and my hands with dishwashing powder. Then I took a pen and napkin and wrote to Esmerelda Only I would pay her back everything, and put that letter on her table, next to the note to Margie. I had put something else in the trash that could not go down the garbage disposal. It was the bowl. For who could ever serve people food or eat from a bowl once so filthily heaped? I had cleaned it and thrown it away, as one does a can.

That's what I did.

I heard snickering or sniggering outside the back door, like neighborhood children might be out there, and simply walked outdoors. It was a clear night with no moon and spits of individual clouds were racing overhead from the sea. No children. I thought I saw somebody standing against the back corner of Esme's shed where the Corvette was parked, but if there was someone there he faded back around the corner. A rush filled the air, a whistle and hiss, and I looked skyward as the rocket exploded into a long showering ball. One lone firework. A big man lay on his back on the lawn, with his feet towards the house. The showering firework lit him.

Margie was out of the house in a bathrobe and waved at me urgently to come to her.

"Light me," she said. She put a cigarette in her mouth and I lit it using a lighter she gave me.

"Keep it," she said. She was all there. It was hard to accept how it could be.

Another, smaller, lower rocket whistled up and lit the man on the lawn.

"Who's that?" she said and walked over.

I saw her bend over and look in his face, then she ran back to me. On my hand holding the Zippo I could still smell the hollow cockroaches after everything I had done. I could find the perfume on my lips.

"Who is that?" I said.

She blew past me back into the kitchen and up the stairs and back with a quilt. I followed her over to the man lying there, gazing at the stars. His eyes were moist, universally moist. Margie spread the blanket on the ground beside him and sat down on the blanket and pulled me down next to her. She said to just sit still and wait for the fireworks. She looked at the stars and all around us. I looked all around and down at the man beside me, and saw him finally as the caretaker. No sound came from him, just an awestruck intelligence. It was certain, incredible, like every other real thing is. . . Margie rolled out and got to her feet fast as any wrestler or football player, and stood at his head.

"Take his feet!" she said.

"Why?"

"Roll him over!"

We jointly rolled the gazing man onto the covers, onto the quilt. He was heavy and limber.

"Get down on your knees!"

We knelt beside him and rolled him into the quilt three or four times, wrapped him in the quilt like a human tortilla or burrito. I laughed.

"He's gonna wake up!"

"He's dead!" she said.

I smelled my fingers. They smelled of strawberries. On his shoe was a mashed strawberry.

We carried him to the shed and laid him on some hay bales that were stacked against the wall like cushioning in case somebody pulled in too fast or hard. The Corvette was gone. Margie sprinkled some loose hay over the human burrito and, reaching as high as she could into the raftered attic of the shed, pulled down an old tarp or army surplus pup tent and unfolded it over him. She stood there a moment thinking and rubbing her hands on the front of her robe. We heard thunderous running and Margie blocked me into the blackest recess of the shed. Children with sparklers ran past the mouth of the shed like cave men with magic shining sticks. She kissed me, and the front of her robe was moist with blood from where the caretaker's head had pressed against it. But nothing stops the hands and mouth, not even death, especially. The dirt insatiable after blood and knees and buttocks and elbows and mucus. The sparklers hard sticks of gunpowder fusing the night of independence. The caretaker. Stardust and moondust and one dust. The weeping of the incredible sources of each time ungalaxied, reverb. Begotten. Final. But on her back a beautiful soft hot mountain, and on her face the bottom of a beautiful soft hot mountain, and in the heaven out the square door of the shed comes the shadow of a person who drops a light thing on a necklace into the entrance dirt. And

I pull out and step up there with the blood on me to see coiled on a light dog-tag chain a fuzzy thing and a pointed thing, a tooth and a furry bone like a skinny rabbit's foot. Margie picks it up and puts it in her robe pocket and goes back inside to the kitchen table, where she sits down on a chair and takes the amulet out of her pocket and places it on the napkin-note that I wrote to Esme.

"A puppy dog's tail and a golden tooth," she said.

The chain was pulled through a hole drilled through the bone, and the tooth was set in a polished bit of bone, like a shark's tooth or a sharp acorn, but it was human. It was Jonah's. Margie brought down a shoe box from Italy, and I put these possessions in it. The lid fit snug as a shoe, and Margie tied the coffin shut with a lavender cord made of braided ribbon she found in a drawer full of hammers and hinges and nails and screwdrivers and wrenches. . .

"This was the Knights," she said.

"Same ones cut Juliette's tongue off."

I nodded. But I was a fool, then and now. Like a dashboard ornament with a spring connecting my head and tail. The road sagged or rose and I nodded compliance.

"Fuck yes," I said.

She stood up and bent and licked the strawberry gumbo off the vodkanated hair of my head, and it all started over again with the opening of a garment and the sloshing of the sea against my face. . .

. . . Things go on. The world keeps turning though you see it's impossible. Seeing is thinking. Believing is true philosophy snuggled between the breasts of a woman, in between the legs of a man. . . Crazy bewildering fact crowds memory out like some son of a bitch breaking up a dance, tapping on your shoulder... "May I?" "Of course": politeness takes over where courage falls away from duty for the fear of losing teeth, of embarrassment, of tears... If I could only just really go back again to Esme's kitchen and just fucking write down what goddamn happened! Yea, though I walk through the Valley of the Shadow, the Vale of Soulmaking, the Canyon of Margie's breasts, the riverbanks of her quiver forested peroxide blonde... No vulgarity except between the eyes where the brain is like a penis that can't feel for all the armor of bone God gave us to think about things and live, survive... I keep wanting to say I am sorry to all the children reading this map of my Nehi-Woodcock-AP-Big Oak-back to Woodcock-Huisache Mott legend in fine print down in the corner, printed over the shadowy tan figure of a nodding sea horse or a sand dollar spinning out of control, a map on a menu of every seacoast, a map on a Treasure Chest placemat made of paper...

The Giant Contessa had beautiful hands and the love of a man called Jonah. Her mother was a normal, beautiful woman who taught school in Corpus Christi and got in trouble and had to quit and moved to Woodcock where, fulfilling a life-long dream, she opened a gift shop called the Countess Eileen. It was across the street (Beach Road) from Chet Evans' mother Glory's place called Fallen Apples, and she was the first woman I loved. Eustacia Lopez was the first person with whom I ever had sex. I also loved her. I and Chet-Who-Loved-Her called her U-U. U-U saved me from being lynched as a scapegoat on the night of July third 1964 after the black Eagle died running on fire from the burning school bus into the sea with his kitten he could not leave home in Waxahachie. You wonder why. Don't you? You think maybe his father would have smothered it or flushed it down the toilet in a set of swirlies had he left it at home? My own real mother told me of a man who threw his dog against the side of his house until it was dead. My grandfather told him he should not do it, while he was doing it. But the man was insane and told my mother's real dad to Fuck Off quietly, and in front of children and my stone mason grandfather who played the violin, a fake Stradivarius, threw the dog against the wall till it was dead. Then I met Margie, the Beautiful Blonde Walrus of Whaling Love and Cruelty, who buried the caretaker under the hay and a tarp in the Corvette barn, assigned to protect me by Esmerelda Only. That takes us down to now. . .

The Giant Contessa had beautiful hands and the love of a man called Jonah.

Stud came to the front door of Esme Only's with Esme Only unconscious in his arms. He was so strong he could carry her like a baby, and she a grown big woman with honey brown hair. He was wet all over, and so was she. They looked like they had been swimming in the sea with their clothes on. Behind them ranged up the other girls who worked and stayed with Esme except Juliette. Stud's facial look was realistic and tired. He wasn't a kid anymore. His big steel watch was waterproof. Even soaking wet, he looked rich and powerful innately with big arms and thick wrists cradling his one true love. Margie had said his wife was too drunk to fuck most of the time, and lost in some kind of dream world where things like Bambi belonged.

"Where's Juliette?" Margie asked Stud.

He looked at me and back at her and shook his head. A dying cicada bumbled through the door above Stud's head and all the girls shrieked except Margie who pulled me to her. I loved her too. Stud walked carrying Esme past me.

"The spa," he said.

"She's at the New Geronimo Spa."

Margie laughed a little snigger of surprise at the deeply anchored absurdity of this here world. Stud sank onto a huge red velvet Victorian couch with thin ankles, with Esme asleep all the way on his lap, in his cradling, loving, tender, hairy arms. I wished more than anything in the world, more than memories of Trout and Merkel, that he was my father.

"Where's New Geronimo Spa?" Margie asked. She had gone to get a hot wash rag to clean Stud's face, and she was wiping his eyes and nose and lips and neck and fingers with a gold band still there. He closed his eyes as if going to sleep vigilantly. Margie looked at his torso bulk and knelt to take off his Wallabees. They were brand new ankle-high Clark's Wallabees and they slipped off easily. Margie smelled his feet and licked them. His eyes quivered, waving inside under the weary automatic lids like in a dream, but slowly. Margie sniffed up her sinuses and rose to her feet and took me to the kitchen for some ice cream.

It was Fourth of July, and on that night the women had a big all-you-can-eat ice-cream bash among themselves at the house after the Dimple fireworks. It was an extreme privilege to sit among them shoulder to shoulder in the kitchen, the only male, and share the ice cream. There were three kinds of homemade and two kinds of store bought: peach, strawberry, and pineapple (homemade); Neapolitan and French vanilla store bought. A redhead who looked vaguely pregnant finished first and lit a cigarette and asked who made the ice cream.

"Stud," one of them said. "Stud and Kokomo."

"Who's Kokomo?" I said. It was wrong. I should not have said anything, for speaking made me suddenly visible. I felt a little wave of shock like discomfort you would give out to an invader or unwelcome guest. Margie rolled her eyes and pointed with her spoon over her shoulder, towards the shed. Then she shook her head almost indistinctly at me and scowled and swallowed and, finally, delicately cleared her throat to shut me up.

"The caretaker," Margie said.

"I want you to go outside and wash out the buckets and rinse the cranks free of salt with the hose," she said to me. "Just go along, now, by yourself. It's okay now. You're clear. Stud and Chet covered for you and the little colored Boy Scout's in Heaven, so you just get your kitteny ass out there and get them buckets clean."

The girls, in the middle of their day, smiled at me, and Margie was in charge with Esme out in the parlor. Margie dipped herself a huge salad bowl full of homemade strawberry mixed with French vanilla and Neapolitan and from the refrigerator took out a square Tupperware dish of walnuts, peanuts, and pecans and shook out a layer of these onto the mountain of ice cream in the huge salad bowl and then pretended to look for a cherry.

"Anybody got a cherry?" she asked. She and all of them laughed pleasantly enough.

"Not a cherry in the house," a Yankee-voiced miss from New Orleans said. She winked at me. Margie's face flattened out, and she wiggled her dry spoon in her fingers. The New Orleans-style girl was half her size but unafraid, and she walked past Margie to the back door out to the porch. I went, too, because that was where the buckets were.

Stud came out a few minutes later with Esme still cradled like a long, lank, beautiful baby he loved asleep or unconscious in his arms and set her down on the grass—a deep, old, Victorian-old sod of St. Augustine—and laid her down carefully. You could smell the sea water on her lank hair that fell groundward in clumps or planks like planks of taffy, saltwater taffy, and he approached me and took the garden hose from my hands and gently washed his fingers to test the temperature of the water then gently doused her hair like a squatting beautician would the hair of a baby, carefully, a holy thing, a thing action of real unfucked-up human holiness.

"God," New Orleans commented. Uttered.

Esme did not wake up. Nothing in Woodcock or along Walnut Street where Esme's house was, stirred. Nothing. Not even a burning star. Over the roof of the car shed a bumbling cicada smashed head and tail and wing and piercing lip for insect love, for love, real love unfakable you will sleep seven or thirteen years for, and from a stooping position Stud swirled around at the stars over the shed and slung his arms at the insect... He lost control in himself and shouted at the bug to Shut the Fuck Up.

It did. But it just came to rest atop the point of the shed. The car shed was like a little barn.

New Orleans went back inside the house and Stud continued to bathe his love. He was crying. I had never seen a grown man who was not a pervert cry. My whole heart caved in like a city on wheels where everybody was gone but the homes remembered. Every smell in eternity in the backyard of Esmerelda Only registered. We had no sound again. Again. It was like a heart of vacancy, the heart of vacancy pouring into the grass and the various blades of grass were paintings of the sea. Then, the cicada on the roof brewed up a noise like a death rattle and Stud pulled the hose out its full length till the tall spigot bent and he sprayed the roof of the shed to get rid of it. It was like he was putting out a fire.

In a minute Margie came out with a bowl of ice cream for me and an open can of sardines for Stud. Stud slapped it out of her hands. Quickly, a cat from under the house pounced upon a sardine that had hit the porch. Another came and licked the oil. Soon, a dozen cats wove and jumped across the lawn to get the delicacies. One of them touched Stud's foot because there might have been oil on it and Stud kicked it away. It had spooked him.

"Come in," Margie said.

"Leave him," Stud said, calmer, not weeping. And he looked at me. Margie did not exist for him, nor did his wife or any woman. Not Misty George he could never know, nor any bartending waitress. He just looked at me. I thought he had lost his mind, but he was beyond anything.

"Come here," he said.

Crossing over was worse than being at home, at Nehi, with Dad, for just a second, just half a footstep. His mitlike hand, removed from the garden hose, was light upon my shoulder. He spoke like a child crushed in a man's voice.

"Why didn't you take my shoes?" he said. "My Wallabees?"

His head tilted on the axle of his life of feeling and memory and he wept from his whole face, his whole pinched being.

"Sir, they didn't fit."

"Horseshit!" he screamed. He was right.

"Yes, sir."

He turned from me and re-entered the dismal halls of Heaven. He squatted down beside Esme and washed her hair with the gently running hose. His hand passed over her hair; I called myself Mingus. . .

"Get me some soap. She likes her hair shiny clean."

I started for the kitchen, where there was soap at the sink.

"No!" he said.

"In the closet."

I had no idea whatsoever on God's green and frightened earth what my real father meant. Everything He said was new. I searched frozen with my eyes like an idiot.

He pointed with the hose to the other side, the unexplored side of the house, where some shaggy dead palms let grow their beards. I went around there in the Fourth of July darkness and felt along the boards of the house with their chipped and peeling paint thick in curled-up slabs. A half dozen cats scattered from the black floor of dirty grass, dead Augustine, down holes under the house. A stray Roman candle exploded in a red fizz way overhead and I could see a lean-to fix-it shed not original to the house standing with a sloped roof, maybe seven feet tall inside, against it. More confidently, I reached out for the door of the shed and found it was cloth, an old, heavy tapestry rug or curtain hung across the six-foot span of the closet. It even had deep waves in it, like a jalousied curtain or hanging rippled tapestry. I heard a gurgling sound made by a bird overhead and looked to the sky for a Roman candle, hopeful, and one burst whitish yellow, gold, and greenish blue above the torso of a crow.

Man, you couldn't see shit on the door as far as pictures or weavings. Nothing gold. I placed my hands on it the way Stud touched Esme's hair, and pulled back the curtains. I reached up and pulled on a string tied to a broken chain and a bright lightbulb came on. It blinded me for a second and I heard meowing. At my feet were kittens in a box that had been cut in half. They crept toward me. I saw a box of rat poison open against the back wall, which was the wall of the house, tipped it into a corner and, using a trowel, buried the granules under dirt. The kittens barely had vision. I heard a *ching* and the light went off. "I found the soap," I said brightly, turning to face Stud, but it wasn't Stud. I felt warmth on my head, then on my face, a cranberry flavor, and fell back into the shelves. As he ran away I could feel his palms hot against the flat flesh of my chest. The kittens were mewing. Meow. Meow. And Stud came and turned on the light. I had no soap in my hands. I looked up at him. His hair was slicked back and he peered down at me with great concern. He swallowed. He took my hands and pulled me to my feet and walked me outside and stood me against the side of the house. I could see his face.

"Did you see who did this?"

I did not see what he meant. I had failed. It was simple. But he had asked me a question. Time was passing. He looked scared. He took my shoulders. He pushed me down to the ground and went around back. A big cat leapt from a palm tree to the ground and took a seat, and licked its lips. Its white pinny teeth showed. It was the only one came anywhere near. Stud came with a flashlight and camera and took my picture several times. He went back and got the hose and stretched it back around towards the closet and sprayed me as well as he could in a sternly pointed jet of water that bounced off the house and showered me from above. He went back and turned up the water as hard as he could and came back and sprayed it at my head. It hit my eyes. I screamed out. "I'm sorry!" he shouted, then rushed to me. A clump of candied matter had fallen from my head onto my lap like a featherless bird that had been set there. It had slid a wing across my lips and had no cranberry taste. It had no flavor at all. Stud picked it off my lap and the big cat went away. "A sparrow," I said. It looked like a featherless sparrow, headless and full chested. Stud's thumb moved. Then its weathered head popped out and had no eyes. Stud's eyes lit like a flower of horror blossoming under the moon. A firework showered above his head, far, far above, like a cheerleader's pom or a golden helmet riveted by blacksmiths in ancient times.

On his knees, Stud poured the pickled item from one palm into the other, and sniffed it. He tasted the tiniest bit of the liquid off it on his fingertips. He winced. . . He wanted to tell me something, then. . . A mighty firework rumbled rebellious and goddamn near loud as thunder above the house and shook the palm trees like sticks of old false hair. A small, roaming child ran past with a sparkler. He doubled back and looked down at the thing in Stud's hand. He pointed with his unlit hand, stiffened and shrieked "Peeee-*PEEEEEEE!*" so loud and shrill he shook all over, used all his breath, ending as the trees behind him flashed in the concussion of a firework shaped like a fleeing jellyfish or a bonnetful of golden snow.

The girls turned on the porch light behind the house and startled Stud who got to his feet and carried the mass quickly, like a hunter, to the back of the house to check on Esme. He stood uncertain for a second in the new, harsh light. A harsh light compared to the stars. He turned the flashlight on the mass in his hand and dropped it into the grass. A big cat leapt upon it like a leaping rat on a stage. Stud watched him. Since the meat was dead, the cat did not play with it, but deftly carried it away to the shed. Stud saw where he took it until it was too shadowed over to see. Then he returned to the closet, turned on the light, found a bar of soap, and washed his hands. After washing his hands, he went to Esme and washed her hair. The rhythm of the water made a beautiful song. Then he came back to me and pulled me to my feet and walked me around back and sat me on the edge of the porch and very gently washed my hair.

The water flowed across my shoulders and torso. He rubbed the bar of soap on my back, into the cloth of my shirt, and scrubbed it with his fingernails. He washed a little of the top neck front of my shirt where it was unbuttoned and gave me the soap and told me to stand up and scrub myself clean with the soap through my clothes. All of me. And when I had I was clean and he rinsed me off.

In all this time none of the girls came out, nor did he move to pursue the wrongdoer. Nor had Esme moved. Not even a twitch. You could see her eyelashes and the shadow of her chin upon her breast in the porch light. He lifted my arm to rinse under it and I asked him was Esme dead. He said he couldn't know. It was a spell.

"Rinse your teeth of the pickling," he said, and held the water to my mouth. I drank my fill, with my hand also on the hose, until I thought I might float away.

A phone rang upstairs and Margie came out to get Stud. Esme's room had the only phone in the house. Stud asked Margie who it was and she said she did not know but he was laughing when he asked for Esme. Stud went up there. Margie stayed with me. She was clothed, now, and we looked at Esme. On the grass she looked like a goddess you would call Belladonna Lonely. Stud came back down in a dead hurry, like a stick man in a movie animated under blankets of big muscle, a healthy, wealthy stick man, and took me by the wrist like you would a child much littler than I was, up inside the house to Esme's room.

It had a blank TV in it reflecting the world of a whore. Stud turned on the TV to a loud blank fuzzy channel with nothing on it, and shut the door. He opened the top drawer of a manly dresser painted a light, bright color, and took out a host of snapshots small in size. They were smaller than Brundetti's of Mom and Chet Senior, of Chet Junior's mom and the blank black devil, the unsigned Goose Island Bridge pictures I could barely see. When I tell you that I don't know why I tell you that ever again. The words were delivered to me on the smile of a dolphin.

Delivered silent, negative on the smile of a dolphin, the film of this lovesong, dreadfully delicate developing on the water, like the long lost sigh of a daunted gondolier, thirty years learning the melody, forgetting the words, with Jonah and the Mrs. in the boat. Black Knight, Big Artemis. The sigh of the erstwhile gondolier dread Sperry sang of, how beautiful, in his perversion heavy as water, his tongue through the cell bars flashing black of brown rotten teeth in human water. Heavy as water, the sigh of the ghostly gondolier. Forgiving all he cannot remember, my Grand Master's eyes on love, that channel without fuzz, without flip, adjusted to the recompense and fretless ongoing compensation love is when it's buried in the shoulder of a woman born illegitimately noble, and raised that way, of a normal, schoolteacher mom who got into trouble in Body of Christ and had to quit teaching school and started her store selling old things and new things and, really, few things, in Woodcock Texas. Heavy as water, the dolphins breathe the film of the ocean sea. Developing now, Brundetti's blue-I-don't-remember eyes pearling shut without closing as the fiddlers picked them to their sifting music before whoever it was dragged the photog's twin up from the bay and dumped him under Fallen Apples' shade, the slant of morning cool on that side, west, I wonder why, the day they found the sea horse in his. . . ear. . . The picture I threw into the bay south of the cabin showed a woman who looked like Chet's mother looking back over her shoulder at a hazy black figure intercoursing her. You could see his hand on her hip and that he wore a suit coat. If the flash was blinding, you just couldn't tell. Her ecstasy was whiter than light but the light had not illuminated him. Just all I can tell. Just all I can word. Just a picture. . .

Stud hands me the pictures and I thumb through them, traveling through time. Through time. Blank. Stupid. The TV applauding in foreign waves. Stud reached down and adjusted the portable on its golden stand on vertical so it would not wave. The picture insisted, and moved sideways. He pounded the fuck out of the TV and Margie came into the room. She was bigger than Stud but knew where she was and she backed off. He said, "Tend to Esme." She went away.

"What do you think?" he said.

"I don't know these people," I said.

It was the same sort of snapshot-stealing, pictures-of-different-periods-of-life photographs parents take of children, children of parents, people of pets. The paper on which the pictures rested was yellow and gray and white. One was brown. It had a burnished sepia tone like an old doorknob. It was genuinely older than I was and not something you'd buy to fake or decorate a wall of gingham. The man in it was Jonah Hutchin. Faded brown as a salamander with age, he stood alone in a nice gold suit, smiling calmly, like an executive. I cannot bring out the color of his suit. I wish I could swear to the fact it was a palm tree beside him because then I'd know the green had faded to gold, but may have been a huisache in the winter. He looked happy and calm. He had a thumb hooked in a watch-fob pocket.

"That's the Muleskinner, sure as hell."

"No sir. That's a man in a suit."

I looked at Stud like a fool boy lying to escape and couldn't act like Chet. So I told the truth again, looking straight in his eyes:

"That's a man in a suit."

He could have the pervert sheriff in a car with Sperry and the King of Darts downstairs. They all hung out at the bar he owned. I had not seen his attempts to defend the safety of Chet the day they whooped his face Oriental at the Conspicuous. He was my father. I felt ashamed. I laughed.

He took the pictures out of my hand and shuffled through them teasingly or pokingly-fun-at-me, almost panicky, glancing at me like an amateur entertainer, and drew one out by pushing it out with his thumb. His fingernails were absolutely clean and perfectly manicured by himself.

"You know this one," he said.

I took it and shookenly faced it. It was the curtain of my eyes opening onto a stage.

"Yes," I said.

It was the Contessa Eileen, standing naked in a tear-shaped clearing. Indefinable trees surrounded her, black as two gathered hands forming a chapel. She was alone except for the camera, like Artemis finally succumbing. Had she not been finally succumbing, she could not have stood for the picture so milky thighed. The edges of the snapshot were jaundiced as if by smoke, and God if there wasn't a pinhole at the top. I could tell you exactly what she looked like, each pudge and shadow town, but it would not be what you see. A curd. . .

He pulled the picture from my hands and tossed the pictures back into the drawer and we went downstairs, saw Esme covered with a sheet, and got into Big Stud's Lincoln and sped away. . .

"Why didn't you answer the phone?" I said.

"It wasn't for me," he said.

The phone had just lain on its side, the black receiver, with no sound coming out of it, on Esmerelda's bed.

Margie had said the phone was for Esme.

Stud lit a cigarette dry from the dashboard. He looked ahead at Beach Road toward death in the beams of his headlights. He looked to me, because he had no audience, like the picture of success. An insurance salesman in the Million Dollar Club.

We drove to THE CONSPICUOUS ABSENCE OF WISDOM OF ANY SORT bar and saw a horde of men sprinkled with women standing like an amoeba in the space between the bar and the bait house behind which I had found U-U parked in Esme's Vette. Stud drove right up to them, and into them, till they separated like the Red Sea and we saw all the way up the dock of the yacht basin to where down at the end stood the sheriff of Refugio and the Model. The Model now had on work khakis like the sheriff's.

Stud got out of the car but left me in there, walked up the dock to its end, stayed a short while, then returned to the fascinated edge of the crowd of the ignorant, and they turned around to face the headlights of the powerful Lincoln as he waved at me, signaled me to come on. I looked for Sperry or the King and saw them not, so I got out and did his bidding and would have anyway. Respect.

Up at the end of the dock stood the Model and the sheriff with Stud Mingus. Where they hang big fish for pictures and weigh them on a scale hung the head of a human being without a face. The face had been eaten off by crabs and picked by fish. Some flags of its skin hung adrift in the still harbor air hardly ever still. The weighing hook was up under the back of the head. Model had a flashlight he swept nonchalantly at the head and around the planks framing the concrete base of the scale like he was searching for clues. I want to make him as real as possible, like everything yearning in the unsung alphabet of our little worlds: he wanted to be just like Big Stud Mingus. . . The boards around the scale showed bits and pieces of scale, flesh and fin slashed, cut off, or exploded. Tatters of it. A huge jewfish had hung there earlier, the winner of the Shotgun Lodge Independence Day Tournament that day, caught beyond the island and brought there for weighing and documentation. The Model showed me a fresh photograph of a tall, skinny boy like Ichabod Crane in jeans and black tennis shoes, with a crew cut and short-sleeve shirt with the short sleeves rolled up a notch, standing next to the jewfish hoisted on the scale beside him.

"He would have to be standing where I'm standing now," the Model said threateningly. He had worked for hours, filing and polishing his nails.

Without lowering the photograph from the light beam, Model flipped the picture and showed it officially stamped by Shotgun Lodge, signed by Darla Mingus and witnessed by Papa Lopez. The fish's weight exceeded all but the biggest people; I want to say over five hundred pounds. The tall fisherboy's name and height have been lost. These things have a certain appeal to the treasure hunter, but I am not a treasure hunter. They say Jean Lafitte's treasure is buried on La Vaca Island.

"What time is it?" I asked the Model.

His wristwatch did not glow, so he lit it with the beam. His watch had rubies on the hour and minute hands but nothing jewelled the sweeper hand as that would throw off time. I tilted the butt of the flashlight in his fist so that the crystal would not glare. The open calendar window magnified the day. It was now July fifth.

"A new day," I said to him.

It felt all new. I smelled bits and pieces of the record fish, knowing that the skinny boy's record could not be un-Darla'd. It made me happy. The record was forever in pictures, memory, and print. Turquoise ink. Papa Lopez never lied. Everybody knew it and loved him. His poor poverty-stricken honest hardest-working ass.

I stepped backward and slipped on a piece of flesh. A tall, thin man in his forties walked up from behind me and with him had the boy from the photograph. The boy wore an oversized baseball cap centered on his head and had his fingers in his front jeans pockets. He clung as near his father as he could get without falling against him or falling down. The boy looked like an old man, as if sickly.

"My boy's fish is gone and I want to know who's responsible."

The Model and the sheriff and Stud Mingus knew. They all knew Sperry. They didn't speak. I turned around and in the people moiling saw Papa Lopez crying. I asked Stud why Papa was crying. He didn't answer me. Stud looked directly hound-dog sad at the tall boy's father. The tall boy was there, and somehow the meaning of everything, but I don't think anybody could look directly at him. They looked at his father. The boy had been crying. His being was slouched down behind his father in the shade thrown by the flashlight still held by the Model. You heard him crying. O the sad whimper, worse than a puppy missing its tail not yet healed over. You just wanted to kill him so he could go to sleep. But then there's his proud father. O Jesus.

"What's the matter with your boy?" Model said.

Stud looked at Murphy.

"You go away," he said.

The sheriff cleared his throat of the something that had clogged it, and the Model handed me the flashlight. The Model backed away and stood erect against the railing of the platform. I flashed the light at the foot of the weighing scale and saw a thumbnail or the prehistoric scale of a fish. Most of the blood had been washed off the concrete slab the scale was planted on. Stud for some reason put his hand on my shoulder. My knees were giving as the sheriff grabbed the flashlight from my hand and the light beam swung out over the yacht basin crammed with sleepy dark yachts and a light blue shrimper. When the light was entirely confiscated I looked directly at the boy. He was dying of love. He had a father's love and God's.

The father stepped forward and worldly wise faced Mingus. The father was still for a second.

"It cost a thousand dollars to catch that fish."

Stud took out his wallet and counted out ten one-hundred-dollar bills that were still wet with sea water into the wronged man's hand. Then he took the picture of the tournament winner and placed it on the money. Then Stud stepped forward and took the young man's hand and shook it. In no wind I could feel, the raw head spun on the weighing hook in the harbor-lit darkness like a shadow box above the shoulders of the hidden and the apparent policemen. The Model piqued, turned to face the sea, placed his hands on the railing of the platform, bent slightly, whispered something, and quick as a swordsman spun to sniff the air around the turning head. He put his nose close to where the mouth would have been. He raised his spread fingers and touched the cheek. Then the boy said clearly, "Is that my fish, Daddy?" Everyone who heard turned eyes to him. He wasn't a sick boy at all. He was mentally retarded. He looked away from the sluggish waters of the bay, where he had been patiently studying some kind of dream, and with humored eyes gathered gently the remnant of the human head. His father readjusted the new cap his son had gotten for the tourney. It seemed to have shrunk. It fit him. His eyes floated. His father said no. Noiselessly he began to cry like a person must when the whole world is gone.

. . . I remember I walked across Beach Road away from the others, and up the hill. Darla Mingus sat among the deer with a little shiny ceramic deer with white spots on her lap. What she had on was a flimsy bathrobe with the collar turned up around her face and her face was beautiful, done up like a painted whore's or a young girl's with too much makeup. I said hello to her. She smiled distantly in peace up at me, very big luscious lipped.

"Do you want to fuck me like Stud fucks her?"

I walked past her to the thicket of priestly oaks obeying voiceless Nature and blessing the living ground with little leaves. I stood around. To get my bearings on life, I stood around. I turned back toward the beach, the deer, the sea, and saw her walking toward me. No hurry. Her robe gradually fell off and all that clothed her whiteness was the spotted deer baby she clutched to her bosom. If a thousand of her floated my way. . . I just let the female essence of the sea go by without alarm. . . You just drown and ride it out, a cowboy on a bucking sea horse. Her big velvet eyes were like the eyes of the sea horse in Brundetti's ear. But I had no leanings towards her, then, and little thoughts, with all the wives I already had, two: Eustacia and Margie. Mrs. Mingus blew gently past me, and danced with her baby in the trees. The nickel moon looked humped like on the buffalo nickel, and serious like an old Jefferson. For some reason, I thought about six-man football.

"The Refugio Buffaloes," I said. I perhaps laughed without changing my face.

Up the field behind the trees, where the trailers and recreational vehicles were parked beside water and electrical hookups, past a community gas grill some fucked-up kids were trying to light, children of late campers, I came to the burnt-out school bus the Boy Scouts had arrived in, and looked it over, up and down. I went inside and sat down in the drivers seat and fondled the magic handle of the levered door and finally shut the fucking thing, working it.

I got up and searched for the kitten. The kitten that wasn't there. But I found a dead kitten in a shoe box full of old socks under the back farthest seat. I picked it up and rattled it around. It slid around like a burnt slipper. I cried because the black boy had actually turned his face to see me go by. It was magical Fate and bravery that he had made Eagle in a white troop.

Happy Hutchin would have smiled. Like Happy, but dead, he had made things right. A healer. The remnant of a plaid shirt, his burnt badge, was under my foot. I picked it up with my toes. The weekly called *The Bend* would lie. He had not made it to the sea and drowned in flames doused in salt. Fuck. He had made it home to the bus, though, to his cat. Fate like Margie, moving, hot, a bus of a woman...

"Fucking been himself. Fucking was." I wished so bad I had a Shiner, to toast him.

The remains of the kitten were tenderly in my hands. A tiny log, a little weight. Love me, love me, they said. Wet, heavy, light, sandy, dusty, muddy, gray. Wet from a firehose, wet from the sea. The town and Stud pumped firewater from the sea. Whorled hair, planetary eyes, pliant ribs. I pressed these to my face and put the ashes in my pockets. I wrapped the remains of the kitten in the remnant of the shirt and placed it back inside the box curved like a harp from the water...

Back on the road I caught a ride with someone I didn't know and never talked to back to Dimple where Eustacia's uncle Leon lived and knocked on his door. A big man in suspenders and a white tee shirt opened the door and asked me what I wanted in English. I saw the shoe-box cavalcade of home life at night on parade in the darkness his shoulders hoisted. His thumbs poked a picture of velvet Jesus Christ. He opened the screen door and got near my face and said, "You're that white boy my baby's been seen with. I don't want that. All you want is a fucking whore. A brown piece of tail."

I couldn't talk.

"Now fuck off. I see you back around here I kick your ass boy."

It was all done quiet.

"What if she's pregnant, Mister, pregnant by me?"

He laughed and spat upon me, a fine mist through the screen.

He latched the screen and went back to bed. I knew things. I knew things about the whole world. She wasn't there. My wife was gone. Snake-bit beauty. Dwindling thoughts like little sweat flies on Whiskey's ass. I backed away from the house of my love to record it forever in my mind. You hate it to end but it does. A lone green sex-mad cicada burst into flight and dive-bombed the house, bumbled in circles in the dirt the Mexican kids crunched with their toes, and marched into the grass like a wounded pilot. I took some ashes from my pocket and sprinkled them on the dirt at the gate where a fence used to be. I saw where they hit like burnt-out stars and fingered the dust fine as face powder.

On home, now...

At Nehi I heard a whining and found my puppy shaking in a pile of shirts in my closet. Or maybe it was Merkel and Trout's closet. Dad had put her there. She strained her golden face with liquid little chocolate-covered raisin eyes bursting and her new pink tongue stunk of puppy ass blood where her tail was cut off, probably with pinking shears, by my dad. Wadded up behind her, and behind the shirts, was the bloody baby blanket Dad used to hold her still on his lap. He would wad up a dog like a pig-in-a-blanket with just its tail sticking out, then gradually snip it off. It took work and time and sounds impossible, but he was strong from shaking so many debtors' hands. To show her I loved her and Always would, I licked her tail wound myself and kissed her precious weepy eyes and placed her upon the pillow of my own bed. Over her, I fluffed a quilt off Trout's bed my mother had enshrined. . . and the puppy Contessa stopped whining. Her soft infant music like a baby's coo you will Always know and love last puffed from her puppy nose into my God-blessed, God-knowing ear. I took a little of the kitten dust and let Contessa smell it. She put her little tongue out, a pink leaf at work on the tree of God. There was salve in the medicine cabinet I thought about putting on but thought better not to because it was not to be eaten. Let it go. I kissed and patted her head. I lay down beside her to let her know I was her father and though I might have to leave her someday I would always love her more than anything ever in this world. She opened her mouth and shut it three or four times the way the long-tongued, thumbless beings do, and put her head upon her mitteny paws and went softly to sleep. Then I covered her entirely and left her side to go somewhere I knew not where, and before I stepped foot through my bedroom door to the hallway windowless, pictureless, mirrorless, and meaningless, I heard her whine and turned back to see the quilt hill beneath which she was buried bob and bob and bob, for she had gone back to work. . . In my parents' room I took a picture of them off his dresser and using a loafer smashed it to pieces facedown on his pillow. The black back of it with its legs sticking out was the backside of Satan I kept smashing into my father's face. This was hope. . .

What sweeps you out the door sometimes you don't know, but love is a great motivator. You leave behind the dust and the animals for a life of spirit exactly equal the supreme reduction of stillness in a road toward Father and not Mother or Lover or God, because it is he who sits in the "livingroom" of the Spa... in his big fat transported easy chair recliner, like a word you'll never use again but could never remember, in a fresh shirt and tie, wearing his reading glasses which must be new because never seen before, from Frost's in Corpus...

"Hi, son."

He is smiling his bullshit insurance smile, and what's this?— smoking a cigar! He stares out entertainedly at the hot spring beyond the glass. The new spotlights installed at Mother's expense shine down on a person's humped back sticking out of the water at the midpoint of the hole of gray artesian water.

"All loved out," he said.

"All loved away."

He was proud and happy. He had on new shoes and his feet were crossed. The crease in his pants was perfect, sharp, like it was cut by a knife from inside his britches. He put the cigar in his mouth and reached down carefully for a snifter of brandy he had hidden in the shadow of the chair.

"Aren't you awfully pleased with this place, son? It will be famously a father-and-son venture."

He extended the big snifter of brandy out to me.

"I wouldn't do this normally," he said, "but this is indeed a special time for us as a family, a brand-new chapter."

I went out a sliding-glass door to the entrance down steps to the water, the perfectly motionless gray water, and entered it past my pockets where the kitten's remains were turned to light mud in transit. I felt vaguely glad, like a hot tulip in my chest, that my first wife nor Juliette was there. I felt of the mud floor gingerly. Perhaps they had been. The person's humped back was a sport shirt bloated or bubbled up. As I disturbed the water, deeper out, the arms and head turned toward me without lifting, and I could see hair. Father came to the door and asked me what in the world I was doing. "What has entranced you so?" he said. The hump reversed, away from me, like a person looking at night for something or anything underwater. "The man has polluted my spring," he said, "leave him be, let him drown." Father returned to his chair. I took the outstretched hand as it spun near my chest, and pulled him near. I took him by the chest and pulled him nearer. "Look, son! Look!" Father yelled from inside. I looked up and saw a yellow Roman candle or rocket just exploded shower down like a little thin umbrella impaling the earth or sky with quiet wishes. "How about that!" Dad exclaimed. It lit the eyes of the man whose mouth was slightly open like the door to a bedroom ajar. Death had taken off his living mask and I couldn't tell who he was. I don't think he had found anything in the spring. His hair was feeling fully curled. Short ringlets from birth. I stepped on something hard and pushing him away dove down for it. It was a camera. The corpse would not face the moon, so I placed the device upon the hump of his back, where it rode. . .

EPILOGUE

By daylight, the sheriff and dandy came and hauled the man ashore, using a heavy chain the dandy lobbed across his back without having to enter the water. . . The King of Darts took pictures with an old Brownie camera. . . The Giant Contessa had beautiful hands and the love of a man called Jonah. Her mother was a normal, beautiful woman who got into trouble and had to quit teaching school.